measure of the heat sliding through her at the
joining of their skin he didn't reveal in the
eyes crinkling at the corners that were both
amused and er

'We do.'

He smiled with

her faint

Author Note

When Justin Connor first made his appearance as Philip's friend in *A Debt Paid in Marriage*, he captured me with his charm. It's his determination to succeed, to rise above everyone's low expectations of him, that I chose to explore in *A Too Convenient Marriage*. In doing so I introduced him to Susanna, a heroine who learns that she is so much more than what other people think. Together they support one another, and overcome all obstacles to find the love they deserve.

Many times in our lives we reach a point where we have to throw off the expectations of others and have faith in ourselves in order to achieve our dreams. It isn't always easy—especially when things are difficult and we want to quit. Justin and Susanna's story is about doing what it takes to reach a goal—never giving up and learning to ignore people's negative opinions. It's also about drawing strength from those who love and support us and remembering to cherish them.

I hope *A Too Convenient Marriage* inspires you to keep striving, to continue loving and always to believe in yourself and what you want to achieve.

A TOO CONVENIENT MARRIAGE

Georgie Lee

MILLS & BOON

Published in Great Britain 2016
By Mills & Boon, an imprint of HarperCollins*Publishers*
1 London Bridge Street, London, SE1 9GF

© 2016 Georgie Reinstein

ISBN: 978-0-263-91678-2

Printed and bound in Spain
by CPI, Barcelona

A lifelong history buff, **Georgie Lee** hasn't given up hope that she will one day inherit a title and a manor house. Until then she fulfils her dreams of lords, ladies and a Season in London through her stories. When not writing, she can be found reading non-fiction history or watching any film with a costume and an accent.

Please visit georgie-lee.com to learn more about Georgie and her books.

Visit the Author Profile page at millsandboon.co.uk.

To my husband, who believes in me and my dreams.

Chapter One

London—May 1818

'Marry you?' Helena Gammon sat back from Justin Connor, her ungloved hand stilling on his chest beneath his shirt. A horse snorted from somewhere outside his chaise where it sat parked in a long row of conveyances in front of Vauxhall Gardens.

'I'm quite serious. We get on well together, especially at night,' Justin murmured against the buxom little widow's neck. 'Soon, I'll have the resources to establish myself in the wine trade. I'll need a wife who can manage as well in my business as in my bed.'

She shifted out of his embrace and laid her hands in her lap as though they were at tea. 'There are other matters to consider.'

Her lack of enthusiasm wasn't how he'd imagined this proposal unfolding.

'Such as?' Justin leaned back against the squabs, sure he wasn't going to like what he was about to hear.

'You aren't likely to make a go of it.' She shrugged as though his failure was predetermined. 'Not after what happened with the last one.'

'The storm sank the ship.' *And my business.* He pulled his gaping shirt closed. He thought everyone understood that little fact. Apparently he was wrong. 'There was nothing I or anyone could have done to prevent it.'

Despite months of careful planning, researching, investing, hiring the most capable captain and the sturdiest ship, his first foray into business had dropped to the bottom of the English Channel, taking with it a considerable amount of his money. He hated ships.

'Even if you did manage to make a go of it, I'm tired of being some unpaid servant to my husband's ventures. I worked myself to the bone with Mr Gammon. Now I want to be free of such concerns.' She tugged her bodice up higher over her ample breasts. 'Mr Preston asked me to marry him this morning and I accepted.'

'You did what?' He hadn't realised the old furrier was sniffing around the widow, much less falling on his knees in front of her in infatuation.

'He's rich and has people to take care of his business for him.'

'He's well over sixty and not likely to keep you amused in the evenings.'

'That's why I'm here.' She laid her hand over the open flap of his breeches. 'I thought we could continue.'

He caught her fingers. 'After a year, you should know I won't dally with another man's wife, or help a woman break her marriage vows.'

She pulled back her hand. 'When did you become so serious about anything except Mr Rathbone's business?'

'I tend to be serious when there's the possibility of violence,' Justin growled, seeing Helena's true colours for the first time and despising them. He'd thought their convenient arrangement was based on some measure of respect and affability. He'd been mistaken.

'Well, if that's how you're going to be.' She

flicked her skirt down over her calves and ankles. 'Mr Preston is waiting for me inside.'

'You'll regret marrying him.' Justin pushed open the chaise door. 'He might be making a lot of promises now, but once you're his wife, they'll all disappear.'

'You know nothing of the situation.' Mrs Gammon hopped down from the chaise and stormed off across the walk and into the gardens.

Justin slammed the chaise door shut and slumped against the squabs. It galled him to think she'd waited until he'd proposed to reveal her true impression of him, though he supposed it was better now than after the parson's mousetrap was sprung. Justin roughly stuffed his shirt back in his breeches and did up the fall, not bothering to button his coat or redo his cravat. Outside, the excited chatter of ladies and gentlemen passing too close to the chaise as they filed into the gardens filled the air.

Then the door swung open. He jerked upright, thinking Helena had come back, but it wasn't her.

A stunning woman with eyes the colour of the emeralds he'd once handled as collateral fixed her gaze on him, not with the coy calculation of a vixen, but determination. She opened her full lips as if to say something, then changed her mind, pressing them tight together. Gold earrings swung from the small lobes as she raised her foot to step inside the chaise, then paused, as she took in his partial undress and began to back away. Male voices outside the carriage caught her attention and, in a sweep of chestnut curls, she looked to the sound of the noise, then climbed inside and pulled the door shut behind her.

'Drive away, at once,' she commanded, pressing herself against the squabs and out of view of the window.

'No.' Justin pushed open the door, inviting her to leave. Whatever nuisance this was, he wasn't in the mood for it, no matter how pretty it might be.

'Please, you must.' She leaned out of the chaise to pull the door closed, bringing her face much too close to his. A few freckles dotted her nose and her eyelashes were thick and dark above her vivid eyes. She licked her lips nervously, making the red buds glisten in the low light. Her jasmine perfume encircled him like the cool night slipping in through the open door. She was tempting, but she was trouble, he could feel it.

'I've had enough female companionship for one night and don't intend to pay for more.'

She closed the door and sat up across from him with unwarranted indignity. 'I don't want your money, or anything else.'

She waved a bare hand at him, making the gold bracelet adorning her wrist slide down.

'Then what do you want?' He dropped his elbow on the sill of the window and touched his fingers to his chin, more intrigued than annoyed. She wasn't dressed in the flamboyant colours of the night birds, but in a silhouette of shimmering green material which hugged her high breasts, the tops of which rose in lush half-circles above the bodice.

'To be away from here, as fast as possible.' She could barely sit still, but still he didn't give the order to the driver.

'Why?'

'It's none of your business.' The irritation mingling with anxiety in her eyes made them sparkle even brighter.

He levelled one finger at her. 'You're in my carriage, so I think it is my business. Besides, you don't strike me as the kind of woman whose family approves of her jumping in a strange man's vehicle.'

She glanced out of the window, a new panic dimming the slight sweep of pink across her fine nose. 'You don't know the half of it.'

'Enlighten me. I have nothing else to do this evening.'

There was no time for her to tell him as the door swung open again. Two men stared inside, too finely turned out to be whore minders. The older man sighed and clapped his hands over his eyes. The younger man heaved like a bull as he studied first the woman, then Justin and his undone cravat and coat.

'How dare you.' The bull reached in and grabbed Justin by the lapels, hauling him out of the chaise.

Justin's boots hit the step before he regained his footing. He brought his arms up between the bull's and knocked them aside, then pulled back his fist and rammed it into the younger man's face.

The bull dropped to his rear in the dirt, sending up a puff of dust. Stunned but not beaten, he hauled himself to his feet, staggering as he glowered at Justin. 'You'll pay for that.'

'Why don't you stay down?' Justin moved

one foot back for balance, then raised his fists. 'It'll hurt less.'

The man rushed at Justin, who slammed his fist into the bull's stomach, making him double over. Then Justin brought his elbows down on the man's back to knock him face first into the dirt. He groaned and rolled over, clutching his middle.

Justin straightened one cufflink. 'I warned you to stay down.'

'No, Father,' the woman yelled from behind him. 'It's not what you think.'

Justin whirled around to see the older man rushing at him with his walking stick raised. The woman jumped between them, spreading out her arms to stop them, her steadying hand meeting Justin's chest. He looked down at the lithe fingers spread out over his loose shirt, her thumb just slipping into the open V to kiss his sweaty skin. It was the lightest of touches, but it could have knocked him across the garden.

She turned her piercing eyes on him and they opened wide with a shock to match his. Tense breaths raised and lowered his chest beneath her palm as he waited for her to pull away, the danger from the other men fading beneath the subtle press of her skin against his. Helena's touch had never rattled him to his boot heels like this woman's, which was igniting him like a reed set to the coals.

'Then what exactly is it?' the older man demanded, lowering his stick, but not easing the hard glare he fixed on the woman.

At last she pulled back her hand and it was almost a relief as the tension between them ebbed, although not completely.

From the ground, the bull coughed and hauled himself to his feet. He staggered over to stand beside the older man. A nasty bruise marred his cheekbone and he failed to fully straighten as he continued to cradle his stomach.

'Is this the man you've been compromising yourself with?' the bull wheezed.

'I've never seen this woman before in my life,' Justin spat out, levelling his gaze at both men and daring either of them to pounce again. Whatever connection he'd experienced with the strange woman was gone.

'This isn't him. I forced my way into his carriage to hide from you.' The woman threw an apologetic look at Justin over her shoulder before turning to face her family. 'I wasn't here for a tryst. I was waiting for Lord Howsham. We were to be married, but he never arrived.'

Her defiance began to wilt beneath the truth and her father's condemning stare. Despite his stinging knuckles, Justin felt a twinge of pity for her. He knew a little something about disappointed hopes.

'Then who is he?' The bull pointed at Justin.

'Who the hell are you?' Justin shot back. This whole situation was growing tiresome.

The older gentleman stepped forward, asserting his authority the way Justin had seen his own father do so many times. 'I'm Horace Aberton, Duke of Rockland, and this is my son, Edgar, Marquess of Sutton, and my daughter, Miss Susanna Lambert.'

Justin raised an eyebrow at the hesitation which met Lord Rockland's admission of the woman's relationship to him. Justin supposed if he gave a fig for what the upper classes got up to when they weren't trying to thump him outside Vauxhall Gardens, he'd understand the hesitation, but he didn't and therefore didn't care.

'If you expect me to be impressed, I'm not.' Justin had helped collect enough debts from men like Lord Rockland to not be cowed by their grand titles and lack of manners.

'How dare you?' Lord Sutton stomped forward, ready for another beating.

'Stop.' Lord Rockland's booming voice pulled him back, muzzling but not completely checking the bull's anger. 'I think we've had enough fighting for one night. I believe an apology is in order, Mr—?'

'Connor.' Justin jerked straight the lapels of his coat.

'I'm sorry for offending you this evening and for holding you responsible for an inappropriate situation in which you were not involved.' Lord Rockland laid a large hand on his chest, his diamond ring flashing in the lantern light. 'Surely you understand how easy it was to make such a mistake.'

'No, not particularly.'

'Then perhaps you can understand the need for discretion.'

'It's not my discretion you need to worry about.' He flung a look at Miss Lambert, who boldly faced him. He had to give the woman her due; she was no cowering miss.

'True, but I'd like us to come to some understanding about your tact in this matter. If you'd be so kind as to pay a call on me tomorrow at noon, I believe I can make it worth your while.'

Justin wanted nothing more to do with this trio, but he did need money to finally put his last venture behind him and start again. He recognised opportunity when it came crashing through his chaise door. 'I believe you can.'

'Good. Until tomorrow.' Lord Rockland bowed to Justin before ushering his wayward progeny away.

'He doesn't deserve—' Lord Sutton sputtered.

'After the beating he gave you, I recommend you shut your mouth.' Lord Rockland's admonishment silenced any further protest.

Only Miss Lambert dared to turn and watch Justin as she strode away with her father and brother. It was a plaintive glance, but Justin wasn't in the mood for extending more pity or forgiveness. With his plans for the evening in tatters, he stepped back into his chaise and made for home. With any luck, tomorrow would be better. He'd receive a tidy sum of an apology from the duke, the kind he needed to repay Philip for the money he'd invested and lost in Justin's last venture, and secure the necessary merchandise to establish himself in the wine trade. Nature had defeated him last time. It wouldn't happen again. He'd succeed, no matter what Helena or anyone else thought.

'What did you think you were doing?' Lord Rockland roared at Susanna from across the coach as it spirited them away from Vauxhall Gardens.

'Acting like a slut,' her half-brother sneered. 'What else do you expect from a bastard?'

'Shut your mouth, Edgar.' Lord Rockland trilled his fingers on his knees. 'Well, Susanna? Why were you throwing yourself and my promise of your dowry away?'

To have a home, life and family of my own instead of constantly being reminded of how grateful I should be to you for nothing, she thought, but she didn't dare utter it. She was too ashamed of her foolishness to make the situation worse with the truth. 'I told you, I went to meet Lord Howsham. We were to leave for Gretna Green.'

'With the rumours of debt circling him, I'm not surprised he ran after you, or I should say your dowry. Did he compromise you?' Lord Rockland pressed, though she didn't know why. Her father wasn't about to force the earl's hand, not for his bastard daughter.

'No, I'm not as stupid as you believe,' she lied. The truth would see her banished back to the country with all hope of escape lost. Thankfully, the darkness of the carriage kept the shame from lighting up her face. She'd been a naive fool to believe Lord Howsham's false compliments, but she'd been so lonely and he so attentive and insistent. Lord Howsham hadn't cared for her. He'd only been after her dowry. She pressed her fingertips to her temples, chastising herself more than her father ever could.

'If I'd known bringing you to London to try and make a good match would result in you throwing yourself at the first man who flattered you, I'd have left you at Rockland Place.'

She wished he had, but remained silent. It was best not to provoke him. Instead, all she could do was play the dutiful daughter, bite back her anger at his and his family's treatment of her in what they considered the name of generosity and humble herself once again. 'I'm sorry, you're right, I didn't think.'

'Indeed you didn't. Whatever he might have promised you, Lady Rockland told me this morning he's marrying the Earl of Colchester's daughter in a fortnight.'

'Seems he'd rather have a nobleman's wife and her considerable inheritance than a bastard and her meagre dowry,' Edgar mocked.

Susanna balled her hands in her lap, wanting to pound on her thighs, the carriage, her father's chest and her half-brother's swollen face. Lord Howsham hadn't just abandoned her for a woman with a more robust lineage and fortune, but he'd told her the deepest of lies a man could tell a woman. She'd fallen for them like some kind of country simpleton, allowing Lord Howsham to press himself on her in the hope he might love her. In the end, it'd gained her nothing but more scorn.

'You'd better hope Mr Connor and Lord Howsham are both willing to keep their mouths shut about this. If not, what little I've been able to achieve on your behalf will be gone,' her father threatened.

Susanna almost wished it was gone. For all the effort he thought he was extending on her behalf, she'd seen very little love or true concern about her and her future. All he and his wife, Augusta, seemed to care about was getting rid of the taint hanging about their house in the form of her.

'I can't believe you're going to entertain a common man like him.' Edgar rubbed at the dark bruise forming on his cheek. 'If I were you, I'd have him thrown in jail for what he did to me.'

'If I were you, I wouldn't want such an embarrassing beating made public for all of London to read about in the papers,' their father answered. 'As it is, I believe Mr Connor can be of some use to us.'

'What could he possibly do for us?'

'He might be the solution to the new problem Susanna has presented us with.'

Susanna's stomach tightened as it had the morning after her mother's funeral when Lord Rockland had stepped through the door of their simple wine shop and looked down his aquiline nose at her. She'd known by the way he'd studied her, as he did now, her life was about to change. The little love she'd enjoyed with her mother, who'd done all she could to protect her daughter from the taint of being a bastard among their friends, relatives and neighbours, had ended. Instead of leaving her with all the people she'd ever known, although

they weren't any more loving than the Rocklands, Lord Rockland had taken her into his
household to have her moulded into heaven
knew what. She'd never been like Edwina, her
half-sister and his legitimate daughter, coddled
and dressed and paraded through court and the
ballrooms. Instead she'd been a barely tolerated companion and chaperon who was now
being thrust into society in the hope her family might foist her off on someone else. Lord
Rockland should have left her in the wine shop.

'Whatever you have in mind, I want no part
of it,' Susanna said and was scolded with a
cold glare.

'You'll go along with my wishes or you'll
find yourself cast out of my house, with the
promise of the dowry rescinded and you left,
like any little whoring bastard, to fend for
yourself. Do I make myself clear?'

'You do,' she answered with feigned meek-
ness. Tonight was a setback, but it wasn't the
end of her plans. Her father wouldn't decide
her future as he had when she was thirteen,
nor would he get his way. She'd make a life for
herself somewhere, somehow, get her thousand
pounds of dowry and be free of the Rocklands
for ever.

Chapter Two

〜〜〜〜〜

Justin stepped into the Rocklands' ornate Grosvenor Square entrance hall, unfazed by the painted cherubs and knights peering down at him from the gilded ceiling. This wasn't the first time he'd been in a grand man's home. In the many years he'd helped his friend and employer, Philip Rathbone, collect debts, there'd been a few titled men who'd defaulted. They'd face Philip and Justin to either return the money or hand over whatever cherished family silver or priceless paintings they'd set up as collateral.

'Good day, Mr Connor, and thank you for coming,' Lord Rockland greeted Justin as the butler showed him into the wide study situated near the centre of the house. The books lining the many shelves held little interest for

Justin. The experience he'd gathered from his years as Philip's assistant was more practical and valuable to a man interested in trade than a book full of theories or pretty poetry.

There was no sign of Miss Lambert as the duke led him to a pair of wingback chairs in front of the fire. Between the chairs stood a table laden with a selection of liquors. Now here was something Justin could appreciate.

'What will you have?' Lord Rockland asked.

'Something expensive.'

The surprised arch of Lord Rockland's eyebrow didn't trouble Justin as the older man picked up the decanter with the silver brandy tag hanging on a delicate chain around its neck and poured out a healthy measure. He handed the thick glass to Justin, who took a taste, impressed. This was fine drink, not the rotgut he usually endured when he was sent to extract information from common men regarding the suitability of Philip's potential clients.

Lord Rockland poured himself a glass, then motioned for Justin to take a seat across from him. Once both men were settled, the duke wasted no time getting to the matter. 'A man like you with such a fine chaise must do well in business.'

'I do well enough,' Justin answered with a shrug. The chaise was Philip's. Justin had been forced to sell his to repay a few investors after the ship had gone down. The loss of his fine vehicle and the matching grey horses had hurt almost as much as the loss of his business.

'And what exactly is it you do?' Lord Rockland enquired.

'I'm in business with a man who loans clients money. I investigate the quality of their collateral and assist my employer in obtaining payment if their debt goes unpaid.'

'It certainly explains your skill with your fists.'

He pinned the duke with a sharp look. 'I don't extract payments in such a way. I use it to defend myself against uncalled-for attacks.'

'My apologies again for last night.' Lord Rockland swirled the brandy in his glass, then took a sip. 'Our emotions were running high after my daughter's ill-advised adventure. I'm afraid neither my son nor I was thinking straight.'

'I see.' Justin didn't, but he could play along. 'I don't intend to continue in my present occupation. I mean to establish myself as a wine merchant, once I have sufficient funds.'

It wasn't a subtle hint, but he wanted the man to come to the point. He didn't have time to lounge in Grosvenor Square, drinking a duke's brandy all day.

'I see.' The older man tapped the side of his glass. 'Then allow me to propose an offer, one, as a man of business, you're sure to appreciate.'

Justin took a deep drink, savouring the rich liquor, then set the glass aside. 'I'm listening.'

'As you might know from gossip, Miss Lambert is not my legitimate daughter.'

Justin hadn't known, nor did he care. Half the people he dealt with were born without the vicar's blessing. It didn't matter to him.

'Before her mother died, I promised to give Susanna a thousand-pound dowry if she married a gentleman I approved of,' Lord Rockland explained.

'How very generous of you.' And worrying. He was starting to wonder what exactly Lord Rockland intended to offer him.

'I'm a man who takes responsibility for my mistakes.' He enjoyed another sip before continuing. 'Susanna, as you might have noticed, is a headstrong woman who often acts before she thinks. It's made finding her a respectable husband difficult, even with the promise of her dowry. She nearly threw away the money last night with her impulsive behaviour and now I must hurry to rectify the situation before all is lost.'

'For you, or for her?' Justin asked, suspecting it wasn't the young lady Lord Rockland was worried about as much as the taint her escapade might leave on his family.

'For both of us, and you. I'm prepared to give you Miss Lambert's thousand-pound dowry if you agree to marry her.'

Justin stopped the glass halfway to his lips and stared at the man from across the aromatic brandy. 'You want me to marry your daughter?'

'Assuming you're not already married.'

'I'm not.' Justin frowned, the memory of Helena's rejection stinging as much as his knuckles after the beating he'd given Lord Sutton last night. Justin took a long drink, barely tasting it as it burned past his tongue. It was her loss, not his.

'Good. As a man of business, I'm sure you won't dismiss such a tempting offer so lightly and will keep the details of last night private. I possess grave concerns about Lord Howsham's ability to remain silent on the matter.' Lord

Rockland sighed as though they were discussing a troublesome horse which wouldn't trot properly and not a young woman and her future. 'It's only a matter of time before Susanna's reputation is called into question and all chances of her making a more advantageous match are gone.'

Justin opened his fingers over the glass, then closed them, one by one, trying to ignore Lord Rockland's unintended insult. Justin was no nobleman's son, only the common son of a man who'd served Philip's father the same way Justin served Philip. Despite the way Justin's father and Helena derided him for wanting to be more, he wasn't about to make something of himself off the back of some young lady. 'She doesn't need a husband. She needs a better chaperon.'

Lord Rockland's chiselled cheek twitched. 'I don't think you clearly understand what I'm offering you.'

'I understand exactly. Money and a connection to the Rockland family. I know what these things are worth. I also understand the price your daughter would pay for me to obtain them. I won't ask it of any woman.'

Lord Rockland gaped at Justin as though

it'd never occurred to him Justin might refuse what he considered a magnanimous gesture. 'I assure you, she's quite amenable to the idea.'

'You don't know me, she doesn't know me and neither of you know what kind of man I am.' Although Justin was coming to understand clearly what kind of family this was.

'From what I've seen, you're a man of honour and integrity who'll treat my daughter as well as any man is expected to treat his wife.'

Lord Rockland's love and concern for his child was enough to make Justin sick. 'No.'

'Perhaps if you were to speak to her, you might see how much you have in common?' Lord Rockland rose and strode to the door leading to an adjoining room and pulled it open. 'Susanna, please join us.'

'I'm afraid you're mistaken.' Justin stood. He had better things to do than sit here and humour this ridiculous idea.

Then, in a swish of silk skirts the young woman appeared and whatever it was he needed to do today was forgotten.

If Miss Lambert's eyes had captivated him in the dim light of the lanterns hanging from the trees above Vauxhall Gardens, in the sunlight, they blazed with a green which nearly knocked him out of his boots. She strode closer, sparing not a glance for her father, but focusing entirely on Justin. The rich chestnut hair framing her face bounced a touch with each step, making the soft ringlets graze the long line of her neck and high cheeks. He envied the curls, especially the one resting over the swell of her breast. The creaminess of her skin was just visible beneath the fine netting of her fichu while the rest of her supple roundness was covered by a brown-silk gown in a tone to match her hair. It heightened the colour of her skin with a warmth he longed to bury his face in and inhale.

Despite the allure of her full curves, it was her eyes which continued to command him. They were intelligent, quick, hiding her thoughts, but telling him they existed, and not one was concerned with the frippery of dresses or gossip. She was playing the demure, dutiful daughter for her father's sake, but Justin caught the steely resolve beneath the polished manners. It was the will of a woman with a plan she was as eager to implement as Justin was to establish his wine business. She'd been foolish last night, but Justin sensed it was a momentary weakness, like his proposal to Helena or the five pounds he'd spent on a bottle of wine last week, or what he was very near to agreeing to do.

He settled his shoulders, determined to resist the fleeting temptation of an attractive woman, confident she couldn't change his mind about this match, even if the part of him low down wanted her to win him over.

'I'll leave you two to discuss the matter,' Lord Rockland offered.

The duke's words broke the spell cast by Miss Lambert's eyes.

'And then cry foul once the two of us are left alone. No, thank you,' Justin protested.

It wasn't the first time a father had tried to get him alone with his daughter in an attempt to snare her a husband.

'I won't cry foul. She's been compromised enough already,' Lord Rockland flung off as he slid the doors closed behind him.

'Quite a charming father you have there,' Justin remarked.

Miss Lambert dropped her hands from where she'd been demurely holding them in front of her and rolled her pretty eyes. 'He's the envy of the *ton*.'

She walked over to the small selection of

drinks and picked up the brandy. She splashed a tiny drop into a glass, then tossed back the contents, shivering as it went down.

If this was meant to shock Justin it did, but there was something in the confidence of her movement, the surety with which she was executing what he felt was a clear plan, he had to admire.

'Shall I pour you some more?' she asked.

'No.' He needed a clear head for this encounter. 'I gather you're in favour of your father's suggestion.'

She set the glass down with a clunk. 'How very intuitive of you.'

'It's part of my job to guess what people will do before even they know. It helps me to avoid trouble.'

Her full lips turned down at the corners. 'I'm not the trouble my father has made me out to be if that's what's worrying you.'

'I'm not worried about anything, since I have no intention of marrying you.'

'But you will.' She crossed her arms under her breasts and the slight rise of the full mounds was distracting.

'I assure you, I won't.' Justin forced himself to focus, surprised by the ease with which Miss Lambert affected him.

'I don't think you fully comprehend the benefits of the agreement.' She rolled one graceful hand in the air between them, her nails short and neatly buffed.

'Oh, Miss Lambert, trust me, I understand very well the benefits.' He caressed her lithe body with his eyes, following the faint trace of a small waist and rounded hips beneath the flowing dress. He took the last fortifying sip of brandy to ease the heat rising inside him. He needed to reason with his brain, not his member.

She squared herself at him, sure in herself and her goal. Her confidence was currently her most appealing and annoying trait. 'I heard most of the conversation between you and my father. I know you think I don't want this marriage, but I do.'

'You don't even know me. For all you know I could be a drunk who likes to beat women.'

'You aren't such a man. You have too much integrity. If you didn't, you'd have accepted my father's offer without bothering to talk to me, set a date for the wedding and rushed through to the bedding as fast as possible.'

Justin tipped his empty glass to her. She was flattering him, a somewhat effective tactic. 'Perhaps, but even with you standing here demanding we wed I won't take you.'

'What if I could be of use to you?'

He winked at her. 'I don't need to be married for that.'

She frowned then, the small pursing of her lips as tempting as the subtle rise and fall of her chest.

'I mean in business. I can make my father increase his offer, especially since he's so eager to be rid of me.' A pain Justin recognised rippled through her eyes. She wasn't alone in enduring the condemnations of a demanding and stubborn father. Justin knew a little something about it, too. 'A word of support from him will have clients lining up at your door.'

'I'm aware of this, Miss Lambert, but it's not so much the clients I'm worried about as it is my wife.' He set his glass down. 'I don't want to look around one day and find you back in Lord Howsham's bed or in some other man's.'

For the first time since she'd entered the room her eyes dropped from his and a flush of red washed over her creamy skin. Her shame didn't last as she raised her head to meet his gaze again with a will as seductive as the faint scent of jasmine gracing her skin. 'I don't blame you for being suspicious of me and my motives, so I'll be as honest with you as you've been with me. I didn't run after Lord Howsham out of lust. I did it because I believed he'd offer me the things Lord Rockland never has, the freedom of my own home and a place as something more than a bastard. You're worried I'll chase after every lord who comes my way. The truth is I want nothing more to do with any of them, not even my father. If you agree to the marriage, I will maintain contact with my father in an effort to help you. I could be quite an asset to your wine business.'

'What do you know of trade, Miss Lambert?' She didn't look like one to sit behind a counter all day or wander through a cellar in search of a bottle.

'My mother's family owned a wine shop in Oxfordshire. I assure you, I didn't spend my girlhood learning to draw on plates, but to manage customers, inventory and accounts at my mother's side. She was an excellent negotiator. It's how she managed to extract Lord Rockland's promise to support me, even after she passed.' She swallowed hard. Justin pitied her and wanted to reach out and take her in his arms to soothe her. His grief for his own mother was as raw as hers, but he didn't move. 'I can garner for you the same type of deal.'

'Can you now?' She was certainly more experienced in the wine business than he'd imagined. He wondered what other surprising traits and talents she possessed.

She strolled over to him, allure and innocence wrapped up in the slow swing of her hips. 'Judging from your willingness to start your own business, you're a man not averse to taking risks. A betting man as some might say.'

'I've been known to wager from time to time.' Justin remained still, as intrigued by her offer as he was tempted by her full lips and what they would feel like beneath his.

'Then let me offer you one now. I'll prove to you today I can be an asset to both you and your potential venture. If you're suitably impressed, you'll agree to my father's offer.'

'And if I'm not?' He was ashamed to admit it, but she was already halfway to impressing him up the church aisle. However, he wasn't ready to tie himself to this strange woman, not yet.

'Then you're free to go. I'll leave the decision up to you.'

* * *

Susanna waited for the tall gentleman with the brown hair to answer, ignoring how her chest caught every time his amber eyes caressed the length of her body. Lord Howsham's hurried, fumbling touch hadn't made her insides melt as they were doing now with Mr Connor standing mere feet away. He smelled of leather, sawdust and musk, a more masculine scent than the lemongrass preferred by the society fops. It wrapped around her, drawing her to him until she almost forgot it was she who was here to win him over. She was close, her victory revealing itself in the hold of his eyes on hers and the twitch of his jaw above his cravat as he struggled between detached uninterest and desire. For all his rejection of the proposal, he wanted her as much as Lord Howsham had, only this man possessed the self-control to deny himself. She wished Lord Howsham had done the same and not pressed her into an intimacy she hadn't truly wanted. However, if he'd shown some restraint, she wouldn't be in this position, with her freedom only a conversation away. 'What do you say, Mr Connor? Are you willing to accept my challenge?'

He settled his muscled thighs covered by buckskin breeches against the edge of a small table and crossed his arms over his wide chest, his ease of manner both annoying and rousing. He reminded her of a tiger she'd once seen at the Tower lounging in the sun, relaxed but laced with an edge of danger one could almost touch. 'How do you know I won't simply say I will and then walk away?'

'Because you're the kind of man who keeps his word once it's given.'

He tilted his head in silent agreement. 'Are you the kind of lady who keeps hers?'

'I am.' She raised her chin, determined, in spite of the actions which had landed her in this muddle, to demonstrate her integrity. She might have made a drastic misstep with Lord Howsham, but she wasn't a woman to cuckold a man or break her vow once it was given. 'I promise you, when I change your mind, you won't regret it.'

He tossed a cocky smile at her which made her toes curl in her half-boots. 'No, I don't believe I will.'

She held out her hand to him. 'Then we have a deal?'

He eyed her fingers with the same amusement he'd demonstrated during their entire discussion. Embarrassment eroded her confidence as her hand hung in the air waiting for him to take it. For all his glib lightheartedness, she sensed the serious streak lying just beneath the humour. He was considering her offer and whether or not she was worth the risk. He wouldn't be the only one taking a chance with this challenge. She would be, too, but it was worth it if it meant ending her time with the Rocklands and escaping the taint of being a mistake and an unwanted intrusion.

At last he slid his hand in hers, his hold hot and hard. Her heart began to race and she took a deep breath to steady herself, willing her body not to tremble. If he experienced any measure of the heat sliding through her at the joining of their skin, he didn't reveal it, his eyes crinkling at the corners with an enticing smile. How the woman who'd leapt from his carriage last night could have walked away from such an alluring man Susanna didn't know, but she was thankful she had.

'We do.' He smiled with a wickedness to nearly make her faint. 'Now do your best.'

Reluctantly, she let go of his hand and strode to the double doors, struggling to make each step sure and to not peek back at him. It felt too much like something Edwina would do in the presence of the Earl of Rapping, gazing longingly at him from across the theatre, making a fool of herself as she all but drooled over a man who barely acknowledged her existence. The same couldn't be said for Mr Connor. Without turning she knew he watched her and it gave an even greater purpose to her goal. If she succeeded, there'd be no need for all this girlish mooning about. She'd have the rest of her life to stare at his sharp cheeks and strong nose. It wasn't an unpleasant thought.

She gripped the brass handles hard, as much to steady herself against Mr Connor's influence as to prepare to face her father, and opened the doors. Everything depended on the success of what she was about to do. 'Father, please return, we have a few more things to discuss.'

'You've both seen the sense in the proposal, then?' Lord Rockland asked as he returned, appearing quite pleased with himself.

'Not until you agree to raise the dowry to two thousand pounds.'

This startled her father out of his usual imperiousness. 'One thousand pounds is a very generous offer.'

Clearly he hadn't intended to engage in a negotiation, but to hand her over to Mr Connor with little trouble and no further thought. She wouldn't allow him to get off so easily. He was the man who'd helped make her a bastard, now he'd make her a legitimate woman, but not without some pain.

'One thousand, five hundred, and you'll purchase the wine for Lady Rockland's masque from Mr Connor and see to it we're both invited so Mr Connor may make the connections necessary to ensure the growth of his trade.'

'Lady Rockland will never allow such a thing,' her father scoffed and she wasn't sure which he dreaded most, his wife's wrath or the thought of connecting himself so publicly with his potential merchant son-in-law.

'If you agree to this, in writing, I'll marry Mr Connor and create no stir which might result in a scandal where Lord Howsham is concerned.'

Tense silence settled over the room as her father mulled through the points of her demands. She slid a glance at Mr Connor. If her negotiations couldn't open his eyes to the ben-

efit of having her as a wife and a partner in
his business, nothing could. His admiration for
what she'd done showed itself in the impressed
half-smile he offered her. Freedom was within
her grasp.

'All right, I'll do what you've asked.' Lord
Rockland looked to Mr Connor. 'Are these
terms amenable to you?'

She waited, hands tight at her sides for him
to answer. It wasn't so much the thought of
freedom which captured her now but the sun
from the window illuminating his hair and falling over the tan wool of the jacket covering the
width of his shoulders. She shivered a little at
the sight of him, tall, solid, a rock of a man
next to her father, yet with a humour to soften
his edges. She'd witnessed his strength last
night when he'd flattened Edgar, but he wasn't
all unthinking, uncompassionate brawn. When
her pain had welled up during their discussion,
sympathy had whispered through his eyes. For
reasons she couldn't explain, she knew he understood her loneliness, not in the mocking
way Lord Howsham had pretended to understand, but in the way of a man who had shared
something of the same kind of experience. If
they married, she would come to know both

the serious man and the one smiling at her father now, the one she desperately hoped would accept the offer.

'They are,' Mr Connor said at last. 'I will marry Miss Lambert.'

Susanna unclenched her hands, relief sweeping through her followed by a new anxiety that tightened her neck. Her course was set, for good or for bad. Mr Connor was right, she knew nothing about him, but he was now her intended and no matter what, she must make the best of things, although being with him would surely be better than staying here.

Mr Connor turned to her, gracious in his surrender. He reached for her hand, bending his tall frame as he slid his fingers beneath hers and brought them to his lips. He pressed the firmness of them against her skin, raising a chill which raced up her arm to crash inside her against the fire his gentle touch ignited. She'd never experienced such a reaction to a man and she rocked a touch before the squeeze of his fingers steadied her.

'I'll call for you later this afternoon for a carriage ride,' he offered, his breath whispering over the back of her hand.

'Please do.' She could barely utter the words

through the dryness in her mouth. It wasn't like her to want a man so powerfully, not after the awkward way Lord Howsham had introduced her to the physical side of love, but Mr Connor was no Lord Howsham. There was tenderness beneath his teasing, something she'd never experienced with the earl. This man wouldn't be rough with her. It would be smooth and easy like sliding into the warm water of a bath.

'Until this afternoon.' At last he released her and with reluctance she lowered her hand, wanting him to take her from this house now, tonight, so she could delight in the fire filling his eyes and the comfort of his good nature.

Mr Connor left with more confidence than he'd entered with, when she'd watched him through the crack in the door, listening eagerly for what he might say.

'Well, there's one matter resolved,' her father sighed with relief once they were alone. Then he turned to her, his expression clouding with the disapproval he'd meted out to her last night. 'Now you've accepted Mr Connor, there'll be no calling off the wedding, no matter what happens, or I'll cast you out of this house without a penny. Do you understand?'

'I do.' She stared at Mr Connor's empty

glass and the faint outline of his lips along the rim. In her desperation to escape the Rockland house, she'd misjudged Lord Howsham. She hoped she hadn't misjudged Mr Connor. If he proved even a tenth of the man she gauged him to be, he'd make a good husband. She'd do her best to deserve him and put all of the unfortunate incidents of the previous day, and her life, behind them.

Chapter Three

'Was your meeting with Lord Rockland a success?' Philip asked as Justin strode into his friend's study.

'You have no idea.' He explained to Philip the events of the interview. When he was done, he leaned back against the French door, feeling the sun warming his back through the glass. 'I suppose you think I'm crazy.'

'I'm the last person to judge a man for taking a wife so quickly, or for the most ephemeral of reasons,' Philip admitted from where he sat ramrod straight in the chair behind his desk. Philip had proposed to Mrs Rathbone after she'd held him at gunpoint demanding the return of some collateral. It'd been a strange start to a very successful marriage, one Justin hoped to emulate.

'Mr Connor, your father would like to see you in the morning room,' Chesterton, the Rathbones' butler, announced with more apology than efficiency. This wasn't the first time Justin's father had come here in search of him.

Justin looked at the liquor on the side table before eschewing the drink. Smelling alcohol on his breath would only give his father another reason to criticise him. 'I'll be back.'

He strode down the panelled hallway of the Rathbones' house which was situated in Bride Lane just off Fleet Street. Across the street, the bells of St Bride's church began to toll the noon hour. In a matter of days, he'd have his common licence and a date fixed at the church. It amazed him how the green-eyed hellcat had managed to snare him in a matter of minutes, though he'd rather be back with her than preparing to face the man pacing across the Rathbones' fine sitting-room rug.

Mr Green, the young man Justin paid to reside with his father and keep him out of trouble, sat on a bench near the front door. He jumped up at the sight of Justin. 'I'm sorry, Mr Connor, I tried to talk him out of it, but he insisted on coming here to see you.'

'It's all right, Mr Green. You do your best.'

Justin waved the young man back on to the bench. It was hard for anyone to deal with his father, much less dissuade him from any course, including ruin.

''Bout time you came to me,' his father grumbled as Justin approached. 'Thought I was going to have to wait here all day.'

'And a good afternoon to you, too, Father.' He should have taken the drink.

'I waited all morning for you to come and tell Mrs Green to stop shoving those damned tonics on me, but you never showed.'

His father's housekeeper was a saint for putting up with him, as was her son.

'I'm sorry I failed to arrive for our appointment. I was meeting with a young lady and her father to finalise the details of our engagement.' There was no other way to make the announcement except the direct one. His father wasn't one for polite conversation, though once he'd been charming and suave, able to talk a stranger into buying him a drink as well as putting down the pistol when he and the elder Mr Rathbone had arrived to collect a debt.

'Finally making that little widow your wife, heh?'

'No. She's accepted a proposal from another

man. I'm marrying Miss Susanna Lambert, the Duke of Rockland's illegitimate daughter.'

Shock lengthened the deep lines of his father's face before he drew them tight into his usual scowl. He marched up to Justin. He was a good head shorter than his son, but it didn't stop him from waving one thick finger in Justin's face.

'So a widow of your own class ain't enough for you—you want to raise yourself up. Think you're too important for your station and the life I've given you. Well, you aren't. Reach too high and you'll fall fast enough.'

'Your faith in me is astounding.' Justin laced his fingers behind his back. The insulting man was his father and he'd honour him, but no commandment could make him like him. The most he could do was tolerate him, much as he'd seen Miss Lambert tolerate her father. He'd admired and revered him once, but his father's acerbic tongue had killed those feelings ages ago.

'What have you ever done to give me faith in you except drink, lay about with easy widows and squander your money on ridiculous shipping schemes? How much of my blunt did you lose in that harebrained venture of yours?'

'Not one ha'penny. Now, as much as I'm enjoying this conversation, I must ask you to get to the point. Mr Rathbone and I have business to attend to this afternoon.'

'Well, la-de-da.' His father made a mock curtsy, his hands trembling as he held them out. It was lack of alcohol which made them shake, a situation he'd soon remedy. 'Knew sending you to school was a waste. I've come for money, since you think me too great a fool to manage it myself.'

Justin withdrew a few coins from his pocket and handed them to his father. He didn't bother to point out he was acting in his father's best interests. The older man wouldn't understand any more than he understood Justin's desire to emulate Philip and be more than another man's assistant.

'Taught ya' everything ya' know and this is how ya' repay me, handing out a pittance as if I was a child.' His father scowled as he plucked up the coins and shuffled into the hall. 'Come along, you,' he barked at Mr Green. 'No-good son of mine thinks he's better than his old father.'

A trail of mumbling curses followed him out

the door until Chesterton closed it and brought the noise to an end.

Justin turned his hand over, studying the dark bruises on his knuckles. He wasn't sure he should subject Miss Lambert to his father, but judging by the brief treatment he'd seen meted out to her by Lord Rockland, she more than anyone might sympathise with the necessity of managing a difficult relative.

'Is your father gone already?' Mrs Rathbone stepped into the sitting room, concern for Justin in her caring eyes. Her infant son slept on her shoulder, one small hand curled tight by his tiny mouth.

'Not even pleasant company with me could keep him from his other errands today,' Justin said glibly, hating to be pitied. This wasn't the first spat Mrs Rathbone had witnessed between father and son. They were a regular occurrence.

'You must recall the better times and ignore his taunts,' she urged, rubbing the sweet baby's back.

'I do.' He sighed out the lie, barely able to remember his father from before his mother's death. Afterwards, his father had turned to drink, growing more callous and quarrelsome with each passing year. It'd come to a head last summer when Justin had taken over the management of his father's finances after the older man had woken up in a ditch in Haymarket with no memory of the night before and a nasty bruise under one eye. His father had been so enamoured of his son's desire to help him, he'd turned on Justin like a wounded dog.

'I know he still loves you.' Mrs Rathbone laid an encouraging hand on his arm. 'But he has his demons to struggle with.'

'Don't we all?' Justin flashed Mrs Rathbone a wide smile, stamping down on the anger and pain chewing at him.

'On a happier note, I understand congratulations are in order.' Mrs Rathbone beamed as her son snored lightly.

'Indeed they are. I'm about to join you and Mr Rathbone in wedded bliss.' Although the idea he might not enjoy a union as happy as theirs taunted him. Hopefully, the force to be reckoned with he'd witnessed this morning wouldn't turn into a haranguing fishwife once they were married. He could only tolerate one person calling him a failure at a time.

Mrs Rathbone tapped a finger to her chin. 'I understand it was a most peculiar proposal.'

Justin matched her sideways smile with one of his own. 'It wouldn't be the first in this house now, would it?'

'Certainly not.' Mrs Rathbone laughed, the cheerful sound driving away the curses still ringing in his ears and making the baby let out a small cry before he settled back to sleep. 'I only hope Jane doesn't surprise us like that some day.'

'If our examples are anything to judge by, I wouldn't be surprised if she did.' Jane, Philip's fourteen-year-old sister whom he had raised since their mother's death, was too precocious and sure of herself for her own good, just like her brother.

Philip stepped into the room, dressed in his redingote and carrying his walking stick. 'Shall we be off?'

'We shall.' A vintner had fled back to France to avoid repaying a loan. They were going to seize his stock, the wine which Justin would purchase from Philip and use to establish the business his father and Helena had so callously dismissed.

'Be careful,' Mrs Rathbone cautioned, squeezing Philip's arm.

'I always am.' Philip laid a kiss on his son's

little forehead. Then he pressed his lips to his wife's, in no obligatory peck, but a deep meaningful kiss. Philip, the most rational man Justin knew, had raced headlong into his union and all had been well. Hopefully, Justin would enjoy the same luck in his hastily negotiated engagement.

Chesterton handed Justin his gloves and he tugged them on. He flexed his fingers beneath the supple leather and pushed away the memory of Miss Lambert's hand in his. She'd transfixed him as much with her ability to bargain as with her presence and the faint catch of her breath when they'd touched. As much as he enjoyed the charms of women, they usually didn't have such power to sway him. If they had, he'd have failed to seize half the collateral from Philip's clients. Yet with a few glances from beneath her dark eyelashes, and a walk to mesmerise him, she'd wrangled him into one of the most binding contracts he'd ever entered into. He looked forward to discovering more of her hidden charms.

He tapped the pistol in the leather holster beneath his coat, the agitation biting at him fuelled by more than the task facing him and Philip. He didn't usually relish the physical aspects of his position as Philip's assistant, but today he wouldn't mind if a man took a swing at him and he could swing back. It would take a row, or an hour at his pugilist club, to work off the frustration from his encounter with his father, and the more pleasant tension roused by Miss Lambert.

He followed Philip to the waiting carriage, ready to be done with business and enjoy his drive with Miss Lambert. He wished to discuss with her tonight the vintner's inventory and his plans for it. She'd wrestled a duke for his support of Justin's venture while his own father and previous paramour had dismissed it. If nothing else, it was a positive omen for what their future life together might entail. She'd share his success and he would succeed, despite what anyone else believed.

'I think French silk would be beautiful for the dress,' Mrs Fairley, the young modiste, suggested as she draped a sample of the fine cream-coloured fabric over Susanna's shoulder.

'English silk will do,' Lady Rockland barked from her place on the sofa where she watched the fitting. Lady Rockland had grudgingly summoned the modiste at Lord Rockland's command to discuss Susanna's wedding dress and a suitable costume for the masked ball. If only he'd ordered her to be pleasant. 'The future wife of a merchant won't need such an expensive gown.'

'Yes, Your Grace.' Mrs Fairley folded the sample and laid it with the others in her case. Lady Rockland hired Mrs Fairley to dress Susanna while she and Edwina patronised a much more fashionable and expensive French modiste.

Susanna exchanged an awkward glance with the comely Mrs Fairley, who blushed on her behalf. It wasn't the first time the kind young woman had witnessed this sort of conversation, but it would be the last. Even if Susanna's desire for freedom had made her misjudge Mr Connor, surely the life of a merchant's wife must be better than a duke's unwanted bastard daughter.

'I don't see why you're buying her a new dress for her marriage when one of her old ones will do for a wine merchant.' Edwina, Susanna's half-sister, selected another sweet from the box on her lap and popped it into her round mouth.

'He won't even be a merchant until he's received your father's money,' Lady Rockland was kind enough to point out, looking down her nose at a man she hadn't even met who probably had more honour in his right hand than she possessed in her entire stick-thin body.

'Then why are they coming to the masque?' Edwina whined, her exasperation as annoying as the way she chewed her sweet. 'We've invited no other common people.'

'It doesn't matter if they come. Everyone will be wearing masks—no one will recognise them anyway,' Lady Rockland explained, as though Susanna were not standing in her suddenly too-tight stays and chemise right in front of them.

'I hear Cynthia Colchester is going to have the finest French silk gown and a ceremony in St George's in Hanover Square.' Edwina licked the tips of her fingers with a smacking noise before smiling smugly at Susanna.

'She's having it because her family can afford it, unlike her husband-to-be. Lord Howsham is up to his neck in gambling debts and on the verge of losing his estate.' Susanna bit down on her irritation at her half-sister. It was she and not Lord Howsham who'd gained the most from him breaking his promise. He'd wanted her money; now he had someone else's.

'He still has his title, as does his wife, which is more than some people possess.' Edwina smirked, her pudgy face squishing up with her arrogance.

'Edwina, leave us,' Lady Rockland commanded.

'Whatever for?' Edwina rubbed a bit of marchpane from her cheek.

'Don't question me,' the duchess snapped.

Edwina, who was only one year younger than Susanna's twenty, stomped from the room like a toddler.

Lady Rockland didn't dismiss Mrs Fairley, who knelt on the floor packing up her box. The woman was too far beneath Lady Rockland's notice for her to believe whatever she was about to say needed to be kept from her.

Susanna prepared herself, imagining this exchange would be no more pleasant than any of their previous encounters. Her expectations weren't disappointed.

'Given your behaviour with Lord Howsham, I assume I needn't tell you what will pass between you and your husband on your wedding night,' Lady Rockland blurted out with all the concern of a fish.

Mrs Fairley paused in her packing before returning to her work.

'My mother was kind enough to explain it to me when I was thirteen, before she died,' Susanna answered, the idea of this woman acting in any kind of motherly way as revolting as her haughty attitude.

'Yet another of the many mistakes she made in regards to you, mistakes others are now forced to endure.' Lady Rockland screwed up her face as if smelling something foul. 'When you and Mr Connor are wed, and after the masque, don't think you'll be allowed back into this house. I've endured the shadow of Lord Rockland's marital weakness and been forced to parade it in front of all of society for the past seven years. I won't do it any longer.'

'You needn't worry. I won't pollute myself with the taint of society by coming back here as a married woman.'

The duchess's lips drew back across her teeth. 'Oh, you'll come crawling back eventually. Men of Mr Connor's class never forget where they can obtain money, but you've both

got all you're going to get out of Lord Rockland. I'll see to it you don't get a shilling more.'

Her imperious dictate given, Lady Rockland
gathered up the hem of her skirt and swept
from the room.

Susanna let out a low, frustrated sigh. If she
could pack up her things and make for Scot-
land tonight. she would, but Mr Connor had
been guaranteed her father's help and she'd
make sure the duke kept his word. Then she'd
do everything she could to help Mr Connor
succeed and prove Lady Rockland's nasty pre-
diction wrong. She only needed to bear this
a little while longer, then she'd be free of the
woman for good.

'Congratulations on your engagement,' Mrs
Fairley offered as she rose. 'Did Lady Rockland say you were to marry a Mr Connor?'

'I am.'

'Is he the associate of Mr Rathbone, the
moneylender?'

'I believe so.' They hadn't discussed many
details of their lives and, in fact, she knew very
little about him except for his ambition in the
wine trade and his willingness to accept a deal
on which both of their futures hinged.

'I'm familiar with the man and his employer

and they're both very honourable gentlemen.' She picked up her case, holding it in front of her. 'You'll be very happy with him.'

'Thank you. I'd like to retain your services, if I can, when I leave here.'

'I should like that.' With a polite curtsy which made her light-gold curls bob, Mrs Fairley took her leave.

Susanna slipped on her banyan and began to pace. It boded well that Mrs Fairley thought highly of Mr Connor. During the fittings in which Lady Rockland had been absent, Susanna had shared many confidences with the young woman who understood as well as Susanna what it was like to be looked down on by a duchess. The modiste was the closest person to a friend Susanna possessed. Lady Rockland had seen to it there were no other people on whom Susanna could hang the title.

Despite the fact she'd lived with the Rocklands since her mother's death, they'd only grudgingly treated her as a member of the family within their home. Outside of it, she was virtually ignored. At the few teas or country parties she'd been allowed to attend, the duchess had always given her strict instructions to keep her mouth shut and make herself as invisible as possible. It wasn't the most ideal way to forge friendships with other young ladies, though most daughters of the other country families didn't deign to talk to her. They were too afraid the taint of bastard would rub off on them to attempt so much as a discussion of the weather with Susanna.

She went to the wardrobe and began to rifle through her dresses, looking for one to wear for tonight's ride, as eager to see Mr Connor as she was to escape this house for an hour or two. She'd thought of little besides him since he'd taken his leave this morning, and had eaten even less at nuncheon than she'd been able to choke down over the last two weeks. It wasn't just his commanding presence or the deep roll of his voice, which was both powerful and playful, but what the agreement they'd entered into meant. She'd be his wife, his property as much as a helpmate in his business.

Her body would be his, though she doubted he'd fall on her as Lord Howsham had done in the forest at Rockland Place. There'd been something distasteful in Lord Howsham's pressing need for intimacy and the speed with which he'd slaked his lust and left her confused and wanting. Mr Connor wouldn't rush through the bedding; she'd felt it in the smooth slide of his hand beneath hers, the gentle pause when his lips had met the back of her hand and the drawing humour in his eyes which had invited her, instead of forcing her, to think of what was to come.

She clutched the dress to her chest, shivering at the idea of his broad chest and flat stomach against her skin, wondering what it would be like to linger with him in the dark, the sheets tangled around them as their bodies melded together. Though there was more to a marriage than the bedchamber to consider. The hours between rising and sleep were long ones in which a man could ignore his wife, much as Lord Rockland did to his, giving rise to a bitterness of spirit Susanna had felt the brunt of many times.

She sagged down onto the edge of her bed, releasing her tight grip on the muslin. With any luck, the isolation she'd known at Lady Rockland's hands and the indifference of her father were about to end, assuming Susanna hadn't made a grave mistake. Even if she'd chosen poorly and Mr Connor turned into a monster, she'd have to stand beside him at the altar or find herself penniless on the London streets.

Rising, she rang the bell for her lady's maid, ready to dress and face her intended. This wasn't a poor choice, but the best she could make. She'd have a home of her own and a respectable husband and at last a station in society where people couldn't look down on her or whisper behind her back. She'd already proven to Mr Connor she could be useful to him and had gained something of his admiration. If he never grew to love her, or even cherish her, she'd at least earn his respect. It was the most a bastard like her could hope for in a marriage. If something more came of their union, it would be a gift of providence, although providence had never been so generous to her before.

Chapter Four

'I believe you have no more business here with the family, sir.' The balding butler looked down his crooked nose at Justin as though he'd been discovered sleeping on the Duke of Rockland's front step. Apparently, between this morning and this afternoon, the family had failed to inform the man of Justin's change in status or his appointment to ride with Miss Lambert.

'Miss Lambert is expecting me.' He tried to step around the lanky man who shuffled to stay in front of him. This wasn't the first time a servant had tried to rebuff him at the front door. Usually it meant their master was slipping out the back with the best of his goods, where Justin's men were sure to be waiting for him.

'Let him in, Netley. Mr Connor and Miss Lambert are engaged.' Lady Rockland's voice slid out from behind her dedicated servant, the announcement made with as much enthusiasm as if Justin had arrived to clean the chimneys.

Netley offered no congratulations, but grudgingly stepped aside to allow Justin entrance.

Justin dismissed the overly pompous fop whose pedigree was probably no better than his and approached the duchess. She stood on the landing in the middle of the grand marble staircase like a crow on a gable, her dark dress as thin as the risers were high. 'Your Grace.'

He swept off his hat and bent into a deep, well-executed bow. When he straightened, she arched one eyebrow at him, betraying her surprise at his manners. More than likely she'd expected to find a lout with the grease of his cart and the smell of fish clinging to his coat. Ah, the better sort were such a charming lot. 'I've come to take Miss Lambert for a drive.'

The woman's gaze shifted from Justin to the large windows on either side of the door. Outside sat Philip's curricle with the hood down, the chestnut horse pulling it held by a well-tipped boy. There was nothing about the vehicle to bring down the tone of the house or the occupants. Again Lady Rockland's eyebrow twitched and Justin wondered if she'd swoon from the shock of having her lowered expectations so utterly confounded. An examination of the tall woman with the rigid back, square chin set in a long face and hair arranged in tight rows of curls against the front of her head told him she wasn't a swooner, but a silent striker. Like a snake, this lady would take a quick bite, then slither off to let her wounded victim suffer a slow death. A most charming woman.

'Good afternoon, Mr Connor.' A more melodious voice carried over the crow's stony silence as Miss Lambert came down the stairs. The pale blue muslin swung about her thighs as she moved and the pastel colour heightened the subtle hue kissing her cheeks. Pert breasts gave shape to the fitted bodice of a matching blue spencer which was cut away at the chest before dipping in to fasten just under those tantalisingly full mounds. Elegance marked her movements, but something of Lady Rockland's lineage was missing, betraying a childhood spent among more humble people, her airs and graces learned too late to make them completely natural. Still they captivated Justin, weaving a spell around him which took away his speech and all awareness of Lady Rockland eyeing him as though he were a rat about to be smacked with a broom.

'Miss Lambert.' Justin bowed again, but more shallowly this time, unwilling to cease watching her.

She paused and reached for the banister as if to brace herself before she pulled back her hand and resumed her steady descent. With each drop to the next step, the curls along the arch of her neck just peeking out from beneath her bonnet shivered and he flexed his fingers, envious of the way the locks brushed her smooth skin.

Lady Rockland was not so enamoured of her ward's regal entrance and scowled at her as Miss Lambert passed by on the way down. Miss Lambert met the woman's contemptuous sneer with a challenging glance of her own. To Justin's astonishment, it was the duchess who flinched first.

Justin nodded his silent congratulations to Miss Lambert. She lifted her chin a touch, taking on an air of confidence, but the shift of her green eyes betrayed the vulnerability he'd caught in his conversation with her earlier. In a flash, compassion rose up to overwhelm his desire. He'd been like her once, trying to appear brave while struggling to stand firm against those who wanted to tear him down, especially his father.

'Shall we?' Justin proffered his elbow when she reached him.

'Please.' Miss Lambert laid a gloved hand on his arm, the expectation in her wide eyes helping him to dismiss his sour memories. He'd learned long ago to laugh and not care what others thought.

'Try not to embarrass the family while you're out,' Lady Rockland warned as she snatched up the edge of her skirt, flung it behind her and flitted off to whatever business consumed her day.

'I'm sorry,' Susanna mumbled, the excitement fading from her bright eyes as they left the house. The door nearly slammed shut behind them, Netley clearly as eager as his employer to see the back of them.

'Don't be. It's not your fault her curls are too tight.'

Miss Lambert hid a subdued laugh behind one gloved hand and Justin was heartened by the return of her cheer. Whatever her treatment at the Rocklands' hands, it hadn't destroyed her spirit, or her sense of humour. It would be an interesting challenge to draw it out fully, as intriguing as the promise of her alluring curves beneath the straight dress.

The sunshine piercing the trees along the front path spread over Susanna, melting away the chill of the Rockland house. Despite having more fireplaces than servants, the stone mausoleum was never warm and neither was the company it kept. In the fresh air, Susanna felt as if she could breathe at long last, though Mr Connor's arm beneath her hand and his tall figure beside her made each breath shallow and unsteady.

'Lady Rockland is quite the charming lady,' Mr Connor remarked as he helped Susanna into the vehicle.

She gripped his hand tightly, more to steady herself from the surprise rocking of her body in his presence than at the twitching springs of the chaise. 'She was practically polite today, though once we're wed, I don't think we'll have many dealings with her.'

If it wasn't for the promise she'd extracted from her father to help Mr Connor, she doubted she'd ever see her father again after the wedding. It wouldn't surprise her. Her grandfather and uncle had breathed a sigh of relief when Lord Rockland had arrived to take her away the day after her mother's funeral. They'd washed their hands of her, just as Lady Rockland would. Susanna didn't give a fig about the duchess, but her grandfather and uncle's utter rejection, after she'd been raised in their presence, had nearly shattered her already mourning heart.

'I assume, then, we won't have to entertain august guests at Christmas?' Mr Connor climbed in beside her, raising her mood despite the old pain biting at her. It felt good to laugh with someone who wasn't afraid to poke fun at her dour relations. It was a refreshing change to the parade of sycophants who usually wandered into the house.

'I don't think we'll tarnish our dining room with their company.'

'Good, because I hadn't intended on purchasing a new dinner service this year.'

He winked at her, then snapped the reins over the horse's back, urging the fine animal into motion. While he focused on the traffic filling the street, she studied him. A fawn-coloured coat and matching hat set off those teasing brown eyes which had nearly made her stumble on the marble staircase. However, it was the approving nod he'd tossed at her when she'd silently challenged Lady Rockland's sneer which had filled her with more delight than the sight of his light grey breeches stretching over his strapping thighs. This near-stranger had supported her more in one moment than anyone had in the seven years she'd lived with the Rocklands. She drew her spencer a little tighter over her chest, chilled to realise how narrowly she'd missed being tethered to Lord Howsham, who held as little regard for her as anyone else in her life. The promise of freedom from the Rocklands must have been overwhelming to make Susanna ignore all of Lord Howsham's faults. Hopefully, it wasn't blinding her to Mr Connor's.

'Speaking of dining, my friends, the Rathbones, have offered to host the wedding breakfast. We're to join them for supper tomorrow night. They're eager to meet you.'

'I'd be delighted to meet them.' And nervous. As much as society looked down on her, those of the class she'd been born to were usually more vocal in their disapproval of her. For Justin's sake, she hoped his friends would at least be grudgingly cordial and save their most cutting remarks for after she left. It didn't matter what they said about her behind her back. She was used to the whispering and it had lost most of its sting long ago.

'They aren't the only ones I intend to introduce you to before the wedding.' He shifted his feet against the boards and for the first time in their brief acquaintance, she suspected he might be nervous. It didn't seem possible, and yet if she were permitted to wager on it, she felt sure she would win. 'I'd like to introduce you to my father.'

She wondered what it was about his father that disturbed his ease, though she could well imagine. There was little chance of mentioning anyone in her family without it setting her teeth on edge. 'I'd be honoured to meet him. I'm curious about the man who's given you your jovial attitude.'

'It wasn't him. That came from my mother. She died when I was fifteen and my father's good nature died with her.' The small lines between his eyes deepened with a pensiveness she hadn't thought possible as he explained how he'd gained control of his father's affairs and how ungrateful his father had been afterwards.

Then the story ended and with it Justin's

seriousness, which was replaced by a devil-may-care attitude which piqued her curiosity. To all, it appeared as if he didn't possess a single concern, but no amount of flippancy could completely conceal how deeply his father troubled him, or the hole his mother's death had left in his life. She knew about such grief; she still lived with it, too. 'You'll see what an amiable fellow my father is when you meet him. Prepare to be charmed. He's more Lady Rockland than Father Christmas and I won't be shocked if he makes you cry off.'

Her hands curled tight over the edge of the seat as he merged the curricle into the crush on Park Lane. 'I won't cry off and you needn't worry about me meeting your father. I'm used to dealing with difficult relations, Mr Connor.'

'I'm glad to hear it because I need you.' He slowed the horse as they made a wide turn on to Kensington Gore. 'And please, call me Justin. Mr Connor reminds me too much of my father.'

'And you may call me Susanna.'

He slid her a charming smile. 'A pretty name for a pretty woman.'

His compliment shocked her, adding to her

alarm as he turned the curricle into Rotten Row. 'No, we can't go in there.'

'Why not? You're a duke's daughter. I thought the toffs loved to see the high born's progeny paraded about.'

If it weren't for the boning in her too-tight stays, she'd have slumped with her displeasure. 'Not the illegitimate ones, at least not without his Grace present to keep the daughters' tongues firmly in their heads.'

His curricle joined the stream of carriages entering the park and driving down the wide, dirt path. Mr Connor sat up straighter in the seat, motioning at her to do the same, seemingly oblivious to everything but the direction of his horse and the ribbons in his wide gloved hands.

Susanna tugged her small hat a little further down over her forehead, wishing the brim curled like a poke bonnet instead of up to reveal her face. At least then she might tilt her head and hide behind the straw.

'If you continue to pull on your bonnet, you'll tear it,' Mr Connor chided her good-naturedly.

She let go of the brim. 'We shouldn't be here. People are staring.'

She had no desire to be made a spectacle of, especially not with Edgar riding by and scowling at them as though they were beggars who'd happened in on his supper and didn't belong here. She didn't. She didn't belong anywhere.

'I'm not surprised since I'm alongside the most beautiful woman in the park.'

Her heart fluttered at the compliment. It wasn't flung off or studied as Lord Howsham's flattery had been when he'd worked to seduce a naive young woman starving for attention.

Then four young married women passed by in a landau, gaping wide-eyed at her before dipping their heads together to whisper.

'Ignore them. They mean nothing to us,' Justin instructed.

'Then why are we here?'

'I want you to enlighten me about these people. I know many wealthy merchants. It's my acquaintance with the better sort which is lacking.'

'I'm not sure what I can tell you. I don't really know them any better than you do.' Invitations weren't regularly extended to bastards, no matter how influential their father.

'I'll wager when you're sitting silently in your fearsome stepmother's midst, she talks past you to her husband, or her friends as if you weren't there. During those conversations, some interesting things must slip out.'

'Careful, you lost our last wager,' she warned with a smile.

'I don't see it as a loss, but a very interesting gain.' He turned the horse to avoid an oncoming phaeton with its hood open and its springs strained by the very rotund Lord Pallston.

'I thought these people meant nothing to us,' she challenged.

'Their sensibilities don't, but their business does. If I can claim one or two great men as clients, it might ensure our success.' It surprised her how easily *our*, instead of *mine*, rolled off his tongue. 'Now tell me, who's the round gentleman driving the phaeton as ruddy as his nose? He looks like a man whose thirst could make a wine merchant rich.'

'I thought you already possessed means.'

'I used to possess a great deal more before my last venture sank.' The humour in his eyes hardened, telling her all she needed to know about his last attempt at business. It was admirable of him to keep trying, despite what must have been a considerable setback, and it was more than those around them were capable of doing. It was another trait she and Justin shared—the ability to pick themselves up and continue on. The alternative was too upsetting to consider.

'He won't make you rich. He's Lord Pallston and he doesn't pay his debts. Few of these great men do. They pride themselves on owing almost every merchant in London.'

Justin rubbed his chin thoughtfully. 'I know something of collecting debt. I haven't let a man run out on Mr Rathbone yet.'

'It's not worth the effort or the uncertainty. My grandfather was foolish enough to deal with men like Lord Pallston. All they did was drink the wine while we watched our dinners grow thinner and the bills go unpaid.' She hated to disappoint Justin's ambition, but if the business was to be hers, too, she knew better than to build their hopes for success on the fickleness or insolvency of the peerage. A need for money often played a part in all these people's decisions, including Lord Howsham's, whose debt was about to consume his family estate. She hoped it did. He deserved to be ruined.

Susanna warning him off pursuing the nobility as clients wasn't what Justin wanted to hear. If the voice saying it wasn't so sweet he might have disregarded it, but he understood her reasoning. Philip employed the same logic, rarely lending to great men. When he did, it was only after they'd laid out the silver for Philip to hold until their debt was paid. Justin wasn't likely to convince any lord to leave a soup tureen as collateral for wine, not when there were a hundred other merchants willing to risk bankruptcy to supply a peer with his Madeira. He'd planned on using Lord Rockland's influence to bolster his name and perhaps even match Berry Bros. in their success. Now it was clear this part of his business plan might not work as he'd expected.

With one avenue to expand his trade quickly narrowing, the idea he might not succeed in this venture as his father and Helena believed drifted over him like the faint notes of Susanna's jasmine perfume, only rather less pleasant. He flicked the reins and guided the horse past a lumbering town coach. No, he would succeed and damn his father and Helena. Justin's desire to capture the business of the *haut ton* through Susanna might come to nothing, but it didn't mean he didn't have more plans or other possible clients. There wasn't a pub owner or merchant near Fleet Street he hadn't had some dealings with and most of them were pleasant. He'd make a go of this if he had to call on every man who owed him a favour from here to Cheapside.

'Does your grandfather still have his shop?' Justin asked with some hope for his own venture. It might be good to have contacts outside London.

'I don't know, though if he and my uncle were on the verge of sinking, I'm sure they'd deign to write to me begging for money, and to remind me how much I owe them for all of their years of *kindness*. They'll get nothing if they ever show up on my doorstep.'

'They sound as warm as mounting blocks.' Justin laughed.

'Just like the Rocklands.' She sighed.

'I'm curious—why did Lord Rockland take you in instead of placing you with another family?' He pulled on one rein to make the horse turn at the end of the row. 'I have a difficult time believing Lady Rockland was amenable to the idea.'

'I've never really asked.' She shrugged. 'Out of gallantry, perhaps, or a desire to prove he's so far above everyone else he can claim paternity to any child he's sired no matter how much it irritates his wife or shocks his peers.'

'I imagine Grosvenor Square was alight with other grand ladies warning their husbands not to follow Lord Rockland's lead.'

'And children of questionable parentage all over London breathed a sigh of relief at not being thrust into this world, always hovering on the fringes, a lady and yet not a lady, a duke's daughter and his bastard all at the same time.'

'You aren't to refer to yourself in such a way. Do you understand?' He refused to hear her speak so meanly of herself.

'But it's what I am and how everyone here and in Oxfordshire has always seen me.' Her green eyes clouded with a loneliness he understood. He knew what it was like to be derided by those who should care for you the most. 'It's how Lord Howsham viewed me.'

'Hang Lord Howsham and all these idiots. It's not how I see you or how I want you to view yourself. You're my affianced and very soon to be my wife, a respectable woman who no one has the right to look down on.'

She tugged at the bonnet ribbons beneath

her pert chin. 'About Lord Howsham. I think I should explain.'

'No, I don't want to know. Neither of our past amours interest me.' He gathered her time with the earl hadn't been good and, despite never having met the man, Justin wanted to pound his face for the insults he'd heaped upon Susanna. How he could have abandoned such a woman, especially after the promises he'd made, he didn't know. It didn't bode well for his honour, or that of any other man of his class.

Justin settled his shoulders and his hackles, allowing the more pleasant sensation rising beneath to come over him. He wished he had a man to drive them so he could sit with Susanna and bask in her intelligent eyes and the way she admired him with respect and interest no other woman had ever shown.

If they weren't sitting in view of all of Hyde Park, he'd lean across the bench, take her parted lips with his and shock everyone passing in their carriages. He was tempted to bring the curricle to a halt near the line of trees, place his hands around her trim waist to help her down, and then feel the curve of her breasts against his chest as he led her behind a tree while he freed her hair from the bonnet. It was a giddy, boyish desire, one she'd sparked the moment she'd appeared at the top of the stairs. He hadn't experienced a craving like this since his youth and it filled him with an anticipation he'd never known with a woman before, one he wasn't about to act on.

Soon she'd be his wife and they'd be free to take their pleasure at their ease. He'd make her sigh with passion instead of sadness. She wasn't a jaded widow or spurned paramour, but a lonely woman in need of affection. He'd see to it she had what she needed both in body and spirit. He looked forward to drawing out the bold woman who'd faced him yesterday, instead of the unsure, hesitant one sitting beside him today.

Susanna stared out at the passing carriages, thankful Justin didn't intend to press her or judge her for her mistake with Lord Howsham. Justin's lack of interest in the matter wiped the slate clean. If only she could brush away the nasty chalk marks of her illegitimacy and the way it tainted her in the eyes of everyone riding past. Justin might urge her to think more of herself, but after a lifetime of being reminded of a sin of which she was not guilty, she couldn't simply put it aside. The taint was too much a part of her, like her hair colour or eyes, although perhaps in time, with his help she could forget it.

She slipped Justin a curious look, admiring how straight he sat on the seat, the edge of a smile drawing up the corners of his mouth until it seemed he might whistle in delight. Despite his joy, he wasn't some silly lout with more fluff than brains, or a thug for his employer who thought of nothing more than his own pleasure. There was a depth to him she'd caught earlier in the mention of his father, and again just now, a sense of honour and loyalty to those in his charge, including her.

'When do you think we'll wed?' She was eager for the date to be set and the vows to be spoken, suddenly afraid something would rise up to take this opportunity and the happiness it offered away from her.

'Eager for the wedding night, are we?' His subtle, teasing words curled around her and sparked an excitement deep inside her she hadn't experienced since the time she'd stood alone in the woods with Lord Howsham. With the earl there'd been an edge of uncertainty and danger. With Justin, it was like craving the cool rush of water over burning skin on a hot day. It made her bold and she tilted her head, eyeing him through her lashes.

'Among other things.'

'Such as?' He glanced at her from beneath the shadow of his hat and she licked her lips. She *was* eager for the wedding night, though she didn't want to appear like some hussy and admit it, not in the middle of Rotten Row.

'Having my own house,' she announced wistfully. 'It'll be nice to belong somewhere instead of being made to feel as if I'm some unwanted guest by the Rocklands, and even by my mother's family.'

The admission itself shamed her as much as the ease with which she'd made it. It wasn't like her to air her grief because there was never anyone there to listen, or to care, but something about Justin made it difficult for her to be reserved.

'You'll never be unwanted at my house, though it isn't as grand as your father's.'

'It could be a hovel for all I care.'

'It's not quite so humble.' He laughed, his good mood lifting hers. 'But it needs a woman's touch.'

'I don't wish to intrude on your space.' Outside of the colour Lady Rockland and Edwina's rooms were painted, her father had rarely allowed Lady Rockland any say in the decor or even the management of the four houses he owned. It was another of the many things which stuck in the woman's craw and increased her bitterness.

'Intrude all you want, except in my study.' He slowed the horse as they made a turn, his mastery of the ribbons as appealing as his confidence in the seat and his openness with her. 'A man has to have his space, just as you'll have a room of your own to do with what you please. I want you to be happy with me and for us to work together in both our home and the business.'

'Thank you.' She settled her hands in her lap, fingering the fine embroidery on the back of her glove. Of all the things she must soon become accustomed to, his concern for her, not just his physical desire, would be the most difficult. She would offer him the same regard, although it wouldn't come as easily to her as it did to him. She'd spent so many years hardening herself against attacks, it was difficult to imagine letting down her guard enough to trust another person with her life and possibly her heart, but she must. He offered her a future free of guilt and derision, a future she never could have imagined before today. She would do everything she could to be worthy of it and embrace the life he promised her.

Darkness began to settle over the city as Justin strolled with Philip through the warehouse set on the banks of the Thames. They examined the casks and bottles they'd seized from the vintner earlier in the day. There hadn't been time before Justin's appointment with Susanna for them to take stock of what was about to become Justin's first inventory. Mr Tenor walked behind them, listening and observing as always. Before Justin's ship had faltered, he'd been training Mr Tenor to take his place as Philip's assistant, much to the elder Mr Connor's grief. Justin's father had served the elder Mr Rathbone faithfully, prospering under the family as Justin had done, but Justin wanted more for himself and some day his own son. However, judging by the quality of the casks, it would be a while before Mr Tenor received his promotion.

'The vintages aren't as good as I'd hoped.'

Justin frowned as he held up the lantern to read a label. When the vintner had run off to escape his debt, he must have taken the best of his stock with him.

'There are a few fine ones here.' Philip examined the bottles packed in straw in a crate. 'They should turn a nice profit.'

'Not as nice as I'd like. I can sell the rest to public houses and a few merchants of less discerning taste.' It wouldn't bring in the money he needed. Those funds would come from Lord Rockland's order for the masque and whatever other great men's wishes Justin could fulfil. Despite Susanna's wariness about cultivating some of the peerage's patronage, he hadn't given up entirely on the idea.

'When I have the shop, I'll have you transfer these to it,' he instructed Mr Tenor.

'Yes, sir,' the brawny man answered, scratching at the holster and pistol under his thick arm.

Justin looked over the casks. To his amazement, he was more excited for his upcoming nuptials than this first foray into his new venture. The afternoon with Susanna had been far more pleasant than he'd expected, her humour and plain speaking as charming as it was captivating. He wished he hadn't needed to cut their drive short, but there was as much business to see to as pleasure. Very soon there'd be a wonderful meeting of both.

'When will you have the building?' Philip asked as they stepped out into the misty night and Mr Tenor locked up the warehouse.

'In a few days.' With it would go the last of the money the sea hadn't claimed. If he couldn't make a go of the business, he could sell the building, hopefully at a profit. If his losses were too large, he'd be forced to continue in Philip's employ. It had taken a great deal for Justin to swallow his pride and apply to his friend when failure had beset him the last time. It wasn't an option he wished to entertain now, no matter how much he admired Philip.

'Do you need any assistance?' Philip asked tactfully as they strolled to the waiting carriage. Mr Tenor fell back to the cart where the other men who worked for Philip transferring goods stood smoking pipes and chatting.

Justin rested his hands on his hips and pushed back the edges of his coat, revealing the butt of the pistol in its holster beneath the wool. Though Philip would never allow him to fall into debtors' prison, or worse, Justin wanted to be his own man and emulate his friend's success through his own efforts. 'You helped me enough the last time and lost a pretty penny in the bargain. I won't put your money at risk again.'

Nor would he risk Susanna's dowry until it was absolutely necessary. He wouldn't use it to fund his business, but keep the money safe. It would be a hedge against his losses, protection against total ruin in case nature decided to flatten his business with a grape blight or a sudden fire. Remaining on land was no guarantee one wouldn't be sunk.

'Bastard, you ruined me.' A man's voice rang out from the deep shadows between the buildings.

They whirled to see a man rushing at them, pistol raised. His face was black with grime and his long hair reached down to touch the dirty red soldier's coat with its black shoulder boards.

Justin stepped in between his unarmed friend and the man, brandishing his weapon. 'Move an inch closer and I'll take the top of your head off.'

The man jerked to a halt, fear widening his

eyes. Justin recognised him as a bookseller who'd used Philip's loan for drink instead of paying off his debt and whose business had failed last year. He'd since accepted the king's shilling to feed himself and apparently to buy more gin. Justin could smell it over the stench of the river.

'I'll kill you both for what you did to me.' The man kept the pistol aimed at them, refusing to back down, too drunk to be afraid.

'Drop your weapon and walk away and we'll all forget this ever happened,' Justin suggested, not wanting trouble with either this man or the constable.

'Not until you've paid for ruining me.'

Justin squeezed the trigger of his gun. In an explosion of smoke and noise the ball fired, skimming the man's shoulder and tearing off one black shoulder board, but leaving him unscathed.

The man's face went white in the moonlight as he pressed his free hand to the hole in his uniform, amazed to find himself unharmed.

'You missed,' he jeered with a high, nervous laugh.

'I hit exactly what I aimed for and it wasn't your head,' Justin corrected as he exchanged his empty pistol for Mr Tenor's loaded one and levelled it at the man. 'Now, I'm aiming at your forehead. Put your weapon down, or I'll put a ball through it.'

The man blanched and the end of his pistol began to shake. Justin tightened his grip on his weapon, afraid the man's fear would trigger his gun. He'd drop the man with a shot before risking it if he didn't surrender soon.

At last, reason seemed to overcome the bookseller's muddled senses and he threw the pistol down and bolted into the darkness.

'Should we go after him, sir?' Mr Tenor asked.

'No, he won't be back.' Experience told him when a man had been scared off his taste for revenge. He lowered his weapon and strolled over to snatch up the pistol from the puddle it'd fallen into. Shaking off the water, he handed it to Mr Tenor. 'Unload it, then give it to one of the men.'

'Yes, sir.'

Without a word, Justin and Philip made for the carriage. Once they were inside, the driver set the vehicle in motion.

'Thank you again,' Philip said across the

semi-darkness, his voice as even as ever though a certain strain lingered in his tone.

It was always a challenge to shake off the anxiety after an incident, but it'd never clung to either of them quite like this before. Usually Justin would make a joke or comment to break the tension, but nothing came to him tonight. It wasn't just his future wrapped up in this kind of encounter now, but Susanna's, too. Once they were married, he couldn't be so casual about being on the wrong end of a pistol.

'How do you handle it, now you have a wife?' Justin asked.

'I've surrounded myself with exceptional people. You'll do the same in your business.'

Justin pressed his fist to his chin and stared out of the window as the warehouses along the Thames gave way to the dark shops and houses. One of those bow-front windows glittering with wares would soon be his and it couldn't come too soon. The risks of working for Philip had never troubled him before, not even when he'd been a child. His mother had always been stoic in her support of his father, never fretting whenever he was called away to assist the elder Mr Rathbone. Her bravery had fed Justin's and he'd carried it with him when doing his duty. Now he was about to be wed, it seemed an altogether different matter.

He fingered the smooth handle of the pistol beneath his coat. He shouldn't fret about his position like an old lady, not when the risk of childbirth was greater to a woman's life than an unhinged client. He knew more women, including his mother and Philip's first wife, who'd perished in their travails than he did men who'd been brought down by a man's misplaced anger at the moneylender. Still, the threat he'd encountered tonight, for the first time ever, gave him more encouragement to do well than his desire to prove he could manage a business of his own. In a few days, Susanna's livelihood would rely on his success and he didn't wish to leave his wife and whatever children they had alone. She'd agreed to stand beside him for better or for worse. He'd make sure it was better.

Chapter Five

'How exciting to be dining with Mr Connor and his friends,' Mary, Susanna and Edwina's shared lady's maid, gushed while helping Susanna into her emerald-green silk evening dress. Lady Rockland refused to hire a lady's maid for only Susanna and in a small way she was glad. She'd soon be able to don her clothing without another woman fluttering around her, returning to the days when she was quite capable of dressing herself.

'Yes, very exciting,' Susanna lied, too cautious around Mary to express her concerns as she sometimes did with Mrs Fairley. The young woman with the button nose was more relaxed and open in Susanna's presence than she ever was with Edwina. However, Susanna was never quite sure how much of what she said remained with cheerful young Mary and how much was repeated to the woman's demanding employer.

'The bodice is a little tight, miss,' the maid said as she tugged it flat against Susanna's breasts in order to do up the buttons along the back. 'You must be enjoying too much of the good London food.'

'Nonsense, I've hardly eaten these past few weeks.' There'd been too much for Susanna to worry about with her secret relationship with Lord Howsham, and then Mr Connor. The anxiety had curdled her stomach every morning until she could barely stand the smell of eggs and ham. 'You must not have tied the stays tight enough. Try them again.'

'Yes, miss.' The maid began undoing the buttons and Susanna took a deep breath as the dress dropped away from her body and she stepped out of it. The comfort was short-lived as the maid began to tighten the stays and the cotton and boning pressing against Susanna's breasts made them sting. She rubbed her chest, surprised at the tenderness. It must mean her courses were coming on for her breasts were always sensitive when they arrived, though they'd never been quite so sore.

'There we are, now let's try the dress again.' Mary helped Susanna step into the dress, then raised it over her hips to settle it against her bust.

Susanna turned so the young woman could do up the buttons and it was then she noticed Lady Rockland watching from the doorway. How long had she been standing there, hand on the doorknob, dark brows knitted tight together as she watched the maid struggle to do up the dress.

'How does it feel now, miss?' the maid asked, oblivious to the observing duchess.

'Much better.' Though it didn't fit as well as it had when she'd last worn it in the country a few weeks ago.

'It must have been the stays, then,' Mary concurred.

'Yes, I'm sure you're right,' Susanna said more to Lady Rockland than to the maid, afraid the ill fit of the gown might reflect poorly on Mrs Fairley's skills. While Susanna doubted the imperious woman would send so much as her lady's maid to the blonde modiste after Susanna left, she hated to think of the young woman with the kind eyes missing out on any work. As the daughter of those in trade, she knew how important each order was, especially those such as the Rocklands', which tended to be large.

'Mary, go and see to Edwina,' Lady Rockland commanded and the girl scurried away.

Lady Rockland strode into the room. Her dress hung like mourning crepe on her shoulders and increased the sternness of the dark ringlets arranged over the top of her head. 'You were feeling ill at breakfast this morning, and most of last week.'

'As any woman so close to marriage might be expected to feel,' Susanna asserted. Lady Rockland was probably worried Susanna would take ill and never leave the Rockland house. Even if she were on her death bed, Susanna would find a way to make it down the aisle and away from these people for good.

Lady Rockland came to stand incredibly close to her, far closer than she'd ever stood before, but Susanna didn't move back. She met the duchess's dark eyes as she always did, but this time Lady Rockland wasn't cowed. 'I hope you didn't do anything to jeopardise the wedding, for if you throw off this suitor, you'll be tossed in the gutter where you belong.'

Susanna said nothing about Lord Rockland

having already made such a threat. She didn't want Lady Rockland to learn she and her husband were, for the first time ever, in agreement about Susanna's future. The woman was tiresome in her hate. 'I assure you the wedding will take place as soon as possible and you may have the pleasure of watching me wed.'

'I don't think it necessary for either Lord Rockland or myself to attend such an event.'

Susanna remained firm in front of the woman, despite her sagging spirits, and was relieved when Lady Rockland at last flounced away. For all the gold in England Susanna wouldn't have her stepmother at the wedding, but the girlish part of her which still craved her father's affection wilted. He wouldn't be there to give her away. He'd already done so the morning Mr Connor had accepted the offer and made his proposal.

Augusta marched down the hall to her husband's room. She barged in without knocking, coming upon the duke in his breeches and waistcoat as he held out one hand to the valet who fastened his cufflinks.

She fixed hard eyes on the skinny valet. 'Get out.'

Without a word, Rawlings made a hasty retreat.

'What is it now, Augusta?' Horace drawled, as he finished fastening his cufflink.

'That brat of yours is with child.' Augusta stormed up to her husband, explaining about the tight dress, Susanna's lack of appetite and her suspicions. 'I should have known she'd do something like this, the little whore.'

'What does it matter if she's expecting?' He took up his coat and slid his long arms through the sleeves. 'She'll be married in a few days and the child will be Mr Connor's to deal with. No one will be the wiser.'

'What about her lady's maid? She might suspect something and then how long will it be until the cheap woman tells every maid in Grosvenor Square? It'll taint Edwina. People already wonder why she wasn't married last Season. You never should have brought Susanna to us in the first place.'

'If you'd spent more time worrying about Edwina and less time concerning yourself with Susanna, you might have succeeded in marrying her off.' Horace tugged his cuffs out from beneath the jacket sleeves.

'I've done my best.' Failure struck Augusta, bruising her pride more than any motherly sense of duty. She wasn't blind to her overweight daughter's lack of grace and elegance, but she hated to be reminded of it every time Susanna entered a room and fixed her with those hateful green eyes, Horace's eyes. The morning Augusta's mother had informed her of her own arranged marriage, she'd known Horace's heart wasn't part of the contract, but she'd expected his respect. He'd denied her even that courtesy and there was nothing she could do about it.

'Then do better.' Horace rolled his chin over his collar, straightening the cravat, his signet ring glinting in the candlelight. 'I want Edwina well settled by the end of this Season or you'll have more to worry about than any rumours surrounding Susanna. Do I make myself clear?'

'Yes.' Augusta bit back a more forceful retort. If Horace failed to take her concerns about Susanna seriously, there was nothing she could do, overtly at least. After many years, she'd learned to accomplish a great deal in more subtle and effective ways.

'Good, then send Rawlings back in. I'm expected at my club,'

'We wouldn't want you to be late for your club.' She snorted, knowing very well Horace wasn't going to White's but to Drury Lane to fawn over his actress mistress. At least in this affair he was maintaining some discretion, but if he got this mistress with child, Augusta would insist on a separation before she allowed the filthy little mongrel into her house. She'd borne enough embarrassment among her friends and society because of Susanna. She wasn't about to endure more.

There seemed little difference between Fleet Street and Oxfordshire except for the number of establishments crammed together, their bow-front windows displaying all the items available inside. Were Susanna allowed to, she would have gladly walked through this neighbourhood to the Rathbones' house. She felt more at home among these shops than in any of the ballrooms or salons she'd been forced to accompany Edwina to in the more fashionable district of Mayfair. Instead, she remained in the Rockland town coach, the one without the duke's arms, noting as another person on the street outside paused in the stocking of their cart to admire the maroon coach lumbering by. From inside, Susanna met their eyes, catching a sense of their curiosity as they wondered which grand lady had dared to venture into this section of London.

She was nobody and she settled back against the squabs, giddy to know she'd soon be allowed to travel these streets like a common woman once again. It would be a relief to return to the world in which she'd been raised. Whether these people would accept her remained to be seen. In Oxfordshire, the butchers and grocers had looked down their noses at her for being born without benefit of a marriage ceremony, reserving their greatest disdain for her mother, who had held her head up proudly at her daughter's accomplishments instead of shrinking away with her shame. She wondered if Justin's friends would treat her the same way. He might not wish her to refer to herself as a bastard, but it wouldn't stop anyone else from flinging the word at her.

Worry over what awaited her at the Rathbones' made her stomach tighten, but she took a deep breath, forcing herself to relax. Given the generous way Justin treated her, it was difficult to imagine his friends behaving so meanly, or him tolerating any snide comments, especially after his insistence no one would look down on her. It still baffled her how a near-stranger could regard her with more care and concern than either of her natural families ever had. It wasn't the money making him attentive. She'd seen too many titled but poor men offer only the faintest attention to their wealthy intendeds to think money could make a man love a woman. With Justin, his concern was a genuine part of his character, one which urged her to reveal more to him in their brief time together than she'd told to any of the Rocklands in the years she'd lived with them. She trusted him not to hurt her and he really wanted to know about her.

His interest, and her willingness to confide in him, didn't scare her as much as the plan to become Lady Howsham had. It'd kept her awake the entire night before Vauxhall Gardens. When she'd lain awake thinking of Justin last night, it certainly wasn't worry which had warmed her body, or made her dream of his hands upon her skin. She wanted to see him tonight, to be beside him and indulge in the deep tones of his voice and the power of him beside her.

It was the memory of him smiling at her which strengthened her courage as the carriage turned on to Bride Lane. The old stone church sat on one side, towering over the line of houses and shops on the other and throwing them deep into shadow as it blocked the light from the setting sun. The carriage rocked to a halt in front of a plain but stately home in the centre of the terrace. A moment later, the door opened and Susanna took the footman's hand and stepped down from the coach. It was a peaceful place, with the noise from nearby Fleet Street fading in the rustle of the large trees in the churchyard.

'Shall I escort you to the door, miss?' the footman asked, eyeing their surroundings as if unable to believe it was so genteel and no footpads were lurking nearby to attack her.

'No, I'll be quite fine on my own.'

She moved up the path to the house, eager to leave behind the trappings of her father's status and embrace again the simplicity of the merchant's life, assuming the Rathbones were welcoming. She still had no idea what to expect.

What she didn't expect was for the front door to open and a young woman with auburn hair a few years older than herself to appear in the frame. Not once did her lively hazel eyes flicker to the carriage to gape at it as her grandfather had done the morning it'd pulled to a stop in front of his shop. To this woman it seemed not to exist; only Susanna mattered.

'You must be Miss Lambert. We've been expecting you. I'm Mrs Rathbone. Welcome and congratulations.'

She pulled Susanna into a sweet hug. Susanna stiffened before at last relaxing enough to awkwardly return the greeting. She barely received any acknowledgement at home. She wasn't accustomed to so much affection from a stranger.

'Mr Connor has told us all about you.' Mrs Rathbone held her at arm's length. 'You don't know how surprised we were by your and Mr Connor's engagement.'

Susanna eyed her warily, wondering just how much the woman knew about everything, including Lord Howsham. 'Yes, it was most unexpected.'

'As was mine to Mr Rathbone.' She linked her arm through Susanna's as though they'd been fast friends for years and guided her into the house. While the butler helped Susanna out of her pelisse, she took in the simple yet elegant entrance hall. The Rathbones' wealth was evident in the high polish of the panelling on the walls and the quality of the furniture, although it lacked the ostentatious gilding and overwrought ornamentation the duke and those of his station favoured.

From a door along the side of the hall Justin emerged, accompanied by a tall, slender gentleman with a boy of about two perched on one hip.

Susanna saw only Justin and her feet nearly carried her to him before she restrained herself. The desire to be near him startled her. During her unfortunate yet brief time with Lord Howsham, it had been the freedom he'd offered which had filled her with yearning, never truly him. It was different with Justin. His sweep of her figure with his eyes, the glance both fiery and impressed, and the broad smile which softened the square set of his jaw and lit up his expression called to her more than any promise of a future. His wide chest practically demanded she wrap her arms around his waist and lay her head on his tan coat, the hue of which nearly matched his copper-coloured eyes. She craved the weight of his arms around her and the steady sound of his heart beating beneath her ear. She hadn't expected to feel such a powerful reaction to a man she barely knew, but in all the uncertainty of her life he was in a very short amount of time becoming something very secure.

'Good evening, Miss Lambert, and welcome to our home. I'm Mr Rathbone.' The tall gentleman came forward, his face more severe than Justin's, but with a friendliness which eased his sternness. 'And this is my son, Thomas.'

The boy resembled his father, with dark hair and a watchful expression which took in everyone while he sucked on two fingers.

'Good evening,' Susanna answered with a curtsy, but her attention flicked back to Justin as he approached.

'I see you made it in one piece,' he joked, coming to stand before her as Mr and Mrs Rathbone kissed the boy goodnight and gave him to the nurse to lead upstairs.

'I did, though I'm sure my father's driver was worried we'd be robbed by ruffians once we turned off Fleet Street. He hasn't ventured much further than Hyde Park.'

'Of course he has, he's been with his lordship to Drury Lane,' Justin countered.

'Why would he be in Drury Lane?' A young lady with Mr Rathbone's eyes and something of his stance asked, coming to join them in the entrance hall. Susanna was eager to know the reason, too, though she could well guess.

'There's a certain actress there the duke—' Justin began before a matron who reminded Susanna a little of her mother stepped up behind the young lady and shot Justin a silencing, yet mirthful glare.

'You shouldn't speak of such things in front of Miss Rathbone, or Miss Lambert,' she chided, wrapping her arm around her young charge's shoulders.

Mr Rathbone introduced the young lady as Miss Jane Rathbone, his younger sister. The matron was Mrs Townsend, Mrs Rathbone's mother and Miss Jane's companion.

'I'll be sure to send out some food and drink to the driver for his troubles. Since he may be bringing you into this part of town for the wedding, we want to be in his good graces,' Mr Rathbone announced as he wrapped his arm about Mrs Rathbone's waist. Their unashamed intimacy was touching.

Lord Rockland didn't offer his wife affection in public and, judging by the woman's sour nature, not in private either. Growing up, Susanna had never had a father to show tenderness to her mother. She'd once caught her grandfather hugging her grandmother in the garden behind the house. He'd even smiled at the small bent little woman who had been his wife. The brief moment was the single time Susanna remembered seeing her grandfather happy. What little love and good nature he'd possessed had been buried with her grandmother.

Susanna's throat constricted at the memory of her grandmother's lavender-scented cotton dress. She'd been the only person in the house who'd cherished Susanna as much as her mother had. She used to wrap her gnarled arms around Susanna to comfort her after the village children had taunted her. They were the only warm memories Susanna possessed besides those of her mother holding her, or reading to her at night before she fell asleep. All too soon her grandmother had passed away and a few years later her mother had followed, death stealing from Susanna what little love she'd ever experienced.

Swallowing past the lump in her throat, she looked to Justin. As if sensing her pain, he took her hand.

'Are you well?' he asked with concern.

'Perfectly.' She smiled, hoping with all her being he'd prove to be as caring as his tight clasp of her hand promised.

'Dinner is served,' the butler announced.

It was then Susanna realised everyone was watching them. She tried to let go of Justin but he held her tight. She wondered what everyone thought of her being so bold, but there was no hint of judgement in their eyes. It was as suprising as her hope for Justin's affection.

'Shall we?' Justin shifted her hand to his arm, his solidness beneath her palm settling her remaining worries.

'Please.' These were good people, worthy of being his friends and she would come to know and appreciate them as much as he did.

He led her down the hall behind the Rathbones, as comfortable here as if it were his own home. She possessed little idea of what his abode looked like. Surely it was nothing like this one with its richly panelled walls leading down the hall past an orderly study. Inside, French doors opened out on to a garden where pink, red and white roses bounced on their bushes in the breeze. The company turned left away from the cheerful beauty and into the dining room across the way.

'You'll be sure to tell me about the duke and Drury Lane later, won't you, Mrs Townsend?' Miss Rathbone pleaded in much too loud a whisper from behind them.

'Of course, but not in front of your brother or our guest,' Mrs Townsend answered and the two of them indulged in a conspiratorial giggle before quieting to take their places at the mahogany table.

The dining room proved as refined yet understated as the rest of the house. Blue paper covered the walls, the colour bright with the light of the candles in their elegant silver holders in the centre of the table. On the polished surface sat a set of china, stemware and silver fine enough to make even Lady Rockland take notice.

To Susanna's pleasure, she found herself seated between Mrs Rathbone and Justin, with Mr Rathbone at the head of the table and Mrs Townsend and Miss Jane across from her.

The conversation didn't wane as dinner began and Susanna marvelled at the convivial atmosphere. Here, the knives and forks didn't clank against the plates to echo off the plaster-work, and the sound of chewing didn't replace the conversations as it did in the Rocklands' town house.

'Miss Lambert, Mr Connor was telling us your family is in the wine trade?' Mrs Rath-bone asked with genuine interest. There was no hint of condemnation or criticism in her question.

'In Oxfordshire. My grandfather provides most of the dons and too many of the students at the university with their fare.' It was how Lord Rockland had met her mother, but she didn't say it, not wanting to remind them of her illegitimate status and risk losing their good favour. Though she doubted these friendly people, who probably already knew most of her background and still welcomed her at their table, would be so mean. They didn't strike her as petty like the Rocklands, who tore down even those they considered their great-est friends when they troubled themselves to speak during meals.

'How do you find the wine?' Justin asked as

some topic of Miss Rathbone's choosing drew the attention of the others away from Justin and Susanna.

Susanna took up her goblet and tilted it to her lips. The fine vintage slid across her tongue, smooth and easy, unlike the old swill her grandfather used to sell to the students. She peered at Justin from over the top of the crystal, his interest making her take her time, sensing it was more than waiting for her opinion which kept him enthralled.

At last she set the glass down. 'It's excellent.'

'I chose it.' Justin's already formidable chest swelled beneath his fitted coat. The flickering candlelight caressed his face and danced in his eyes, revealing the small dark flecks mixed with the copper of his irises.

She touched the rim of the crystal goblet. 'If this is the measure of your tastes, then you possess a bright future as a merchant.'

'It's my goal to impress in this...' he lowered his voice and leaned in closer to her, his breath against her cheek as intoxicating as the spirits '...and all other matters.'

She didn't blush, but answered him with lowered lids and the tilt of her head, as though teasing and inviting him all at once. 'I have no doubt you'll succeed.'

The look in his darkened eyes nearly melted her already heated insides. 'I appreciate your faith in me.'

She licked her lips, wondering if he would taste as heady as the wine. 'It's well deserved.'

'Good.' He set his wine glass on the table, the red sparkling like one of Lady Rockland's grand rubies. 'I've secured the common licence and spoken to Reverend Clare at St Bride's. He's prepared to perform the service on Monday morning. Lord Rockland and I are meeting the day after tomorrow with his solicitor to ensure everything in regards to your dowry is in order.'

Susanna touched her napkin to the corners of her lips, trying to maintain some control over her excitement. In three days she'd be free of the Rocklands, and her time with Justin would become much more intimate. She crossed her ankles beneath the table, wishing the ceremony was tomorrow. 'It sounds perfect.'

'Indeed, it does.' He slipped his fingers beneath her palm where it rested on her thigh. The subtle stroke grazed the top of her leg, teasing the skin beneath her skirts. She drew in a deep breath, making her breasts swell against the tight stays holding them and drawing his eyes down for the quickest of moments before they rose to hold hers.

'I must make sure Mrs Fairley is done with my dress,' she stammered, though at the moment, she'd walk down the aisle in her chemise if it meant marrying him and—to her shock— reaching the bridal chamber faster.

'I'm sure she'll be done in time,' Mrs Rathbone assured her, overhearing the conversation. 'She's had practice at doing up a wedding dress in a hurry. She did mine and it was excellent.'

Susanna reluctantly let go of Justin, remembering her place as both the Rathbones' guest and an unmarried woman who shouldn't be touching a man. She should have known better, but under Justin's tempting spell, she'd forgotten herself and where she was.

'She does all of our clothes,' Miss Jane added, as though this alone was enough to recommend the young modiste.

'Mrs Rathbone, you said you and your husband had an interesting courtship?' Susanna asked, her curiosity and the amiable atmosphere making her as bold as Jane.

'Oh, very interesting.' Mrs Rathbone exchanged a conspiratorial glance with her husband, bringing a sly smile to the man's lips and easing the strict set of his features.

Susanna listened in amazement as Mrs Rathbone described how, after she'd threatened Mr Rathbone with a pistol, he'd made a proposal a day later. She'd accepted him on his odd terms and had come to live here with her mother. She went on to explain how her mother, having been a draper's wife, now acted as Miss Jane's tutor, teaching the young girl all she'd need to know to some day become a prosperous merchant's wife, or perhaps the wife of a fellow moneylender's son. These things were told to her as if she deserved to know them because she belonged here and was one of their friends. It was a great pleasure for Susanna to not be judged in their midst, and if her bodice wasn't so tight, she'd have sighed with relief. Instead she listened and chatted and ate, admiring Justin and the small arch of bronze hair curving over his smooth forehead.

'Do you like being a duke's daughter?' Miss Jane bluntly asked.

'Miss Jane, such a question isn't appropriate,' Mrs Townsend gently corrected, although she tilted her head at Susanna as though waiting for her to respond, her curiosity as great as her young charge's.

'It's tiresome,' Susanna answered, wondering what the girl thought when she didn't regale her with magical stories of balls and masks.

Miss Rathbone, proving herself as sensible as her brother, merely nodded, then speared a piece of meat with her fork. 'I thought as much.'

Her curiosity satisfied, she didn't press Susanna further on the subject and she was glad. She wanted to be here with them tonight, not pulled into memories of the shivering loneliness waiting for her when she left this jovial family.

All too soon dinner ended and Susanna expected to follow the ladies into the sitting room and leave the men to their port. To her surprise, Mrs Rathbone didn't rise and it was Jane who dictated the course of the evening.

'Mr Connor, you must show Miss Lambert the roses. They're in full bloom now and quite beautiful.'

'Miss Rathbone and my mother are very proud of the garden,' Mrs Rathbone added, seeming to encourage the idea instead of rebuking the young lady for speaking out of turn as Lady Rockland would have done. 'You must see them.'

'And we will.' Justin rose from his place, as ready as Susanna for them to be alone. What the Rathbones thought of their eagerness to depart to the darkness of the garden, Susanna couldn't say. Given Mrs Rathbone's tale about her introduction to Mr Rathbone, Susanna doubted anyone here would criticise her too harshly for slipping away with Justin.

She laid her napkin beside her plate and rose as Justin slid the chair out from beneath her. He offered her his arm and she took it, following him through the dining room and across the hall into the well-ordered office. Given the masculine furniture and the way not one item appeared out of place, she guessed this was Mr Rathbone's domain.

'Your friends are very kind and welcoming,' she complimented. 'Have you known Mr Rathbone long?'

'I grew up with him. He's like a brother to me.'

She released Justin's arm as he stepped forward to open the French doors. The night air poured in, the heady scent of the roses mixing with the mist of the evening to cover the more pungent smells from the surrounding streets. The dark green leaves of the rose bushes shimmered with the orange light spilling out from the house. Susanna moved past Justin to the nearest rose bush. Taking one full flower in her hand, she dipped her nose down to the centre to inhale its sweet fragrance.

'They remind me of my grandmother's garden behind the shop in Oxfordshire.' Her voice caught in her throat. Too many memories danced in the scent.

Justin said nothing, but stood close beside her listening, the faint moonlight playing along the edges of his shoulders.

'Wildflowers used to bloom there, too, in the spring and she tended them as lovingly as she did her roses, until she died.' She let go of the flower and it bobbed back up to join the others, knocking a few petals off the fading bloom above it. 'Afterwards, I tried to maintain the bushes and the pretty little blossoms, but the work of the wine shop and my grandfather's demands took up most of my time.

Eventually the plants withered. The last time I saw the garden there was nothing but weeds and dandelions.'

Tears stung the corners of her eyes. It'd been years since she'd spoken to anyone of her grandmother, or even her mother.

'My mother loved roses, too. When she was alive, she used to help Philip's mother in this garden since she didn't have one of her own.' Justin took her hand, offering her a comfort the painful memories and years of loneliness had denied her. She stroked the back of his hand with her fingers. Like her, he'd experienced the sharp edge of loss. Unlike her, it hadn't stolen his humour. 'She would have liked you—you have her spirited nature.'

'My mother would have liked you, too. She enjoyed laughing as much as you do. It was the only merriment I ever enjoyed in my grandfather's dour house.'

'My mother and Mrs Rathbone used to get up to all sorts of things here. They might have married serious men, but they both had a wicked sense of humour.'

She offered him a wry smile, thankful he wasn't allowing her to wallow in her grief. 'It explains a great deal about you.'

'And probably Philip.'

'If Mr Rathbone is such a great friend, why do you wish to leave his employment?' Susanna asked, eager to change the subject. Justin was her future and she didn't want the past to drag at her or sour her happiness.

Justin plucked a petal off the bloom and turned it over to examine the slight darkness on the underside. 'If I was content to remain a humble man like my father, to stick to the station in life I was born to as he thinks I should, I'd gladly spend the rest of my days in Philip's employment. But I want to be something more than a hired man and achieve my own success.'

'Your father doesn't approve of your efforts?'

'He hasn't been my most ardent supporter.' He flung the petal away, darkness clouding his eyes at the mention of his father, just as it had yesterday in the curricle.

It made her realise why he insisted she see herself in a better light than everyone else did He was forced to do it, too. They weren't so very different from one another and he, more than anyone else, might understand what she'd struggled against all her life.

'I'm glad you're defying him and I envy

you. I've only ever been the disgraced daughter of a disgraced daughter, someone who belongs neither in a merchant's shop nor a duke's home. They've never seen me, who I am, what I'm capable of. I want to prove to all those people who thought I was nothing better than a little whore, destined to follow her mother into ruin, that I'm so much more.'

'You will.' He brought her hand up to his chest, his fingers entwining with hers. 'We both will.'

With a small tug he drew her closer, then let go of her hands to allow them to lie on the fine wool covering his shoulders. The heat of him wasn't lessened by his clothes or hers and her tender breasts tingled under the pressure of his chest against hers. Lower down, the firmness of him sent a primal shiver racing through her as his large hand touched the small of her back and pressed her closer. She tilted her head and closed her eyes as he brought his face near to hers. The tang of his breath mixing with the heady aroma of the roses made her knees weak and she parted her lips, waiting, wanting and wondering why he hadn't kissed her.

She opened her eyes to see his head tilted to one side, his eyes fixed on the upper storey of the house as though he were listening for something. She followed his gaze, catching a small shadow at one of the windows overlooking the garden.

'The curious Miss Rathbone is watching us.' Releasing her, he caught her hand and pulled her under the small portico off the office.

They slipped into the deep shadow in the corner, where the privacy was made more complete by the large bushes growing in front of this dark, tucked-away spot. Justin turned her, placing himself between her and any curious eyes from the garden or the house. Slight panic welled up inside her. She'd been alone like this with Lord Howsham and the thrill had quickly turned to anxiety and then regret. She shifted on her feet, unsure if she should stay or flee.

'What's wrong?' he asked, his voice a near whisper in the darkness as his hand on her back eased, placing a slight distance between them. 'We can go back inside, if you'd like.'

In the comfort of Justin's embrace, the tenderness with which he held her close banished her fears. He wouldn't treat her so roughly, not tonight or any of the many to follow. 'No, I'm fine.'

She laced her fingers behind his neck and drew him down to her. He caught her lips with his, the moist heat of his mouth against hers making her quiver. Beyond the walls of the garden, a horse whinnied in the mews and the roll of carriage wheels and the call of a driver carried over the house from the street at the front. The sounds faded beneath the beat of her heart in her ears as Justin savoured her mouth. There was more in his kiss than simple lust for their coming wedding night. There was understanding, as deep as the caresses of his tongue, as firm as the press of his fingers against her back. In the brief time she'd been with him he'd shown her a glimpse of her future with him and she was eager to rush to it, though he asked no more of her tonight than kisses. In his restraint, this son of a simple man was proving himself more of a gentleman than Lord Howsham had ever been.

Twining her hands in his hair, she longed to convey to him not only her gratitude but her belief in him and their future together. With him she would enjoy true affection and the companionship of someone more like her than anyone she'd ever known before. The lonely days which had marked her life would end and she'd at last be with someone who cared.

The soft whisper of slippers over the portico stone slid in beneath the rapid beating of her heart. The subtle sound warned her to pull away, but she couldn't. She didn't want to be separated from Justin, to leave this bliss and return to the uncertain world waiting for her, the one where promises were easily broken, affection withheld instead of given and almost anything might come to snatch away her future.

'Mr Connor, are you out here?' Mrs Rathbone's clear voice carried over the night, but there was no missing the note of anxiety in her words.

Was she worried she and Justin were setting a bad example for Miss Rathbone? Had she come here to chastise them for acting like a common street whore and her client? Susanna's heart fluttered with worry. She wanted these people's respect and friendship, not their contempt. If Justin was concerned he didn't show it as he dropped a quick kiss on the tip of her nose, then released her and turned around, his wide body shielding her from Mrs Rathbone's sight.

'Yes, Mrs Rathbone?' he asked with more amusement than embarrassment, making the effortless transition from ardent suitor to deferential employee faster than lightning.

Susanna remained behind him, glad for the shadows, for they hid the blush singeing her cheeks. Here she was wishing for people to think more of her and she was acting like a tart.

'I don't mean to interrupt you,' Mrs Rathbone said with strained amusement, 'but your father is here.'

Justin marched with Susanna to the sitting room, opening and closing his free hand in frustration as he prepared to exchange her soft sighs for the old man's tiresome insults. Mr Green offered him an apologetic nod from where he stood just outside the sitting room. Inside, Justin's father paced back and forth across the carpet, his hands trembling at his sides, his grey hair in disarray, his hat having been discarded on a chair near the fireplace. The felt appeared as rumpled and worn as the old man.

Shaking off the last of the desire which had been doused by his father's arrival, Justin entered the room, his hand tightening over Susanna's when she tried to remove it. Despite what he'd told her of his father yesterday, there was no preparing her for what was sure to be an uncomfortable encounter. Perhaps in the presence of a stranger his father might show some restraint, though he doubted it. The old man would snarl and bite like a badger no matter what Justin did. Susanna had said she was used to dealing with difficult relations—it was time to test her skill, and Justin's.

'Good evening, Father.'

Mr Connor jerked to a halt and turned hard eyes on Justin. 'About time you showed up. Do you enjoy making me crawl and bow before you like some kind of prince?'

Justin exchanged a 'See what I mean?' look with Susanna. 'Father, allow me to introduce you to my fiancée, Miss Susanna Lambert.'

She stiffened beside him and he offered her a slight apologetic shrug. It was best to do this quickly. There was no way to ease her gently into an acquaintance with her future father-in-law.

His father's rheumy eyes jerked up and down Susanna before his lip curled with the usual look of disgust he always wore when it

came to anything concerning Justin. It hadn't
always been like this. Justin could still remember a time when his father had smiled at him,
then thumped him on the back in proud congratulations.

'Mrs Gammon would've been more use to
you than this hothouse flower. Though I suppose this one brought you money. Not sure
what else she could do except warm yer bed.'

Justin moved to respond, refusing to let his
father insult Susanna, but her restraining hand
on his chest kept him still, for the moment.

'This hothouse flower has spent a great deal
of time behind a counter, keeping accounts
and managing inventory. I assure you I won't
wilt under work,' Susanna shot back, refusing
to shrink from Mr Connor's frank appraisal.

Justin was impressed, but not surprised.
Judging from all she'd told him of the Rocklands and her childhood, this wasn't the first
time she'd faced a grouchy old man with a few
insults on his tongue.

Mr Connor's bushy eyebrows rose in surprise and his lips worked to answer, but no
response seemed to come to him. Frustrated
in his efforts to insult Susanna, he turned his
wrath on his favourite subject, his son.

'I've come for me money,' he snapped, then held out his hands to Susanna as though pleading with her for sympathy. 'Look at me, forced by my son to beg like some kind of common street urchin. Would you allow such a thing, Miss Lambert?'

'If it were in a gentleman's best interest for someone else to handle his affairs, then, yes, I would.' Her polite but firm opinion of the situation impressed Justin, but not his father.

'Well, look at the bastard putting on airs,' the old man mocked and no feminine hand could restrain Justin this time.

He grabbed his father by the arm and pulled him into the hall. 'You'll mind your tongue in my soon-to-be wife's presence.'

'Don't you dare order me about.' His father shook out of his grasp, remarkably strong for someone who took no more exercise than walking to the pub.

'Take your money and be gone.' Justin dug a few coins from his pocket and held them out, his hand shaking with rage. 'I have no patience for you tonight.'

With rough fingers, his father plucked the money from his palm, ignoring the coin which fell to the floor as he stuffed the rest in his greasy coat pocket.

'You and your charity can go to hell.' He stomped to the door. Chesterton rushed to open it, but Justin's father shoved him aside. 'Get out of my way. I don't need your help.'

The stench of the misty streets wafted in and with it the faint, sweet scent of gin clinging to his father's coat.

'Mr Connor.' Susanna's patient voice carried over the tense silence in the entrance hall.

Justin's father paused, peering back at her from over his shoulder with one squinty eye. 'What?'

'You almost forgot your hat.' She approached him, holding the hat as though it were a fine Wellington and not a battered old cap. Her stride wasn't clipped or insulting, as though she intended to throw the thing at him so he'd be gone. Neither was her expression condemning, but she smiled, charming him as Justin had charmed many a tradesman's neighbour's wife to ferret out a potential client's situation or solvency. 'Here you are.'

Mr Connor cautiously turned, eyeing her and the hat as if she would strike him if he dared to touch it, his insults seeming to flee from him in the face of her manners. Then at last he took the battered thing, more gingerly than he'd plucked the coins out of Justin's hands.

'Thank you,' he offered grudgingly.

'Our wedding is set for Monday. I'd very much like for you to attend,' she announced to Justin's astonishment.

The white whiskers on the end of his father's chin rose and fell with the way he chewed as he considered Susanna's invitation. Then he pointed his hat at Justin. 'He don't want me there.'

There was certainly truth in that, but Justin held his tongue, refusing to display any lack of solidarity with Susanna and give his father more musket balls for his continued attacks. He intended for Monday to be a memorable day for Susanna, but not for the wrong reasons.

'Then consider yourself my guest,' Susanna offered with all the poise of a duchess.

Mr Connor turned the hat over in his hands, pondering her request. In the gesture, Justin caught for the first time in years something of the thoughtful, intelligent man his father had once been before Justin's mother's death and the gin had done their damage. Then the image was gone, like a shadow chased away by lamplight and the grizzled, mean old man was before him again.

'Ain't making no promises. Never been one for the likes of church.' He narrowed his eyes at Justin. 'Unlike some, I don't give myself airs, or try and look down on others.'

He smashed the hat on his head and stomped out, with poor Mr Green following on his heels.

Chesterton rushed to close the door behind him, his long face expressionless. This wasn't the first row he'd witnessed between Justin and his father, and by far not the most unusual scene he'd been privy to in this house. With the politeness of a deferential servant he slipped away, leaving Justin and Susanna alone.

'What a memorable first meeting,' Susanna observed drily, her humour failing to raise Justin's downcast mood.

'I can't promise it'll be the last.' At least not until his father's taste for gin finally killed his body. It'd already destroyed his personality.

'You needn't apologise. My grandfather was somewhat like him. He and my uncle used to get into terrible rows when my uncle tried to help him. Some people can't be protected from themselves, or laugh over misfortunes such as a broken bottle of wine. They don't face trials with your happy attitude.'

'I'm not always optimistic.' Justin plucked the fumbled coin from the floor, turning it over in his fingers. This wasn't the image he'd intended to leave her with, of father and son fighting like a couple of cocks in a pit. He wanted the man he'd been on the front steps, the determined, confident one bent on success to be the memory she carried home tonight, but the buoyancy he'd experienced when the duke's carriage had rolled to a stop in front of the Rathbones' house was gone.

She laid a hand on his shoulder. 'Are you all right?'

He slipped her hand off his shoulder and raised it to his lips, pressing a kiss to the slender fingers. If they weren't standing in the Rathbones' entrance hall, with Jane no doubt listening at the top of the stairs, he'd wrap his arms around her and forget himself in the delight of her kisses. Instead he did as he always did and shoved down the frustration and torment of his father to flash Susanna a smile as dazzling as a row of lamps along a Drury Lane stage.

'With you beside me, nothing can be wrong.' He wasn't going to wail in her embrace or admit how deeply his father's insults really struck.

The slight disbelieving arch of her eyebrow matched the disapproving curve of her lips. He wasn't fooling her with all his smiles and wit because she knew exactly what this hurt was like.

'Some day you'll tell me what's troubling you instead of hiding it away.'

'Some day, but not tonight.' He took her arm and led her out to the waiting carriage, stopping before the impressive vehicle to embrace her.

She glanced at the driver, who fixated on the reins before Justin turned her face to meet his. He didn't care what the man thought or what he might say to his employer. The only thing concerning him was their last few moments together. He laid a tender kiss on her lips, the promise of something more than merely physical whispering in the soft caress. In three days, he'd savour every curve and supple mound of her. Tonight, he needed her understanding and compassion as much as she'd needed his in the garden.

The bells of St Bride's began to toll the late hour and Susanna broke away from his kiss, her reluctance to leave as strong in her expression as it was in his chest.

'Goodnight,' she whispered, backing out of his embrace to step into the carriage, her eyes never leaving his.

He closed the door, watching her through the open window, reluctantly moving away when the driver flicked the horses into motion. He wished he could keep her here, but he refrained from calling her back. When she'd stood beside him with his father, the man's insults hadn't cut so deep. She recognised the pain he endured and instead of wanting to dismiss it with a laugh, he'd wanted to take her back to the garden and unburden himself of years of torment. It wasn't like him to complain, but realising how much she wanted to soothe his suffering had almost made him reveal it, and the nagging doubt creeping along in the back of his mind.

For all his efforts to impress her with his determination to succeed, the constant reminder of how easily he'd failed before still shadowed him. There was nothing to ensure he'd be any more successful in this venture than he'd been in his last one. He might avoid the sea and all its perils, but he'd seized enough men's collateral to be familiar with the hundreds of other risks merchants faced.

He turned and made for the Rathbones' house, unwilling to entertain further doubts about his business or how much he missed having Susanna beside him already. There were better things to think about, such as Monday and the life he and Susanna would enjoy. She believed in his ambitions like a wife should and would help him achieve his goals. In return, he'd make her see the wonderful woman she was. Together they'd forget the pain their families had caused them. That was a more pleasant subject to ruminate on than his father's insults, or his own past failures.

Chapter Six

Susanna, dressed only in her stays and chemise, stood on the small stool in the room in the back of Mrs Fairley's shop. She laid her hands on her stomach, fighting against the dizziness creeping over her. The stool wasn't very high, but she felt as if she were teetering on the eaves of a house, with any quick turn sure to send her tumbling to the floor. It'd been like this all morning, and she stepped down to sit in the small chair beside the oval mirror, trying to settle her head and stomach.

The queasy feeling had come on after breakfast when Susanna had begun packing in anticipation of Monday. It wasn't nerves over the uncertainty of her future which had made her stomach swim, but Lady Rockland watching her and the maid as though expecting Susanna to slip some silver teaspoons into the trunk with her things. The duchess hanging over her like a bird of prey had exacerbated the tension still nagging at her after a long night spent tossing and turning in bed.

The memory of Justin's lips on hers last night had teased her until she'd jerked awake with the sheets sticking to her sweaty skin. With the dreams of his hands on her fading, the memory of his argument with his father had slid in to dominate her thoughts. Justin might have smiled jovially at her afterwards, but the pain etched in his eyes as his father had left was one she knew all too well. She'd wanted to soothe his hurt as much as she'd wanted to ease the elder Mr Connor's.

It'd been the same way with her grandfather and mother, when her grandfather had thrown her mother's mistakes in her face, flinging at her the same contempt Mr Connor had hurled at Justin. Back then Susanna had tried so hard to make peace between them, until one day, frustrated by her continued interference, her grandfather had aimed his insults at her. She should have known better than to approach old Mr Connor, but there was a pain deep inside of him, too, like the kind she'd witnessed in her grandfather after her grandmother had passed. It had seemed as if there was too much loss in one room for all of them to endure and she'd wanted to banish it with a touch of kindness.

'Here's the wedding dress for you to try on, Miss Lambert,' Mrs Fairley said brightly as she carried in the creamy silk gown, the paleness of it highlighted by the woman's light yellow dress, the hue of which nearly matched the tone of her blonde hair. Blue satin ribbon the colour of the modiste's eyes adorned the small, puff sleeves and circled her trim waist, emphasising an enviable bosom contained by the crossed material of the bodice. 'I altered it according to the measurements I took last week.'

Susanna rose, rocking a bit as she stood. Mrs Fairley reached out a steadying hand. 'Are you well, miss?'

'Yes. I haven't eaten much today and I was up all night. I'm nervous about the wedding.' She fought the swimming room to focus on the modiste. 'You must know how it is.'

'I do.' She nodded with enthusiasm. 'I could barely eat or sleep for days before my wedding to John. Now let's try on the dress and see how it looks.'

She lowered the dress so Susanna could

step into the centre of the silk, then the modiste raised it, pausing so Susanna could slip her arms through the smooth sleeves. The silk kissed the bare skin of her shoulders, reminding her of Justin's tongue against hers last night. He hadn't been greedy or lecherous in his caresses, or pressed her for more than she was initially willing to give. Instead he'd been patient, holding back even as he'd claimed her mouth with caresses to make her knees weak.

Susanna turned to face the mirror, the image of herself hazing a little as her eyes filled with tears.

'What's wrong, miss?' Mrs Fairley laid her hands on Susanna's upper arms and gave her a heartening squeeze.

Susanna wiped her eyes with the backs of her hands. It wasn't like her to be so emotional, but never in her life had she imagined herself in a wedding dress, ready to marry a respectable man who cared for her and her mother's dream for her about to be realised.

'I wish my mother could have seen this.' When she'd been alive, she'd wanted Susanna to have a loving husband, children and a home of her own, all of the things she'd been denied. Her mother had been rigorous in training

Susanna to live a merchant's life, convinced those skills would attract a good man, but also aware it would help Susanna make her way in the world if need be. Despite her hopes for Susanna, she'd feared no one, not even the simple men along the high street in Oxfordshire, would offer for an illegitimate woman. Now Susanna was to marry, and well, and all the hours her mother had spent training her to run a business would be employed at last.

'I'm sure your mother would be proud of you,' Mrs Fairley offered.

'Yes, she would have been.' If only she could be here. It would stifle some of the coldness of preparing for Monday with only the modiste to care about her and assist. Perhaps she should have invited Mrs Rathbone to join her today. Their acquaintance might be slight, but it was deeper than anything she'd enjoyed with her so-called family. Neither Lady Rockland nor Edwina had shown any interest in her coming nuptials. She hadn't expected them to. They were too eager to see her gone and overly consumed with their own affairs to trouble with her. This was Edwina's second Season and already there were rumblings amongst the family, and wider society, over her failure to marry last year. Her half-sister was probably jealous of Susanna making her way down the aisle before her.

'I'll do up the buttons so we can have a proper look at you.' Mrs Fairley began to fasten the long line of buttons along the back. As she reached those at the top, she was forced to pull the two sides of the dress tighter to fasten them.

'It's too tight,' Susanna complained, her breasts sore from the pressure of the bodice.

'My measurements must have been wrong.' Mrs Fairley frowned apologetically at Susanna in the mirror from behind her. 'It isn't like me to mismeasure.'

'My blue dress needs altering, too, it's also snug,' Susanna added, surprised the young lady's work was suddenly so shoddy. It'd always been so neat before. 'And I think I need my stays let out as well.'

Mrs Fairley's eyes met Susanna's in the mirror and then she came around to stand in front of her, looking up into her face with a motherly concern. 'Are you sure everything is well with you, Miss Lambert?'

'I'm quite well, other than a slight bit of dizziness and no appetite. Why?'

The kindly woman studied Susanna, a curious realisation dawning across her round face, as though she was aware of something Susanna was not. The modiste opened her mouth to say something, then seemed to think better of it.

'It isn't my place to pry into your affairs.' Mrs Fairley dropped her hands as she stepped behind Susanna to undo the dress.

'You don't pry, I tell you.' The modiste knew more about Susanna than anyone else, except Justin. Strange he should garner her confidence faster than Mrs Fairley, whose kind patience had relieved some of Susanna's aching loneliness over the last few years. 'You've helped me before. If there's something you think might help me now, please tell me.'

Mrs Fairley shifted on her feet, her cotton dress crinkling with the subtle movement as she silently debated Susanna's request. Then, at last, she spoke. 'Miss Lambert, were you intimate with Lord Howsham, in the married sense?'

Mrs Fairley had been the only other person besides Lord Howsham who'd known about the affair and Susanna's plans to run away with him. Even with the Rocklands paying her bill, the modiste had never betrayed Susanna. Despite the shared knowledge, and Mrs Fairley's discretion, Susanna was reluctant to admit her mistake. She wanted to leave it in the past, as Justin had urged her to do, but she couldn't lie to the one woman who'd been the closest thing to a confidante she'd ever known. 'I was, just once. We were walking in the woods at Rockland Place the day before the Rocklands and I left for London. He kissed me and then insisted on more. I didn't refuse him. I thought it meant he cared for me, but it didn't.'

She rubbed the back of her neck, remembering how the bark of the tree he'd pressed her against had scratched her skin as he'd pawed at her and how much she still regretted her foolishness. She should have known better, she should have pushed him away, but she hadn't.

'When were your last courses, miss?' Mrs Fairley asked, beginning to plant in Susanna's mind the most horrifying of thoughts.

'The week of Lady Day, I think.' So much had happened since then, coming to London, then Vauxhall Gardens, and she'd lost track of time. 'It wasn't long ago.'

Mrs Fairley's eyes widened. 'Miss Lambert, Lady Day was over six weeks ago.'

'It couldn't have been so long.' Yet the modiste's worried expression told her it was.

Susanna racked her mind, trying to determine if her courses had arrived since, but they hadn't. Her hands flew to her mouth as she realised exactly what the modiste suspected. The memory of Lady Rockland watching the maid struggling to do up her dress last night, and then warning her not to delay the wedding, came rushing back to her. Mrs Fairley wasn't the only one who suspected the horrible truth now beginning to fill Susanna. Lady Rockland did, too.

'It can't be. It can't.' The little breakfast Susanna had eaten threatened to come up and stain the skirt of the dress. She held it back, shrugging out of the silk as fast as she could, afraid of ruining it just as she had all hope of a future with Justin.

Mrs Fairley said nothing as she laid the dress to one side and watched as Susanna began to pace back and forth across the small room.

'It can't be. Justin thinks I'm so much more than a bastard, but I'm not and he'll know it. He'll hate me because of it.' The intimacy she'd experienced with him last night, every promise hovering in his kisses, all desire to prove everyone wrong, to enjoy a family and friends who loved and cherished her came crashing down around her. She slouched to the floor against the chair and pressed the heels of her hands to her eyes, determined not to cry, and to face this calamity as she had every other one in her life, but her chest constricted with her sobs.

Mrs Fairley wrapped her arms around Susanna and rubbed her back, her kindness making it impossible for Susanna to stop the tears from coming. A hopelessness she hadn't experienced since the morning of her mother's funeral crashed over her. If she told Justin, he'd break off the engagement and nothing but penury and the dark, ugly streets of London waited for her and the baby. She could interrupt Lord Howsham's wedding, insist he do right by her, but she knew he wouldn't. He'd cast her aside as he had before and Lord Rockland would allow it. He wasn't likely to fight for her, not against another peer.

'What am I going to do?' She moved away from Mrs Fairley and rubbed her cheeks with her hands. Tears and self-pity wouldn't help. They never had before. 'No man wants another man's child foisted on him. I know, because no man would accept my mother because of me, not even my family.'

'Perhaps you could go away to the country,' Mrs Fairley suggested, attempting to bolster Susanna's hope. 'Once the child is born and settled with a good family, you could return to London and marry Mr Connor.'

'I can't. Lord and Lady Rockland would never allow such a delay, and if I tell them why I need to leave, they'll throw me out without a shilling.'

Susanna sat back on her heels and stared at the small cutting of ribbon lying on the floor beneath the chair. Her stomach ached more at the thought of giving up a child than telling Lord Rockland the truth. The stories of families who'd fostered infants with farm couples who'd shown their charges little concern, leaving them to near starve or die of illness even when they were paid well, made her cringe. It was the reason her mother hadn't relinquished Susanna despite her grandfather's insistence. She couldn't subject her own child to such a horrid fate, or the lonely existence she'd endured. Her mother had made sacrifices to give Susanna the safety of a family home, even if it'd lacked true acceptance and love. Susanna would have to do the same, though she had no idea how. Her grandfather and uncle wouldn't take in another bastard, and Lord Rockland wouldn't stand staunchly behind her this time as he had the day he'd brought her to Rockland Park and presented her to his wife.

She sagged against the chair, two tears of despair rolling silently down her cheeks. 'I'm going to lose everything.'

'I've heard of a woman, miss,' Mrs Fairley began hesitantly as she handed Susanna a small scrap of fabric to wipe her cheeks with. 'She offers a tonic of pennyroyal-mint oil.'

'I can't.' Susanna cringed. One of the maids at Rockland Place had tried to end her troubles in a similar way and it'd killed her.

'Then you must trust in Mr Connor.' Mrs Fairley took Susanna's hands in hers. 'I'm sure he'll understand and help you, one way or another.'

'Why? There's no reason for him to care about me.' He'd tried to raise her up last night and in the curricle in Hyde Park. Telling him of the child would lower her in his eyes and turn him, the one person who'd ever thought highly of her, against her. 'There's no more reason for him to marry me.'

'What about your dowry?' Mrs Fairley suggested. 'You two wouldn't be the first to marry, one for money, the other for protection. The better sort do it all the time.'

Susanna snatched at the hope. Even coming to him as tainted goods, she did possess some value, if not for herself and her skills behind a shop counter, then for the fifteen hundred pounds which would be his. It was a depressing, if not practical and uncertain, prospect to hang her future on, and worry gnawed away at the chance it offered. 'What if the money isn't enough?'

It hadn't been the first time her father had proposed the idea to him.

'He's a good man. I'm sure he'll find a way to help you and the child.'

'I hope you're right.' His charity was the only way she and the baby might avoid being cast out on to the streets.

Justin's chaise rolled to a stop in front of Gunter's in Berkeley Square. The sweet scent of the treats inside wafted out of the front door and further turned Susanna's already knotted stomach. It was early in the afternoon and unusually warm for the middle of May. The more fashionable members of society who usually filled the tables inside, or sat outside in their open-topped carriages to enjoy their ices, were missing, leaving the shop to merchants' wives and officers courting young ladies.

Justin had arrived at the Rocklands' at noon to finalise the details of the wedding contract and the disbursement of Susanna's dowry. It'd been a brief meeting in the duke's office, with her father agreeing to the time and place of the wedding and engaging him in a short conversation about Susanna's pin money, doing at least that much for Susanna despite the duchess's disapproving glare. The woman had roused herself before noon to stand behind her husband and their solicitor, never daring to second-guess the men and not once smiling, even at the prospect of being rid of Susanna the next day.

During the entire discussion, and the review of the dowry contract, Susanna had attempted to sit still and not twist in her chair or fumble with her bracelet. More than once the desire to reveal her horrid secret had flitted to the tip of her tongue, ready to be freed, but she couldn't do it. It would make everything Lady Rockland believed about her true and Susanna wanted to deny her the satisfaction, if only for a little while longer, though it was a hollow victory. The harsh way Lady Rockland had regarded her when the issue of providing for future children in the event of Justin's death had been raised told her she did suspect the truth. Susanna had waited while the solicitor had read the wording aloud, wondering if the duchess would say anything, but she'd held her tongue. Like Susanna, she'd allowed events to continue, no doubt more relieved than before to be rid of her bastard charge.

Having failed to reveal her condition in the Rockland study, Susanna had suggested the outing in Justin's borrowed curricle, eager to be alone with him where they might talk. She'd intended to broach the subject while they drove, the open top giving them the illusion of being in public while in the privacy of the conveyance, but her courage had failed her again. Justin had been so enthusiastic in his discussion of the wine-shop inventory he'd acquired, and so solicitous of her advice on how best to sell the different quality vintages, she hadn't wanted to ruin his mood.

'I'm glad you suggested coming here.' Justin flicked a coin at a young boy on the pavement and asked him to watch his horse. As he came around to help her down, the bright sun played off the dark felt of his hat, shading his eyes, but not concealing his pleasure in her presence. His hand in hers was confident and sure, but it did nothing to bolster her own spirits and she bitterly regretted again her time with Lord Howsham. This would be the last time Justin would regard her with such joy.

'Given the warm day I couldn't think of anywhere else to go.' And what Susanna needed to tell him was best said in public. Though she'd come to know something of Justin's character over the last few days, there was no guessing how he might react when she delivered the news she was carrying Lord Howsham's child. She didn't think he'd become violent, or even shout, but whatever his reaction, with so many others around him he would be forced to show restraint and maybe even listen to her reasons why he should go through with the marriage. She didn't want to force another man's baby on him, but she didn't want to lose him either, or condemn her child to the insufferable illegitimacy she'd endured her entire life.

'Are you all right?' Justin studied her with a concern she hoped wasn't as astute as Mrs

Fairley's. She didn't want him guessing her secret before she could reveal it.

'Yes, only I haven't slept well.' It wasn't a lie. After leaving the modiste's yesterday, she'd barely been able to sit still, much less lie down.

'Try and rest tonight for tomorrow night may be a long one...' he breathed against her ear, twining the regret tighter around her stomach. There would be no wedding night and soon he'd discover it, too.

He escorted Susanna inside. A few couples sat at the tables scattered throughout the room, but most were empty. The plump older matron in a bright, white mob cap and an equally clean apron moved from behind the counter to serve two tall glasses of ices to two women sitting together on the far side of the room. The small table in front of the bow front window was empty and Justin guided Susanna there, holding out the chair as she sat down.

He took his place across from her. 'What do you recommend?'

'The orange ice. It's what I had when I was here before.' Then, she'd relished the treat. Today, her stomach was so tight with worry, she could scarcely imagine herself consuming something as rich as an ice. It'd been all she could do this morning to keep down two pieces of toast and her tea. She wasn't sure if this illness was the result of the baby growing inside her or sitting across from Justin, preparing to reveal what she wished she could hide. But she couldn't hide it. He'd been open and honest with her and shown her respect. He deserved her respect and honesty in return.

As she stared across the table at him, struggling to match his smile, the realisation the admiration he held for her was about to be flung into the street like an old broadsheet tore at her.

'This isn't my usual indulgence.' Justin laughed. A young boy pressed his nose to the window to admire the coloured sweets displayed in glass jars before his irritated governess pulled him away.

'Is there a public house you prefer?' Her grandfather had frequented one in Oxfordshire. When she'd been little, she'd wondered at this strange male bastion. Then she'd peeked in the window of the dark timber-and-wattle building to view the plain wooden tables inside and it'd lost all hold on her young imagination.

'No, I spend too much time in those places when I'm collecting information for Philip. To wander into one and pay for a tankard would feel too much like work.'

'Then where do you spend your free time?' Susanna asked, though she wasn't sure why. There was no point continuing to get to know him when she was about to bring their growing intimacy to a terrible halt.

'Philip and I regularly patronise a pugilist club. We've been training there since we were boys.'

'It certainly explains your agility the other night at Vauxhall Gardens.' And the sturdiness of his build. He had the bulk of the men who used to carry in the wine casks to her grandfather's shop, but none of their coarseness.

'That wasn't even my most interesting skirmish.' He held up his fists in mock sparring, his knuckles tight, the strength carrying up to his forearms, which bulged beneath his fitted coat. 'And your brother wasn't much of an opponent.'

The serving woman came to collect their orders, then hurried away.

'Surely you don't spend every night at the pugilist club?' she asked.

He rested his elbows on the table and leaned forward, a hunger for more than ices apparent in his rakish smile. 'If you're worried I won't be home to do my husbandly duties, you're quite mistaken.'

The recollection of his mouth against hers and his tongue caressing the line of her lips made her shift in her seat. She wished she could tug him out of his chair, hurry outside and pull up the hood of the curricle. She wanted to lose herself in the caress of his hands across her back and bask in his compliments and praise, but she couldn't, not when she was about to pull down everything between them like a row of houses in the path of a fire.

She resisted leaning in and answering his invitation to flirt and tease. Instead she changed the subject, fear diverting her from her real purpose yet again. 'Given the state I found you in at Vauxhall Gardens, I gather you don't spend all your time at the pugilist club. Who was the woman I saw leaving your carriage?'

He tapped the top of the table a couple of times, not embarrassed, but not exactly thrilled by her question. 'A friend of mine.'

'A friend?' His clothes had been too dishevelled for her to believe they'd been discussing business. Jealousy pricked at her, the sensation as surprising as it was troubling. Very soon he'd no longer be hers to be jealous of. His past mistakes could easily be walked away from while hers lingered to condemn her.

'Mrs Gammon is a woman I've known for some time, most recently in the carnal sense. The night you saw us, I'd suggested we make our partnership permanent. Apparently, I was only good enough for bed sport. She'd decided to marry another.' He slid back upright in his chair, his earlier excitement fading with this admission. Here was another person who'd failed to believe in him and she felt the sting as keenly as she had every time someone in her life had failed to believe in her.

'You loved her?'

'No. But we got on well together, or so I thought. She didn't have the same faith in my ability to succeed as you do. But enough sour discussion.' At once the seriousness which had marked him was gone and he was again the good-natured Justin. 'How's your dress coming along? Will Mrs Fairley have it ready in time for tomorrow?'

For the wedding which will never happen? 'Yes,' she barely managed to say, not trusting her tongue. The news she was carrying another man's child was not something which could be blurted out across a table at Gunter's, yet in the end it would have to be done.

'Then why the long face? Did Mrs Fairley make the wrong dress?'

'No, of course not. She's an excellent modiste.' Susanna's stomach turned over and she swallowed hard. What she was about to say would heap another insult on him. She wanted to spare him the pain of it, but to lock this sin in her heart for the rest of her life, knowing every time he looked at the child it wasn't his, was more than she could bear. 'Justin, before we meet at the church, there's something I must tell you.'

'About what?' He regarded her with a slightly more serious look.

The room swan around her and she laid her hands on top of the table to steady herself. She opened her mouth to speak just as the matron in the mob cap set two tall glasses frosted by the cold ices inside in front of them.

'Here you are, then.' She laid out two pewter spoons and linen napkins, then bustled off to attend to another couple who'd entered the shop.

Susanna met the eyes of the young woman in the red velvet pelisse striding to a table along the far wall, her narrow-jawed fiancé in tow behind her. She was Baron Holster's daughter and she eyed Susanna as though she were a loose woman who'd crept in the shop to dirty the bright, clean establishment. Any other day, Susanna would have stared the woman down until her delicate sensitivities made her flinch. Today, it was Susanna who looked away first. The woman's opinion of her was correct. Susanna was no better than a cyprian.

'If you're concerned about any lingering feelings I might have for Mrs Gammon, you shouldn't be,' Justin assured her, mistaking the source of her unease. 'Her true opinion of me killed all my feelings for her, as I'm sure Lord Howsham's behaviour did for you.'

'Yes, it did.' If only her time with him hadn't resulted in a new life. She rested one hand on her stomach, remembering how her already weak love for the earl had wilted when he'd failed to arrive at Vauxhall Gardens. If he were as honourable a man as Justin, then she might appeal to him and tell him about the baby, but he'd callously walked away from her before. He'd have no compunction about doing it again and would probably publicly disgrace her this time. Once the Rocklands disowned her, there'd be no reason for him not to reveal the story, for it wouldn't risk offending the duke. No one would be worried about offending her because she didn't matter. The only people she'd ever mattered to were resting in the churchyard in Oxfordshire, or sitting here across from her, unaware she was about to crush his regard for her with the truth.

'Speaking of Lord Howsham...' she began hesitantly, swirling the melting ice in her glass.

'I told you the other day we won't discuss the past,' he insisted, as aware as she of Miss Holster and her fiancé watching them with too much curiosity. Justin shifted his chair, the metal scraping over the wood as he placed his wide back between the couple and Susanna.

'But it's only fair you know—'

'You and Lord Howsham were intimate,' he interrupted in a low voice before she could say the words. 'I'd guessed as much and I don't care. Your time with him is as finished as mine is with Mrs Gammon. There's no reason to discuss it further.'

He jabbed his spoon in the ice, scooped out a healthy portion and stuck it in his mouth with a finality to tell her she wouldn't be able to broach the subject today, and if not today, then never. Tomorrow would see them before the altar.

'Then I won't say anything,' she mumbled, as much to him as herself.

She slipped a spoonful of ice in her mouth. The orange was sharp and she swallowed it down as she did the words of her revelation. Both chilled her, but she forced the feeling aside. She wasn't going to make a public spectacle of either of them by insisting on telling him something he obviously didn't wish to hear. It wasn't a secret she wanted lingering in the corners of her mind, but he'd made her decision for her, just as she'd made her decision to marry him the night at Vauxhall Gardens and again in the Rocklands' sitting room. Her conscience nagged at her, but if he insisted she remain silent about her past then he accepted her as she was and she'd carry the secret the same way she'd carried all the other heartaches and disappointments of her life.

In time, when her child was happy and loved, she might forgive herself, assuming Mrs Fairley's suspicions were correct. She might not be with child, or she might lose it after the wedding. After tomorrow it wouldn't matter. Whether she gave birth to Lord Howsham's child or a puppy, in the eyes of the law it would belong to Justin. No one would ever call the poor little mite a bastard or look down at it the way the baron's daughter looked down on Susanna now. Her child would have the love and care of both parents and a home where he or she would be cherished. It was everything she'd wanted as a child and everything she'd be sure to give to hers. Heaven willing, he'd never discover the truth.

Justin finished the last of his ice, barely tasting the too-cold concoction. Her mention of Lord Howsham, and interest in Helena had turned the sweet sour. He didn't want to hear about her past any more than he wanted to ponder his. He had a future to look forward to and it, not old ghosts, would guide him today.

'I've purchased a shop for the business,' he announced, his spoon rattling in his glass as he pushed it aside.

'Why not lease instead? It'd be cheaper.' She seemed as relieved as him by the change in topic. It settled the storm in her green eyes which had gathered there during the discussion of her past.

'Buying it is a hedge against failure. If the

wine trade doesn't work, at least I'll have the building to rent, or I can sell it and recoup some of the capital.' Unlike a ship it couldn't end up at the bottom of the ocean.

She wrinkled her nose at the last bite of her ice, then dropped the spoon in the glass. 'Once, when my grandfather was doing well, the owner asked if he wanted to purchase the building with his shop. Grandmother begged him to do it, but he didn't want to spend the money. When she tried to insist, he told her not to meddle in a man's work. He should have let her meddle—she was better at business than he ever was.'

Justin reached across the table and took her hand, then slipped his thumb inside the small hole just below the glove's button to caress her smooth flesh. It pebbled under the soft stroke, the tightness of her skin matched by the one in his loins. 'You have my permission to meddle with my business as often as you like.'

Beneath the pad of his thumb the faint thump of her pulse quickened. Her heightened awareness of his skin against hers, even in this small way, increased the need surging through him. He slipped his thumb a little further inside the glove and swept it over the arch of her wrist. Her fingertips beneath his arm pressed into his coat with the same shock which parted her lips in a subtle inhale of breath. He shifted to the edge of his seat, wanting to push the table aside and pull her across the gap to him, but they weren't alone or in some bawdy house. As conscious of his touch as she was, she was more aware of those around them. Her eyes shifted to the other patrons before coming back to him. Someone must be watching them, for the innocent reaction of her instincts faded and she pulled back her hand.

Justin let her go. He wouldn't embarrass her in public, not when tomorrow night they'd be alone and they could both savour her unfettered response to his touch.

'Shall we be off?' he asked, as though a private room were waiting for them and not the imposing iron fences of Grosvenor Square.

'Please,' she choked out, before clearing her throat, gathering up her reticule and rising.

The ride home was no more soothing than their time in Gunter's. Despite the traffic commanding his attention, Justin's focus remained fixed on every shift of Susanna's legs, each slide of her skirts across her knees and thighs. Her voice as she described her mother pierced him as sharply as the faint scent of the orange ice lingering beneath her jasmine perfume. He'd never been so aware of a woman before. Many had amused and intrigued him, but not one had ever exerted such control over his senses without even trying.

At last the noisy streets gave way to the quiet confines of Grosvenor Square. If he could have kept driving right on through today into tomorrow night he would have done it, but he couldn't. Patience was necessary and he pulled the curricle to a halt in front of the Rockland house. They'd have their entire lives together after tomorrow.

Susanna studied the house, blinking against the intensity of the sunlight reflecting off the white stone. Netley pulled open the door and the cavernous entrance hall yawned, ready to engulf her. She wanted to stay out here in the daylight with Justin as the shadows fell from his hat to deepen the rise of his cheekbones. As agitated as she'd been before Gunter's with her secret boiling inside her, the faint caress of his thumb over her skin had increased the tension until she thought she might jump from the carriage and sprint home. On and on she'd chattered at him, trying to dispel her increased agitation. He hadn't demanded she sit quietly the way Lord Howsham used to do, but listened, deftly manoeuvring the curricle through the crush.

'Thank you, Justin.' She made for the house, needing to be alone and settle herself. How she'd get through tomorrow as the smiling bride everyone expected her to be she didn't know. In the meantime, she'd concern herself with the business of seeing the last of her things packed and sent off to Justin's house, wrapping up the unhappy life she'd endured with the Rocklands.

'Wait.' He caught her hand before she could go, his large fingers curling around hers and steadying her against the rocking which was making the street swim.

'Yes?' She wanted to cling to him and his solid faith in himself and her, even if she didn't deserve it. She'd find a way to deserve it, to assist him in all his endeavours in the hope so much good could absolve her of the one wrong she was about to commit. All her behaviour from this day onwards would make her worthy to take his name and enjoy the protection of him as her husband. The sin wasn't just for her own selfish reasons, but for the future of the child. This was her chance to give it everything she'd never had.

He inched closer until his chest was nearly against hers and she could see the faint ash and dust from the street in the threads of the wool coat. As she peered up into his heavy-lidded eyes, temptation almost overcame her better sense.

'I can't linger on the doorstep with a suitor, even if we're meeting at the church tomorrow.' It would only be a matter of time before Lady Rockland scuttled out from wherever she was inside, most likely making a maid miserable, and accuse Susanna once again of being common, or say heaven knew what to Justin.

'Damn them all. I don't care what they think.' He bent down and claimed her mouth.

There was no evergreen bush to shield them from the view of the governesses parading up and down the opposite walk with their charges, or the nosy maid in the window across the street who'd weave what she saw into a fabulous tale to delight her employer and embarrass the Rocklands. Susanna didn't care. Tomorrow she'd leave them and this world behind. Today she delighted in the firmness of his lips against hers. The heat from the sweep of his thumb beneath her glove ignited again until she was sure the trees of the square would catch fire and burn her and everything around them to the ground. She wouldn't be sorry to see it go, only Justin when he drove away. Tomorrow they'd be together and then nothing, not her past, or his, could separate them.

When at last Justin released her, she staggered back a touch, barely aware of Netley coughing his disapproval from his place by the door.

'Until tomorrow.' He raised his hat to her, the sun catching in the light strands of his hair before he settled it back down over his head.

'Until then.' She gripped the iron railing along the front walk to steady herself, admiring the tightening of his breeches over the roundness of his buttocks as he raised one leg to step up into the curricle before placing himself on the seat and setting the horse into motion. Susanna lingered on the pavement, hardly noticing the rough iron against her palm as she watched his curricle turn the corner to be obscured by the trees dominating the square.

With heavy feet she trudged inside, ignoring Netley's disapproving scowl as he swung closed the door behind her. He marched off to see to his duties, and no doubt to tell Lady Rockland of Susanna's blatant indiscretion on their front doorstep. Let him chide and snitch, she didn't care. Tomorrow, she'd be done with them all.

Justin arrived home to find an ordered confusion of men and trunks as they carried Susanna's things into the house.

'Upstairs, first door to the right, mind you don't nick the plasterwork,' the housekeeper, Mrs Robinson, instructed, with all the attendance of a general overseeing manoeuvres.

She'd come to him with this house in Johnson's Court, off Fleet Street, when the previous owner had sold it to Justin in a rush to raise money to keep himself out of prison. It'd been Justin's sanctuary for the last six years, the place he'd retire to after a day of either dodging unhappy perfumers, or after yet another argument with his father. The furniture was left over from the previous owner, some of it fine, other pieces in need of freshening, but that wasn't something he concerned himself with. Susanna could do the place up as she liked when she settled here. To him, it didn't matter what his home looked like as long as it was comfortable.

Leaving everything in the capable hands of Mrs Robinson, he retreated to his study. Its walls were decorated with paintings of spaniels and horses left by the former occupant along with the thick leather furniture. One low bookcase sat under the window with a tray of glasses and decanters on top. The rest of the shelves were empty. The books had been sold last year to fund his venture. He should have burned them for all the money it'd gained him.

He poured himself a measure of the American whisky one of his less reputable suppliers had procured for him. He'd have to see what other gems the man could smuggle in for him for the shop. Justin held the drink under his nose, inhaling the stiff burned-oak scent before tossing it back. The smoky shot briefly eased the tension which had marked him before he'd kissed Susanna goodbye and ever since. Their awkward exchange at Gunter's had been forgotten in her savoury response to his lips against hers, the promise of which he looked forward to fulfilling tomorrow night.

'Quite the flurry of activity here.' A familiar voice slid through the room from the entrance, the notes of it souring his drink.

'Good evening, Mrs Gammon,' Mrs Robinson stiffly greeted her.

Justin carried his glass with him as he came to the door to lean against the jamb, a fisted hand on one hip as he eyed the widow. 'What are you doing here?'

A man carrying a stack of round hat boxes and who knew what other frippery tried to shift around the widow before she stopped him. She lifted the lid on a box and peeked inside, frowning with more envy than disapproval. 'Rather feminine attire for a man of your carriage.'

She eyed him with the same suggestive craving which had invited him into her bed over a year ago. Now, not even years of celibacy could drive him back into her arms again.

'Does your husband approve of you being here?' he asked, taking a slow sip of his drink and wishing he'd brought the entire bottle with him.

'We haven't married yet. He insists on reading the banns.' She dropped the lid and allowed the man to continue on his way.

'Probably too cheap to pay for the common licence.'

Her lips pursed and he knew he'd struck at the truth of the matter. So, her furrier wasn't the pampering prince she'd thought him to be, but a businessman like every other penny-pincher in this part of London. 'What are you doing here?'

'I seem to have misplaced a couple of items since the last time I was here. An expensive ivory fan and a tortoiseshell hair comb.'

Justin had no idea if the items were here, or if this was simply her excuse to come back and dally before the banns were read. Either way, he was about to disappoint her. 'I haven't seen them. Mrs Robinson, have you found a hair comb and a fan left behind by Mrs Gammon?'

'No, sir, I haven't seen such things.' The housekeeper held her hands tight in front of her, arms bent at the elbow like some Egyptian statue he'd seen at the British Museum. She'd never cared for the widow, or her late-night visits. On more than one occasion she'd referred to Helena as a wanton hussy. Justin had been more amused than irked by the house-keeper's mutterings, until Helena had proven them to be true. 'I can't imagine how a lady's items could have ended up in the house of a single gentleman.'

Helena frowned at the subtle dig and Justin restrained a laugh. The widow had never once hesitated to enter his house late at night in her cloak, or to venture downstairs after sunrise for all of the servants to see. It seemed, with her pending nuptials, all sense of decency had suddenly returned, though not enough to stop her from visiting him.

'Perhaps I'm mistaken and they were left at my sister's.' Helena pulled her bright red spencer closed over her ample and too-well-displayed-for-so-early-in-the-day breasts, trying to reclaim her dignity. Justin wouldn't allow it.

'If they're here, we'll be sure to find them.' He exchanged a dubious look with Mrs Robinson before fixing his eyes on Helena. 'I wouldn't want my bride to be troubled by the sight of another woman's things when she arrives here tomorrow night.'

Helena's petulant mouth fell open in shock. 'You're getting married?'

This was fast becoming a very satisfying day, though tomorrow would be even more so. 'In the morning.'

'My, you move quickly.'

'I've learned from the best.' He finished his drink, ignoring her acid stare.

'And who's the lucky woman?'

'Miss Susanna Lambert.' He said no more as he set the empty glass down on a bust stand next to the study door. Helena read the scandal sheets and would recognise the name. He wasn't disappointed.

'The Duke of Rockland's bastard daughter?' She let out a low whistle, betraying her fishmonger roots. 'I'm impressed, Justin. You're marrying into the nobility.'

'Yes, can't you just see me in the House of Lords?' he replied sarcastically, enjoying her jealous astonishment as much as he had his contraband whisky. It proved he wasn't the loafer she'd taken him for in the carriage outside Vauxhall Gardens. Now all he needed to do was make a success of his wine business and prove to her and his father how much they'd underestimated him.

'How did you of all people manage to capture such a prize?' She said it as if no one but she would deign to have him.

'The duke believes in me more than some people do.' He strolled past her to the door and pulled it open before Walter, his valet and butler, could hurry to do it. After his failure last year, he couldn't spare the extra expense for a footman. In time, when his wine business began bringing in money, he'd hire more staff, perhaps even a lady's maid for Susanna. She'd need someone to help her undress at night, though in the meantime he'd be more than happy to assist her. 'If you'll excuse me, I have a great deal to do before tomorrow.'

Shoring up some of the dignity with which she'd entered the house, Helena approached him, pausing to lay one well-manicured hand on Justin's chest.

'If you find your little daughter of a nobleman lacking, my previous offer of the other night still stands,' she purred, her voice like screeching metal compared to Susanna's tender tones.

Justin removed her hand from his chest and allowed it to drop back down by her side. 'That's too kind of you, Mrs Gammon, but I assure you your services will not be necessary.'

Helena whirled around in fury and made for the gig waiting at the end of the pathway. She climbed inside, smacking away the driver's hand as he tried to help her before she settled beside him and they set off.

Justin wandered back to the study, leaving Mrs Robinson and the others to their duties. Despite dispatching the widow, there was more to accomplish before he could claim victory over her and his father's low expectations. He poured himself another drink, not touching the amber liquid this time as he sank into his favourite leather armchair by the fire. Susanna's strained manner at Gunter's made him wary and the unsettling feeling there was something he couldn't anticipate waiting to rise up and crush him nagged. He wanted so much to be successful, but last time, despite all his careful plans, Mother Nature had knocked him down. He hadn't seen the strike coming.

He wondered if a nature more akin to lust was making him blind to a weakness in Susanna. He was normally adept at reading people. It was a skill he'd learned with Philip under the tutelage of the elder Mr Rathbone. If he'd better employed it with Helena, he might not have made a fool of himself outside Vauxhall Gardens. Was he ignoring his better sense with Susanna?

He lifted the glass to the window, observing the labourers, shop assistants and apprentices passing back and forth in front of it through the hazy liquid. Perhaps his father was right about not reaching too far above his station. Maybe he wasn't meant to be anything more than the employee of another. He lowered the glass and knocked back the rest of the liquor before setting it aside.

His father wasn't right. Justin might not have guessed Helena's venality, but all men made mistakes at one time or another. It didn't mean he was any less worthy to strive for something more. Even the nearly infallible Philip had experienced doubts, especially after his first wife had died giving birth to his son Thomas and he'd nearly lost his business. The measure of a man was how he dealt with upsets and setbacks. Justin would face each and every challenge, never allowing his reservations or anyone else's to undermine him, and he would do it all with Susanna by his side. Everyone had their weaknesses and failings; at some point hers would reveal themselves, as would his. There was no reason to brood on them now and sour the honeymoon. Getting to know her and all her little quirks would be as pleasurable as exploring her body and letting her discover his. It was a much more appealing prospect to consider.

Chapter Seven

~~~~~~⸨⸩~~~~~~

Susanna sat alone in the quiet of the carriage outside St Bride's, waiting for the footman to return from inside and tell her it was time for the ceremony. She smoothed her hands over the waist of the silk wedding dress draping her body. The bodice had been altered by Mrs Fairley in time for this morning. While she waited, her father's words as he'd escorted her to the carriage rang in her ears like the church bells in the tall spire overhead.

'I might consent to the marriage, but I can't insult Lady Rockland or my legal children by giving you away. I'm sure there's a friend of Mr Connor's who can stand in my place.'

Susanna hadn't argued or begged him to change his mind. As much as this final insult hurt, not having the Rocklands sitting like a bunch of sour-faced gargoyles in the pews during the service was a relief. In the end they hadn't even bothered to rise and help her dress, leaving her to the lady's maid and her own skills to prepare herself. Despite the cut, it'd saved them all from enduring an awkward goodbye.

Taking in the greystone church entrance with its graceful metal arch over the top, she drew in a deep breath, ready once again to face a challenge alone. Hopefully, with Justin soon to be her husband, this would be the last one. They might not enjoy the grand love she'd read about in novels, but she respected him, though not enough, it seemed, to tell him the truth.

She tugged at the lace along the neckline of her dress, wishing the footman would hurry. The carriage was growing hot in the morning sun and she was eager to leave this last trapping of her old life behind. If only her secret was so easily discarded. It was wrong to enter the church carrying this large a lie, but it would be even worse to bring a baby into the world and see it scorned due to no fault of its own. It would do no good to be tossed with it into the gutter where the baby would either die or endure a life of misery at the whims of the unkind streets. She'd endure anything to ensure an innocent child wasn't subjected to a life of suffering.

At this moment, Susanna felt very alone.

'Miss Lambert, you look beautiful,' a feminine voice exclaimed from the opposite side of the carriage. Mrs Rathbone stood in the open window, beaming at her. Mr Rathbone stepped behind her, his opinion of her dress better concealed, but his expression echoing something of his wife's excitement. 'Mr Connor said important business kept your father from attending the service. Philip has graciously volunteered to walk you down the aisle, if that's all right with you?'

'It is, thank you.' Susanna breathed a sigh of relief as she slid across the squabs to where the driver had pulled open the door.

'It's the least I could do for my friend and his soon-to-be wife.' Mr Rathbone offered her his elbow and she took it.

Around her, Mrs Rathbone adjusted the dress, smoothing out the wrinkles and arranging the short veil cascading down the back of Susanna's head. They were the small services a mother, or at the very least a friend, should do, yet they were left to a kind stranger. Smiling in gratitude at Mrs Rathbone, Susanna knew, in time, these people would mean more to her than anyone related to her by blood, except her mother and grandmother, ever could.

'I'll go inside and tell them you're ready.' Mrs Rathbone hurried off to the church with the good news, leaving her husband to escort Susanna.

Mr Rathbone carried out his duty with all the solemnity of an older brother, setting Susanna at ease despite the formal way in which he stood beside her. Unlike her father might have done, he didn't fulfil this position because it was expected of him, but because he wanted to, and for Susanna this distinction made a great deal of difference.

The moment she stepped through the double doors and into the high space coloured by the large, stained-glass windows, the loneliness she'd known in the carriage disappeared. Mrs Rathbone had taken her place in the front pew beside Miss Rathbone and Mrs Townsend and other people Susanna assumed were Justin's friends. They all turned to watch her as she walked on Mr Rathbone's arm up the aisle to where Justin waited with Reverend Clare.

A black coat covered the width of Justin's

chest, the lapels trimmed in dark velvet. The blue light of a stained-glass window overhead graced his shoulders and caught the faint blue in the darkness of his coat. His face was set off by the contrast between the jacket and the crisp white shirt and cravat, both of which fitted tightly beneath his chin. The severity of his dress was softened by the cut of his wide smile. It echoed in the brightness of his eyes as they took in the length of her before rising to catch her gaze. Under the spell of his charm, it was all she could do not to let go of Mr Rathbone and rush up the aisle. Instead, she moved steadily forward on her gracious escort's arm, trying to maintain the calm reserve expected of a bride. The time to fling off all restraints would come tonight, when she would at last see what lay beneath Justin's staid black and enjoy something of the teasing touch he'd left her with yesterday.

She reined in her wicked thoughts. Now was no time to think of the marital bed, not with Mr Rathbone handing her over to Justin and Reverend Clare observing them from beneath his severe brow.

It was difficult with Justin's hand in hers to keep her thoughts anchored in the solemn surroundings. While Reverend Clare read the ceremony, every inch of her was aware of Justin standing beside her as solid as any of the pillars holding up the church. It was only when the reverend said to the gathered guests, 'If there is anyone here who has cause to believe that these two should not be joined in holy matrimony then let him speak now or for ever hold his peace', that the present flooded over her like wine from a broken cask.

Reverend Clare paused and waited. Susanna's pulse pounded in her ears. She peered over her shoulder at the empty pews, half-expecting Lady Rockland to appear at the church door and announce to all Susanna's condition, snatching away everything, but there was no one there. Any ideas of revenge the woman possessed had probably been overwhelmed by her inability to rise before noon. Late balls made for such a trying life.

At last, Reverend Clare resumed the ceremony and Susanna shifted a touch closer to Justin, her arm brushing against his as she drew from his happiness and strength to bolster hers. Soon they would be bound together and the intimacy she'd craved with him since their time alone on the Rathbones' portico would be theirs.

All regrets from the past, and worries about the future, vanished the moment the reverend instructed them to face one another. With a steady hand, Justin followed the reverend's words and slid the gold band studded with small diamonds around her finger and repeated the vows. She didn't doubt his willingness to stand beside her through better or worse, just as she would stand beside him.

When at last the vows were said, the rings exchanged and the blessing given, Reverend Clare pronounced them man and wife, linking their fates before instructing them to kiss.

She tilted up her head, eager to enjoy the weight of his mouth upon hers, and she was not disappointed. Settling his hands on her upper arms, he pressed his lips to hers. This was not the passionate kiss from the portico or the stolen one from yesterday, but something deeper, meant to convey to her and everyone gathered the intensity of the promises they'd made.

Afterwards, it was a merry gathering in the Rathbones' garden where the sun highlighted the green of the bushes and the blue sky hanging over a fine day. A hearty selection of food was laid out on a table on the portico for the guests to enjoy as they mingled. Young Thomas toddled between the ladies, cooed over by them as his nurse followed after him, and the Rathbones' young infant slept upstairs. More than one ribald joke about the wedding night made the rounds, especially after yet another bottle of wine was opened by a footman. Miss Jane stood in the midst of it all, listening with interest despite Mrs Townsend's half-hearted attempts to shield her young charge.

'Do you like the ring?' Justin asked when he caught Susanna admiring the way the diamonds sparkled in the sunlight.

'It's gorgeous. Where did you get it?'

'It was my mother's.'

Susanna closed her hand, almost ashamed to be wearing it after the secret she'd kept. Then she stretched out her fingers and looked at it again, determined to make herself worthy of the intimate gift.

'If you'd like, we could sneak out the back gate.' Justin tempted her, his hot breath laced with wine teasing her cheek. 'They wouldn't miss us.'

'Of course they would.' After all the effort the Rathbones had gone to on their behalf, she didn't want to be rude by sneaking away, no matter how much she wanted to be alone with Justin. 'I sense Mr Charton hasn't depleted the last of Mr Rathbone's fine port or his store of bawdy jokes.'

As if hearing his name, the lanky man with the red nose approached them.

'Surprised us all with this wedding, Justin. I didn't expect you to settle down. Just like your father. I was stunned the day he escorted your mother up the aisle.' Mr Charton raised his empty wine glass to Justin before wandering off in pursuit of a footman carrying a tray laden with more drinks.

'Your father isn't here,' Susanna said, at last noticing the older man's absence.

Justin shrugged, his lips drawing up into more of a grimace than the smile he'd worn since she'd come up the aisle. 'The plentiful drink might have lured him here, but he'd have to be pleasant, something he's no longer capable of.'

Susanna wasn't so sure and she intended to find out. She wasn't going to allow the wound festering between father and son to continue.

'I hope you aren't offended by Mr Charton, or anyone else's jokes,' Justin asked, his humour returning.

'No, I love it. A society wedding can't compare to this, unless you enjoy sitting around like a statue with everyone bored and watching the clock tick down the minutes until they can leave.'

He brushed the back of her neck with his fingers, sending a chill racing across her exposed skin. 'I'm counting down the time until we can leave.'

She offered him a seductive look, tempting him as much as he tempted her. 'You aren't the only one.'

'Justin, stop fawning so much over your wife or all us husbands will be expected to show our wives the same favour,' Mr Charton called out across the garden.

Mrs Charton laid a steadying hand on him as he lurched a little to one side. 'Careful, my dear, or you'll have all the wives angry at you.'

'Yes, a fate worse than death, isn't it, Rathbone?'

'Indeed, I'd never dream of making Mrs Rathbone angry.' Philip brushed his wife's lips with a kiss, lingering a little too long for the gesture to be called merely playful.

Once witnessing such intimacy would have made Susanna envious. Today she linked her arm in Justin's, knowing she along with the other wives here would soon be enjoying the pleasure of the marriage bed.

At last the shadows of the rosebushes stretched across the gravel path and the chill of the coming night began to fill the air. The Rathbones' coach was summoned and, with the guests lining either side of the front steps to wish Justin and Susanna well, the newly married couple took their leave.

Justin's house wasn't far from Bride Lane, but in the crush of carriages on the street it was some time until it rolled up to Johnson's Court and the simple two-storey dwelling wedged between similar unassuming houses on either side. It wasn't as fancy as the Rathbones' or as large, but simple in a way she admired. After years living in the draughty halls of Rockland Place, she was eager for the cosiness of an unfussy home.

Justin escorted Susanna up the steps and into the entrance hall where his servants stood ready to meet their new mistress. He introduced her to the cook, his valet who was also the butler, and the housekeeper, Mrs Robinson. They all received her warmly, even Mrs Robinson, who didn't seem troubled by a strange woman arriving to displace her authority.

'If you'll follow me, I'll show you to your room,' Mrs Robinson entreated.

Susanna went with her up the narrow staircase. From the height she took in more of the house. No panelling graced the walls and the furniture she could see through the open sitting-room door was from another era, though sturdy and of good quality with the exception of one or two pieces which were stashed in discreet corners. The slight formality of the decor didn't seem to have Justin's mark upon it and yet at the same time it did. It was uncomplicated and comfortable, yet sturdy.

At the top of the stairs, Mrs Robinson led her into a bedroom connected by a door to Justin's room.

'I've seen to the arranging and unpacking of your things. If there's anything you'd like changed, please let me know,' Mrs Robinson offered.

Susanna turned over the brush and comb on

the fine but unadorned dressing table beside the wardrobe. On the wall above it hung the gilded frame with the miniature of her mother. This was such a different welcome from the one she'd received at the Rocklands' house. Back then, nearly everything she'd brought with her to Rockland Place, especially her clothes, had been discarded and replaced. Lady Rockland had been too afraid of the lice which hadn't existed to allow Susanna to keep more than the miniature. Even this had been reframed so it would match the decor of her room. It was a wonder Lady Rockland hadn't pried it out of the frame before allowing it to leave the house yesterday. She'd probably considered the loss of the frame a small price to pay to hustle Susanna out of her life.

Susanna moved around the small but comfortable room. Not a speck of gilding or silk marred the clean lines of the suite or made it so pristine one couldn't touch anything for fear of ruining it. A large bed stood against the far wall and was draped with a fine yellow coverlet which matched the subtle weave in the cover of the chair beside the fireplace. Curtains in a similar cheery hue hung from the single window which overlooked the bustling street in front of the house. A wardrobe stood on the opposite wall, carved in a similar dark-and-burled wood as the bed. Susanna opened the wardrobe and fingered her dresses, which had been arranged by colour. She marvelled not just at Mrs Robinson's efficiency, but at how at ease she felt here, as if this room were made for her. Even in the house in Oxfordshire she'd never felt completely at home, or in any of the Rocklands' estates. In this humble dwelling, with her things spread out by a stranger, it was as if she belonged.

'Is everything as it should be?' Justin asked, opening the door adjoining his room to hers. With him the masculine scent of shaving soap, leather polish and spirits drifted in to overwhelm the more delicate notes of jasmine adorning her space. His coat was gone and he stood in his waistcoat, his powerful arms made larger by the billowing fabric of his shirt. The waistcoat was solid against the flatness of his stomach, the slight taper of it widening his already impressive chest.

'It is.' Susanna fingered the banyan draped over the back of the chair by the fire to warm it, noting from beneath her lashes how he eyed her with an eagerness which made her toes curl. She wanted to see beneath his waistcoat, to lift the linen of the shirt from his torso and trace the hard lines of muscle which must lie beneath.

'Shall I help you undress, Mrs Connor?' Mrs Robinson offered, old enough not to blush with the knowledge of what was about to happen.

Susanna stared at the housekeeper, a little stunned. It wasn't so much her question which shocked Susanna, but the new name, home and the station in life she'd gained, a station which suited her better than any she'd previously held.

'No, I believe we can manage,' Susanna answered, the new surety in her life giving her a true confidence to replace the one she'd feigned so many times in the past.

Without another word, Mrs Robinson left, closing the door behind her.

Once the lock clicked shut, the desire in Justin's eyes ignited Susanna's insides like a hot poker added to wine to boil it. In two steps he brought the high-polished toes of his boots up to touch the satin of her slippers. The nearness of him sucked the air from the room and she looked down at the thick carpet, the confidence she'd enjoyed a few moments before deserting her.

He slid one large finger beneath her chin and raised her face to his. 'Don't tell me a woman of your experience is nervous.'

It was a joke, meant to be light and to break the tension making her stomach draw in, but it fell flat.

'I may not be a virgin, but I'm not as experienced as you believe.' She moved to the washstand near the window and fingered the curving arch of the porcelain handle. 'Lord Howsham and I were intimate only once, in the woods at Rockland Place. He was so eager and I was so stupid to not reject him. In the end it wasn't—' She bit her lip, unsure how to explain.

'—wasn't for your benefit, but for his,' Justin finished, coming to stand beside her, the linen of his shirt brushing against the bare top of her arm.

She crossed her arms in front of her, trying to fight back the chill creeping over her. She looked up at Justin, touched he didn't blame her or call her a whore. She shuddered to imagine what words he'd hurl at her if he discovered the result of her ill-fated encounter with

Lord Howsham and how she'd duped him. She didn't deserve this happiness.

Justin slid his fingers beneath Susanna's, caressing the tender skin of her arm before he tugged her hand away and raised it to his chest. With a reassuring squeeze, he stilled her trembles, but not the unease curling her shoulders and making her draw away from him. He'd been foolish to tease her about Lord Howsham. He wouldn't make such a stupid mistake again.

Justin brushed the side of her face with the tips of his fingers. With her lips pressed together and her eyes wide, she appeared as fresh as the young milkmaid who'd taken his innocence many years ago while surrendering her own. He was no innocent now, but Susanna was, despite her encounter with the earl. He silently cursed the man for having fallen on her like some overeager schoolboy instead of cherishing her enough to take his time and ensure her pleasure as well as his own.

Justin cradled her face in his hands and lowered his lips to hers. The moist softness of her mouth heightened the desire already coursing through him, but he held it back. There would be no hurrying, no cajoling of her favours, but a willingness in both of them to unite their bodies. He gently probed her lips with his tongue and with a sigh she opened to him, her body unfolding beneath his as she uncurled her arms from her waist to wrap them around him. He explored the taste of her as he ran his hands along the row of ivory buttons along the back of her dress. Starting at the bottom, he began to undo them one by one. When the silk gaped open, she gasped, but didn't startle or cling to the modesty the fabric offered. Instead she drew away from him, allowing him to take the short sleeves of the dress and lower it down over the length of her. He admired the subtle point of her toes in the stockings as she stepped out of her slippers to raise first one foot and then the other from the circle of the dress. He laid the silk to one side, then slid a wide hand along the back of her calves, stopping just behind her knee, not ready to go higher.

A sweep of pink spread across the tops of her breasts as he stood to admire the curve of the ivory cotton of her stays. It followed the roundness of her hips up along her waist to where the pliant garment cupped each full breast. Not wanting to leave her exposed and embarrassed, he shrugged out of his waist-coat and tossed it aside, then tugged off his boots. He undid the knot of his cravat and pulled the material out from around his neck. She watched in silence as he undressed and he flashed her a wicked smile when a small gasp of amazement greeted the removal of his shirt. The heat in her gaze as she took in his defined chest made every hour he'd spent in the ring at the pugilist club worth the effort.

'Now we're even.' He caught her by the waist and pulled her into the curve of his body. As their lips met, her hands lay flat against his muscles, singeing his exposed skin.

With deft fingers, he began to undo the laces of her stays, each slip of the strings through the eyelets taunting him to move faster, but he held back. He'd never rushed with a woman, but he'd never moved quite this slow either. The widows he'd enjoyed had known their way around a man enough to keep pace with him, but not Susanna. She'd indulged, but it was clear she hadn't been allowed to enjoy a man's body and he wanted her to revel in his as much as he relished hers.

At last the stays opened and he let go, al-lowing them to drop to the floor. She broke from his kiss, moving back a touch in her hesitancy. The crisp white chemise surrounding her body glowed cream with her skin. Through the fine fabric he could just make out the pink buds of her nipples, pert against the cotton. He knew what his own body was doing to his breeches as she glanced down to his hips, a saucy smile pulling up one corner of her full lips. She caught the sides of the chemise and raised it over her head, revealing inch by glorious inch her supple body and her trust in him.

'We're no longer even,' she purred, standing before him in nothing but the sheer silk stockings with the blue ribbons tied in dainty bows at the centre of her thighs. The candlelight danced over her skin and her full breasts were pert above her stomach which led down to the dark sable at the junction of her thighs.

'Allow me to rectify the situation.' Undoing the buttons on his fall, he slid off his breeches, stepped out of them, then straightened to catch her eyes widening at the sight of him. She bit her bottom lip not in fear, but with a hesitation laced with anticipation, which further tightened his member.

Her soft stomach against his hardness

made him groan as he tangled his hands in her hair, dislodging the pins and sending a cascade of curls spilling down over her shoulders. The feathery strands brushed his chest and he pushed one silken curl aside to cup her breast. With his thumb, he grazed the pointed tip, aware of the shiver it sent coursing through her. She raised her hands to his shoulders, gripping them tight as he continued to tease the hard point, her breathing growing heavy with his. He broke from her mouth and dipped to taste the skin of her neck, inhaling the flowery scent of her. As his tongue traced the line of her skin, she laid one cheek against his hair, the subtle move both innocent and trusting. He wanted to be worthy of it as he sank lower to take the tip of one full breast in his mouth. Her grip on him strengthened as he made small circles around it, suckling as she arched her back so he could taste more.

His hands rested on her hips to steady her against him, but he hesitated to move lower and worship the more intimate part of her, afraid the force of her reaction might undo his control. There'd be plenty of time to show her more. Tonight he wanted her to experience the most basic of pleasure, the one denied to her in the past.

Sliding one hand beneath her arms so the side of her full breasts grazed his skin, he moved his other arm beneath her thighs and raised her up. She wasn't heavy, but fitted perfectly against him, her lips light and teasing against his neck as he carried her to his room. A few candles flickered in the holder beside the bed, but the fire in the grate roared, increasing the heat generated by their bodies. He laid her down on the cool sheets, then stretched out beside her.

'You're beautiful…' he breathed as he traced the curve of her waist and trailed his fingertips down over her hips before sliding between her thighs and into her pleasure.

'Justin, I—' She shifted against his hand, searching for something denied to her as his thumb teased her.

'I know,' he murmured against her arched neck, his ability to hold back with her body tightening around his failing. He wanted her as much as she wanted him and she was ready.

She moaned in frustration as he slipped his fingers from her, but she opened her legs to him and he settled between her thighs.

With languid, questioning eyes she watched him, moving beneath him until his manhood pressed against her need. He paused, noting her silent entreaty for more in the flush of her skin and the faint parting of her lips. The other women he'd been with had been demanding in their desire to be satisfied, but she waited, eager for him to lead her, and he wouldn't fail her. Here was someone who understood him and what it was to endure the attacks of family and the doubts of many. She supported him, believing in him when those he'd once thought his friends refused to, trusting him even in this most intimate of moments.

He slid his arms beneath her back, his fingertips digging into her skin as the softness of her curves pressed into his angular body and he slipped fully into her, bringing her closer to him than anyone had ever been before.

Susanna dug her nails into his shoulder blades as he moved slow and steady inside her, solid against her like a wall. She lost herself in the strength of him as he caressed her hip and trailed his finger over her stomach until he reached between them to touch her. She cried out at the sensation of his fingers working her pleasure as his member stroked in time to his movements.

This was no greedy fumbling or a hurried slaking of his need, but a lingering taste of affection and a deepening of the connection which had been growing between them these past few days. In this as in everything, he was careful and kind to her in a way almost everyone else had never been. Lord Howsham had used her body and ignored her, while the rest had torn at her heart, leaving her to bleed. Justin would never be so unkind.

She entwined her legs with his, drawing him deeper into her body. It wasn't just physical desire driving her on, but a more intense need rising up from the place she'd kept hidden from everyone. For the first time since her mother had died, there was someone to protect her and truly care for her and it touched her more than all the play of his fingers across her back. She was his wife. He would keep her safe and give her more than his body and name and worldly goods.

He took one nipple in his mouth and sucked the tender tip, making her writhe beneath him. The pleasure was too intense, too strong, and she craved the release cresting deep inside her.

Each press of his lips on her exposed skin and the fierce play of his fingers against her continued to drive her higher and higher until at last she cried out, clinging to him. With a few more thrusts, Justin groaned, his pulsing flesh matching the rippling of hers and heightening her release until at last he lowered himself over her, his chest meeting hers with each struggling breath.

After a long moment, the crackle of the fire and the sounds of wagons on the street outside began to fill the room. She released her grip on his back and the cool air danced over her sweat-dampened chest as he shifted away to one side, then drew her close. Her whole body was alive and yet satiated and she let out a long sigh.

His chest rumbled against her ear with a chuckle. 'I assume you enjoyed our evening together.'

She raked her hand lazily through the light hair on his chest. 'Very much.'

'Good, because there'll be many more. I want you to crave them as much as I do.'

She rolled over and settled her chin on his chest, her hair falling down the sides of her

face to spread over him. 'You've certainly succeeded in your intention.'

He brushed a lock of her hair off her face,
tucking it behind one ear. 'Good.'

She laid one thigh over his and shifted closer
to him, her mouth almost touching his. 'Is it
too soon to ask for more?'

He raised one interested eyebrow at her and
his fingers entwined in her hair. 'Not at all.'

Chapter Eight

The chaise rolled down the crowded length of Fleet Street, passing the hundreds of people flitting from shop to shop as they went about their day.

'Where are we going?' Susanna asked, stifling a small yawn behind one gloved hand. She and Justin had enjoyed little sleep over the past few nights, yet for all their long evenings she felt as refreshed as if she'd taken the waters of Bath.

Faint circles hung beneath Justin's eyes this morning as well, but it didn't diminish his natural humour or the teasing smile he flashed from across Mr Rathbone's borrowed carriage each time he admired her. 'You'll see, it's a surprise.'

'Like the one you showed me last night?'

She kicked off her slipper and ran one stocking-clad foot up the length of his thigh.

'Not quite.' He shifted to the squab next to her and took her hand. He turned it over to expose the skin between her glove and sleeve and flicked his tongue against the sensitive spot. His breath against the moisture raised a chill along her arm which reached deep inside her until she almost insisted he turn the carriage around and go back home. 'There'll be time for more later.'

He lowered her hand, both of them conscious of the carriage slowing to make a turn.

Susanna leaned past her husband to peer out of the window, taking in the red uniforms of old soldiers as they walked with their families, and the rosy cheeks of the young hawkers selling pies, apples and flowers. On one corner, they passed a man peddling newspapers announcing a salacious account of the Prince Regent's latest scandal.

Edwina would be eating up the story, tittering about it with her vapid friends, but the doings of the aristocracy were no longer Susanna's affair. She pressed one hand to her stomach, trying to settle it, wishing she didn't carry such a potent reminder of her time with them. It would ruin all the happiness building between her and Justin if he ever found out.

'You're trying to guess where we're going, aren't you?' He tugged her away from the window and down on to the seat beside him to wrap his arm around her waist.

'I am.' She shifted so his hand landed on her hip instead of her stomach, covering her worry with another lie, adding to the one already hovering over her. 'I wish you'd tell me. I don't like surprises.'

'You'll enjoy this one. I promise.'

She hoped so. Most surprises in her life had led to nothing but misery, though she couldn't imagine any of Justin's treading such a dark path. If he made a promise, she believed it. He was too good a man to deceive her. Sadly, she couldn't say the same of herself.

'I need to tell you something, Susanna...' Justin began hesitantly, raising a flutter in her belly which had nothing to do with the baby. 'Until the wine business is fully established, I have to remain in Philip's employ. I don't want us to fall into debt. I've seen too many times the horrors it can wreak on men and their families to risk it.'

'Why make it sound so grave? Working for

Mr Rathbone seems more a pleasure for you than a burden.'

'It is, but it also means there'll be nights, or mornings, or any time of day, in fact, when I might be called away to help him deal with a matter.'

'Like a doctor?' She remembered the one who had lived next to them in Oxfordshire and how many nights she'd been awakened by someone ringing the bell outside his door.

'Rather, but in the past I've never had to concern anyone else with my comings and goings. I don't want you to be alarmed or startled when it happens, or to worry about me while I'm gone.'

'Given the sudden nature of our courtship and marriage, there's little which can alarm me now.'

'Good. I'll rely on you to manage things when I've been called away. I intend for you to be my full partner in this.'

'You'd give me control?' Even when her grandfather had been ill, he'd refused to allow her mother to run the shop, relying on her uncle, even when he was barely a man, to see to the business. She touched her stomach again, wondering how much longer it would be before she couldn't conceal her condition and would have to pretend the child was his. It sickened her to deceive him when he was so good to her, but for the child's sake, she had no choice.

'Who else can I trust to manage it properly if not my wife? Besides, you didn't really think marrying me would mean a life of leisure, did you?'

'Not after the last few nights.' She flicked her top teeth with her tongue, the memory of their pleasure relieving some of her anxiety.

He pulled her against him and claimed her mouth, his wanting kiss making her forget everything except him and the pressure of his tongue against hers. She slipped her hand inside his coat, following the curve of his side beneath the silk before reaching the waist of his breeches. She began to work her hand inside the buckskin when he caught her wrist and broke away from her lips.

'Not yet, my dear. We're almost at our destination.' His eyes smouldered with his need and she knew, if they weren't so close to wherever he was taking her, they'd have indulged in a little sport in the carriage. The mere thought of such a daring intimacy nearly hollowed out her insides with desire.

She laid her hands on either side of his face and rose up to give him a long, tempting kiss. 'Then let's be quick with our business, so we may move on to more delightful work.'

He pulled her to him so each breath made her already taut breasts brush against his firm chest. 'Not so fast, you don't want me to rush.'

'Indeed, I don't.' She hummed, remaining in the circle of his arms, eager to be beneath him and to forget everything in the pleasure of his touch.

The driver's voice calling to the horses accompanied the slowing of the carriage as it came to a stop. Justin's arm around her eased as the carriage tilted a little to one side when the driver climbed down from his seat.

'We're here.' As soon as the door was open, Justin was out and beckoning Susanna to follow.

She blinked against the bright sun which greeted her as she stepped down on to the pavement. People passed by them in a steady stream, hurrying from one establishment to the next, carrying their purchases.

In front of her was a shop with arched windows, the walls holding them painted a shiny red. The name over the door had been removed, but the oblong ghost of it was outlined in faded paint. Brown paper covered the bottom half of the windows, denying all but the tallest passers-by a peek inside, assuming they could peer through the grime covering the square panes.

Justin tucked her hand into the curve of his elbow and pushed through the people to lead her to the front door. Removing a brass key from his pocket, he slipped it into the lock, oblivious to the scraping squeak it made before it released the bolt and allowed them through.

Justin moved into the centre of the rectangular room as Susanna closed the door, blocking out the noise from outside.

'Well, what do you think?' He held out his arms and spun in a slow circle, his boot heels thudding against the wooden floorboards and sending up small puffs of dust which tickled her nose. 'The building is sturdy, the previous occupants didn't take out their anger on the woodwork, or the windows, and it's well situated in a good neighbourhood with a great many prosperous businesses surrounding it.'

'Very nice.' There was nothing in the room

but an abandoned table and chair, a dark fireplace in one corner and a counter in front of the far wall, but Susanna could picture the space filled with bottles and barrels of the finest French and Spanish wines. The panelled walls only needed a little wood oil and dusting to make them shine again and with some washing the windows would sparkle. 'Is there a cellar?'

'There is and it's being stocked with the first delivery of our inventory as we speak.' He banged one heel against the floor and a familiar hollow sound echoed through the room. 'I'll leave it to you to find appropriate decorations for the windows and to arrange this room as you think best. I imagine you've given some thought to a matter like this before.'

'I have.' The same excitement she'd known the morning of the wedding raced through her. 'When I used to sit in Grandfather's shop while he was out with a delivery, I imagined how I could change things to make it more appealing to our customers. I had so many ideas, though I never said anything. There was no point. Grandfather wasn't likely to listen, or to change no matter how much it might profit him in the end. He was incredibly stubborn.'

'Luckily for you, I'm not. This is your chance to employ all your ideas.'

Susanna didn't respond. She couldn't. After doing little more than sitting in corners reading books for the past seven years, to be given real purpose excited her more than even the shop. As hurtful as her grandfather had been, the work of assisting a wine merchant had always kept her busy, distracting her from the pain and loneliness of her life. It would be wonderful to have industry again, to be a useful partner instead of some unwanted adornment.

The familiar thump of a wine cask being unloaded followed by the melodic roll of it down a wooden ramp filled the room.

'Come, I'll show you the cellar.' He held out his hand and she took it, clinging to him as he led her behind the counter and through the door to the room beyond.

The darker, smaller space wasn't as tidy as the front, and the remains of the past business were evident in the papers scattered about the tables or stuffed in the small cubbies along the wall. At the far end, a trapdoor in the floor stood open. Justin pulled her over to stand above it, as proud of the cellar as Lord Rockland used to be of a new hunting dog.

Susanna bent, hands on her knees, to peer down into the hole. The flicker of candles and the daylight from the outside ramp lit up the faded red bricks lining the walls and rising up to arch over the ceiling. The pungent scent of damp plaster and musty air wafted over her, dredging up memories of the many hours she'd spent in the semi-darkness of her grandfather's cellar, counting barrels or fetching bottles. More than once she'd slipped into the cool darkness to cry in the corner behind a tall cask after some rude comment from a neighbour, or her grandfather. She straightened and moved away from the dark hole, back to the sunlight and Justin's excitement, trying to place some distance between the present and those difficult days.

'You think it's too small? I was worried about that. I'm hoping in time to expand the business, perhaps gain the shop next door,' Justin explained, as though seeking her approval. It was something she wasn't used to.

'I think the cellar and your plans are perfect,' she reassured him.

'Except?' he prodded, having noticed the change in her mood. Far from letting it pass to focus on his own concerns, he wanted to draw it out.

'The smell of it reminds me of my grandfather.'

'Not a pleasant memory?'

'No. The students he sold wine to never cared about my background, only how cheaply they could obtain their spirits. It was the neighbours who were nasty and my grandfather and uncle never stopped them. They were too concerned with maintaining their clients to worry about protecting my insignificant feelings. More than likely they agreed with whatever it was they said.'

'Then they and he were wrong.' He brushed a stray curl away from her cheek. 'If anyone throws your past in your face, or says anything degrading to you, I'll see to it they regret it.'

Remembering the way he'd pummelled her half-brother, she didn't doubt he would. As tender as he was with her at night, she'd witnessed the way his hands could turn lethal when it came to defending himself. His protection now extended to her, and if her past was any indication of her future he'd be forced to keep his word. 'I don't think it's a matter of if, but when.'

Justin took her by the shoulders. 'Don't invite trouble. It has a way of finding you—there's no need to seek it out.'

'Are you never bothered by things like your father?'

'Every day, but I try not to regret, or wish things were different. It doesn't do anyone any good.'

'I wish I possessed your optimism.' And his ability to stride away from past troubles and mistakes. Hers grew quietly inside her.

'In time, you will. Now, what do you think? Is the cellar sufficient?' he urged, trying to draw her out of her melancholy mood. She let him, eager to be as happy as he was.

'It's excellent.'

'Good.' He glanced past her out of the window to the yard at the back where the men were unloading the barrels. 'Come and see what I've purchased.'

In the small courtyard behind the building, men laughed and talked as they rolled the casks into the cellar. Susanna approached one of the waiting barrels and read the name on the lid, amazed by the words emblazoned on the label.

'How did you come by such a fine vintage

so soon?' Her grandfather had known many men in the wine trade and he'd never once been able to secure a cask such as this.

Justin leaned his elbow on the top of the barrel and dropped his voice, taking on the sly countenance of a rogue. 'In the course of working for Philip, I've cultivated a number of contacts in, shall we say, more dubious corners of London. Usually, I rely on them to tell me who owes money to whom, what brothels potential clients are in debt to and what other moneylenders they might be avoiding. Since starting this venture, I've used my connections to put it about I'll pay for information about wine coming in on ships. An old source told me about this one and the debts the man owed. I was able to purchase this cask at a fraction of its value and ease the man's more pressing financial burdens.'

He smiled, quite proud of himself. Susanna was impressed.

'How very astute of you, though I wonder if any of these contacts of yours will ever show up on our doorstep?'

'If they do, Walter will handle them. He's quite adept at getting their information and giving them their expected payment.'

'No doubt from years of practice.'

Justin nodded, but said no more.

'Then I won't worry,' Susanna assured him.

'Good.' He picked at the metal band around the top of the barrel, his roguish smile changing to one serious enough to challenge Mr Rathbone's. 'I want you to know your safety is important to me and I'll always protect you.'

'I know.' Guilt chewed at her, but she smiled, trying to bring back the excitement which had greeted their arrival.

'Sir, we'll be needin' you to check on what we brought,' one of the burly men interrupted from near the ramp as he raised his cap to wipe the sweat from his wide forehead.

'Of course.' Justin made his way down the wooden stairs into the cellar, beckoning Susanna to follow.

She hesitated, wrinkling her nose at the dark, but with Justin beside her there was no reason to fear the memories it conjured up. He was right. The past was over and gone, at least most of it. With any luck, the rest of it would stay buried. She pressed her hand to her stomach as she followed the ramp down to where the delivery men were arranging the last of the barrels.

While Justin compared the number and names on the casks to a list he withdrew from his coat, Susanna explored the narrow space. There were sconces in the walls where candles could be placed, but none were there now. They'd probably been pilfered by street urchins once the business had been abandoned. Even in the quiet of Oxfordshire, Susanna had seen more than one shop broken into after the building had been foreclosed on, others picking over the leavings in search of something to steal or pawn.

Moving through the line of barrels, she tapped the smooth tops of each one, as so many things she'd forgotten over the last seven years returned to her—the pop of the casks being tapped, the gurgle of the wine pouring into the bottles, the tedious work of corking and labelling each one. Lady Rockland had tried to drive the common experiences out of her, yet the new ones she'd offered in return had fitted Susanna like a cast-off pair of shoes, more abrasive than welcoming. Here, not at Rockland Place, was where she belonged and she was glad to be returning. For all the bad memories of her uncle and grandfather, she remembered the many hours she'd spent working beside her mother, the two of them talking as her mother shared with her all she'd learned of the business from her parents.

Some day, Susanna would pass on the same knowledge to her child, and to the children who were sure to come from her union with Justin. All of them would possess the love of a father and mother and never experience the sting of being a bastard. It didn't make the deceit she'd played on Justin right, but she'd done it for the child. For this reason, perhaps one day she could forgive herself.

Justin finished his inventory, struggling to concentrate on the list as he watched Susanna move along the length of the cellar. She didn't sneer at the damp, but seemed lost in thoughts which brought a sweet softness to her face. There was something delightful she saw in the casks, not just the harsh memories of a neglecting grandfather, but other more comforting ones. Justin knew the sensation. Sometimes, when he walked into the pugilist club and inhaled the sweat mixed with sawdust and leather, he'd remember not his surly, drunk father, but the barrel-chested man who'd introduced him to the ring when he was twelve and taught him everything his own father had taught him about fighting.

She turned at the end of a line of casks and started down the second row. The light from outside illuminated her face and Justin caught the faint promise of their children in her wistful smile. Some day, he'd escort his own son to the club, show him how to defend himself like a man, both with his fists and his brains. Then he'd bring him down to the cellar and prove it wasn't just brute force which made a man or earned him respect, but hard work and industry, which so many thought Justin lacked. He'd raise his children to make themselves better men than him and encourage them to seek a station in life even higher than his. He wouldn't tear them down or hold them back and neither would Susanna. Her enthusiasm upstairs, and the alacrity with which she'd accepted her duties as his business partner, heartened him more than obtaining this fine shipment. In this stranger he'd found a true partner for both his life and his heart, one who wouldn't look down on him or doubt him.

'Are you done, sir?' the deliveryman questioned.

Justin snapped his attention back to the list,

finished his assessment and dropped a number of coins, including a few extra, into the man's wide hands. 'If you hear of any more shipments, be sure to tell me.'

The man counted the coins, his thick eyebrows rising at the payment before he palmed them, then raised his cap to Justin. 'I'd be glad to, sir.'

The man made for the ramp and climbed up into the daylight, leaving Justin and Susanna alone.

'Why are these separated from the others?' She waved her hand at the far corner of the cellar where six casks were arranged in a small alcove.

'You miss nothing, do you?'

'Observing is nearly all I've been allowed to do these last seven years.'

He moved between the line of barrels to join her. 'The wines near the front are common vintages and should turn a nice profit with sales to merchants looking to enhance their dinner table. These—' he thumped the top of one lid, eliciting a deep sound from the full wood '—are the best of the lot. I'm saving them for your stepmother's masked ball.'

'I wouldn't hold them all back,' Susanna warned.

'You think your father won't honour his end of our arrangement?'

'He will—after all, he kept his promise to my mother, in his own way. It's Lady Rockland you'll have to contend with. She'll whisper about us to the wives of the other peers, I have no doubt about it.' She picked a small splinter off a cask and flung it away. 'Cultivate your own contacts. Don't rely too heavily on Lord Rockland's.'

'Sage advice.' If not a touch disheartening.

'Don't look so grim.' She laid a hand on the side of his face, driving back the sense of failure nipping at him like the damp. 'A man who can secure inventory like this can just as easily shift it to a notable merchant and other prosperous men.'

Justin took her hand and laid a gentle kiss on her palm, thankful for her honesty and her faith in him. Until the shop was on a secure footing, and trade brisk, the risk of failure still loomed. With her by his side he could face it and keep his worries at bay.

'Now come, we should be getting home.' He

led her to the ramp, his confidence restored. 'We have a great deal to plan.'

Justin instructed one of his trusted men to remain behind and guard the store, then he and Susanna made their way home in the carriage. During the drive, they exchanged ideas about the shop, talking over one another in their rush to explain their plans.

They were not more than a foot over the threshold of Justin's house when Walter approached them. 'Mr Rathbone requests your assistance at once with the Jacobson matter.'

'Have you laid out my clothes and other necessaries?' Justin asked as he escorted Susanna upstairs, Walter following behind.

'As usual, Mr Connor.'

They entered his room to see his plain coat draped on the bed, beside which rested the thin leather holster and the lacquered case which held his pistol.

'What is this nefarious matter calling you away?' Susanna asked, her humour unable to completely hide her concern.

'A ship's captain with a considerable amount of debt.' He shrugged out of his good jacket and handed it to Walter before taking up the plain one. 'He gambled the profits from his last cargo away and the one he has now must be seized in order to repay his loan. Keep your fingers crossed there's a shipment of fine wine in the hold.'

'Even if it's bad we can still sell it for a profit.'

'I like the way your mind works.' He dropped a kiss on her lips, lingering a moment to enjoy the sweet taste of her and wishing he could dally, but business called. Breaking from her, and heartened by the answering disappointment in her eyes, he took up the leather holster and slid his arms through it, settling it at his side. He flipped open the lid of the case, revealing the shiny pistol resting on the blue velvet inside.

Susanna's eyes grew wide at the sight of the weapon. 'Will it be dangerous?'

He hadn't been completely honest with her in the carriage about all aspects of his business with Philip. 'Desperate men who owe money are unpredictable. Best to be prepared.'

He checked the flash pan to make sure it was clear of debris. If things with the captain grew tense, he couldn't risk a misfire. Hopefully, the captain wouldn't put up a fight. The thought of risking his life again, especially with Susanna standing tensely beside him, so concerned about where he was going, didn't sit well with him. Soon he'd give up this portion of his life, but not today.

Confident the weapon was clean, he slid the pistol into the holster, then slipped on his jacket.

'Please be careful,' she urged.

He looked at her. 'I'm always careful.'

'Why do I doubt that?'

He came around the bed to stand over her, resting his hands on her slender shoulders.

'Don't worry, the pistol is only a precaution and I'm as skilled with it as I am with my fists.' He dropped a long, comforting kiss on her lips, his desire to remain strong in the pressure of his skin against hers. However, like her he knew he had to go and all too soon the kiss was over. 'I'll be back as fast as I can.'

In a whirl of his redingote, he went out the door and was gone.

Susanna sank a little against the bedpost, holding on as much to steady herself against her worries as to brace her knees against the intensity of his kiss. His ability to affect her so deeply made her as giddy as when she'd sampled the champagne at Lady Rockland's soirées. However, she wasn't drunk now and this was no sitting room.

If business hadn't called him away, she might have provoked him to linger and lost herself in the smell of the leather beneath his shirt and the heat from their time outside. Instead, she'd let him go, understanding his need to remain employed and his loyalty to Philip Rathbone.

His loyalty was one of the traits she admired about Justin the most and one she was determined to match. There was no better time to begin than now. She couldn't sit here all day fretting over him, not when there was so much work to be done.

Susanna made her way downstairs in search of Mrs Robinson. She found her in the kitchen and discussed with her the need to hire a charwoman to clean the shop.

Within the hour, the efficient housekeeper had summoned the daughter of a scullery maid who worked next door and the stout woman with strong arms was engaged. Susanna sent her off with a note to the man guarding the shop to allow her in so she could set to work at once.

This one item seen to, Susanna settled at the desk in Justin's study near the back of the house and began drawing up a list of necessary items for the window. The list was nearly complete when Walter interrupted her with a cough.

'The elder Mr Connor is here, ma'am,' the formidable butler announced with more warning than welcome. 'He's in the study. Should I give him the usual amount Mr Connor does and send him on his way?'

'No, I'll see him.' With Justin gone and not expected back very soon, she might become better acquainted with the elder Mr Connor and discover ways to soothe some of the difficulties between father and son. It seemed a monumental task, but if she could make things even a little better between them, it would be worth the effort.

'Very well, madam. I'll remain close by, in case I'm needed.'

Having seen Mr Connor's temper, she well understood what he meant. 'Thank you.'

Susanna set down her pen and with some hesitation made her way down the short hall to the cosy room at the front of the house. Before she reached the narrow entrance hall she paused and turned to the butler. 'Ask Mrs Robinson to set out a small tea in the dining room.'

'Yes, madam.' Walter hurried off on his errand, leaving Susanna to face Mr Connor alone.

She nodded a greeting to Mr Green, who waited near the front door, his eyes on his boots as though trying not to be seen. With a charge like Mr Connor, she wasn't surprised by his desire to fade into the woodwork. Her nerves weren't exactly calm as she stepped into the bright sitting room to face her father-in-law.

'Good afternoon, Mr Connor,' Susanna called out, refusing to allow his answering scowl to diminish her smile.

'What's good about it?' Mr Connor grumbled. 'With my son out, I suppose I have to come begging to a woman for my money, as though I were a boy in breeches and not a full grown man who earned every one of those shillings.'

'You needn't beg at all.' Susanna clasped her hands in front of her. 'All you need do is ask and I'll gladly supply you with your usual sum.'

Mr Connor scrunched up his face as though trying to come up with an answer to her invitation as biting as the anger eating at his insides. Susanna spoke first.

'First, you'll join me for tea. I'd like for us to get to know one another.'

He eyed her with more suspicion than disdain and she braced herself for a sharp retort, determined not to fling one back. For all her years of living with her grandfather, no matter how hard she'd worked, no matter how sweet and kind and loving she'd been to him, she'd never once cracked the hard shell he'd surrounded himself with. The same might be true of Mr Connor, but the little girl in Susanna who'd tried so hard to gain her grandfather's affection wasn't ready to give up on this old man, especially not when he was hurting Justin, too.

Despite the hardness deepening the lines of his face, the only thing Mr Connor hurled at her was a question. 'Why?'

'Because we're sure to deal with one another quite regularly and it's better to do so as friends than enemies,' Susanna offered, trying to lower the man's hackles. Like her grandfather, Mr Connor was perpetually surly and she could guess the reason why. Her grandmother's death had ended what little cheer her grandfather had possessed. Judging from what Justin had told her of his father, the same grief had settled over Mr Connor after his wife's passing, weighing on him until there was nothing but gin and hate to dull the pain.

'I'll stay if you can offer me something stronger than tea.'

Like his son, he wasn't one to beat around the bush. 'Come and join me in the dining room. We'll see what we can find to slake your thirst.'

Susanna led the gentleman to the dining room, then stepped into the hall to speak with Mrs Robinson. 'Please see to Mr Green. He looks as if he needs a thimble of gin.'

'Or a tankard,' Mrs Robinson replied. 'Leave him to me, madam, I'll see him calmed, though not so much he can't perform his duties.'

'Thank you. And one more thing.' She moved close to the housekeeper, dropping her voice so as not to be overheard by the elder Mr Connor or his minder. 'Bring me a small bottle of spirits, nothing too strong and only a quarter full.'

Mrs Robinson's normally staid expression bloomed with surprise. 'Ma'am?'

'Trust me, please.'

With a 'whatever you wish' nod, Mrs Robinson made for the kitchen, collecting young Mr Green as she went.

Susanna joined Mr Connor at the table where he was already seated and helping himself to a generous slice of lemon cake. Ignoring his lack of manners, Susanna took her place and poured herself tea, not bothering to offer him any.

'This food is much better than the slop Mrs Green feeds me,' Mr Connor complained, tucking in to the cake.

Mrs Robinson's entrance kept Mr Connor's mumbling from expanding into too loud a complaint.

Susanna took the dark green bottle from Mrs Robinson and passed it to her churlish guest. 'Here we are, something a little stiffer than tea.'

He sniffed the open top with a snarl. 'Is this the best you could do?'

'Our merchandise is in the store, not here, Mr Connor.'

'Don't think you can fool me. I've seen my

son carousing enough to know he likes his spirits as well as any man.' He poured himself as much port as the dainty tea cup in front of him would hold. 'Don't suppose a man could get a real glass?'

'Your drink is better concealed in the china.' Susanna raised her cup to her lips, sliding him a conspiratorial glance.

Mr Connor seemed to regard her with a new appreciation and he winked one wrinkled eye at her, then held up his teacup in salute. 'You're a crafty one, I'll give you that.'

'I've learned a thing or two from your son, as I'm sure he did from you.'

'Taught him everything he knows.' Mr Connor sat back and puffed out his thick chest with pride. 'None was as good at gettin' information out of people as me. I could ferret out any man's secret and his debts, and discover where they'd stashed their valuables. I was the one who kept the elder Mr Rathbone safe when his clients didn't want to pay.'

'Justin speaks very highly of your time with him at the pugilist club.' It was a bit of an exaggeration, but it served the purpose of stunning Mr Connor.

'He was the best fighter at the club. Gentleman John Jackson himself once saw him spar and said he could be a professional boxer if he wanted.' Mr Connor's face broke out into a fond smile at the pleasant memory before his expression wilted. 'But he thought himself too good for it, like he thinks himself too good for me. I'm surprised he speaks well of me at all.'

'He wants you to be proud of him.'

'He don't care a fig for what I think.' He drained the teacup, but didn't ask for more.

'I assure you, Mr Connor, you're very wrong.' She laid a steadying hand on the almost threadbare arm of his coat.

He stared at her hand as if this was the first time in a long while he'd been offered any tenderness.

The clock in the hallway began to chime and the quiet moment between them was broken. Mr Connor pulled away his arm and rubbed the whiskers at the end of his chin. 'Best be going before Justin comes back from wherever he's at. He smells liquor on my breath, and we're both in for it. I wouldn't want a pretty thing like you getting in trouble.'

'I assure you, I can hold my own against anyone, including your son.'

'Good. He needs someone to thump some

good sense into him every now and again.' He winked at her and she winked back, happy to be colluding with him. In the gesture she felt a measure of trust and the first small step towards easing the prickliness of his relationship with Justin.

'Please come back any time you wish. I'm sure I can find a little something to make your visit a bit sweeter,' Susanna offered as she escorted him to the door.

'I shall.' He trilled his fingertips together in front of his chest in delight, his look reminding her very much of Justin, especially around the eyes which were the same rich brown as his son's. With a shave and a better-fitting coat, the resemblance between father and son would show even more. 'Now, where's that lousy minder of mine?'

His raised voice carried through the house. A moment later Mr Green came hurrying in from the kitchen, looking slightly more at ease either from one of Mrs Robinson's tonics or just a few moments away from his blustery charge. 'I'm here, Mr Connor.'

'Then let's be off.'

'To the pub sir?' Mr Green asked.

'No, I'm tired and want to go home.' Mr

Connor tapped his hat over his head, oblivious to the stunned stiffness of Walter as he passed him and made for outside.

Susanna watched the two men walk off down the street, aware of Mrs Robinson beside her.

'Well done, ma'am,' Mrs Robinson commended.

'Make sure you keep a half-empty bottle of port handy,' Susanna instructed the housekeeper, whose eyes danced with mirth at the idea. 'I think we may be seeing Mr Connor here quite often for tea.'

Chapter Nine

A myriad things connected to the business kept Susanna busy, both after Mr Connor left and for the many days after. There were curtains to be selected for the front windows, accounting books to purchase, calling cards to order and the design of wine labels to approve. Justin was occupied with his own tasks, taking on an apprentice, two shop assistants and visiting and securing customers. It proved an exciting and challenging week, and with each passing day Susanna felt more at ease in both her new role as a wife and her place in the Connor household. Here, no one made her feel like an unwanted interloper, even when she changed the menu or suggested a different arrangement of the sitting-room furniture. The security of it provided a calm she hadn't known since before her grandmother had died.

Despite her happiness, in the back of her mind she couldn't help but feel something was waiting to end it all. In the past, whenever she'd felt safe and secure, death or a rumour had reared its ugly head to steal her peace. The old worry it would happen again continued to pester her during quiet moments when she studied inventory or reviewed the bills. She tried to shake the feeling, but she couldn't. Whatever foreboding she imagined waiting for her, she suspected it would come from Grosvenor Square. Since the wedding, they'd heard nothing from the Rocklands, but Susanna wasn't convinced Lady Rockland was finally done with her. The woman had little else to do except to see to Edwina and be nasty to her inferiors. Every time a letter arrived at the house for Justin, Susanna feared it might be a missive from her stepmother with some insidious reference to Susanna's secret, one which would plant the fatal seed of doubt in his mind and ruin their happiness.

Only at night when she was alone with Justin in the low light of his room, his body covering hers, was everything forgotten in the bliss of his kisses and the playful caress of his fingers.

* * *

One evening, a week after their visit to the shop, Susanna entered Justin's room where he sat before the fire reading a letter. The sight of it and the stern contemplation dulling his usual humour made her halt. Whatever was being conveyed held his full attention and not for a good reason.

The old crow has finally written. Her hand tightened on the small board she carried. She wanted to drop it and flee, but she held fast. Whatever the letter said, she would face it.

He didn't glance up as she cautiously approached, trying to catch sight of the signature on the letter through the thin paper, but his hand blocked it. The seriousness in his eyes as he read increased the dread sliding through her as she came to stand in front of him. She braced herself and held out the board with the three samples of a bottle label which had been delivered by the printer.

'Which one do you think we should use for the red wine?' she asked, clearing her throat at the unnerving squeak in her words.

He looked up at the labels, then pointed to the one in the centre, barely seeing it or her. 'This one.'

'I agree.' She set the labels on the table next to his chair, still on edge but glad to not see the anger she'd expected. It still didn't calm her fears. 'Who's the letter from?'

'Your father.' Justin folded the missive and set it beside the labels, visibly troubled by the contents.

She dropped into the chair across from his. 'What does he say?'

'He's asked me to see him tomorrow afternoon to discuss the wine purchase for the lovely Lady Rockland's ball.'

She sagged against the back of the chair with relief. However, she wasn't out of danger yet, she never would be. She wished she hadn't made the deal with her father for his support. A clean break would've been best. Instead they were obligated to deal with the Rocklands for a short while longer. Her father wasn't likely to say anything about the child, assuming he knew, but the remaining ties between them risked Justin encountering Lady Rockland and her vicious tongue. She wouldn't put it past Lady Rockland to let her suspicions about Susanna's pregnancy slip, if for no other reason than to be spiteful.

'Do you want to come with me or shall I go alone?' he asked.

'You should go alone.' Lady Rockland was much less likely to approach him if Susanna wasn't there.

With a sharp knock, Mrs Robinson entered, carrying a parcel wrapped in string. 'This just arrived for you, ma'am, from Mrs Fairley.'

She laid the parcel down on the bench at the foot of the bed, then left.

Susanna went to the package and began to untie the knot securing the string.

'I hope you aren't spending lavishly on clothes,' Justin teased from his place by the fire, the return of his good humour helping her to recover hers.

'It isn't a dress—' Susanna tugged at the knot but it wouldn't budge '—but our costumes for the masque.'

Justin came to stand beside her, gently pushed her hands away, then broke the string. 'You're aware I don't dance?'

'At all?' She winced. She sounded as shallow as Edwina.

He leaned against the footboard. 'Dancing isn't a skill a man of my class is required to possess.'

Susanna pulled the string off the package, balled it in her hand and tossed it to one side. 'It's a lot like boxing, with a great deal of hopping back and forth with your partner.'

'Liar.'

'You needn't worry about standing up with me. As much as I enjoy a good reel, I've found it's much more interesting to remain in the crowd and observe.' She lifted the lid off the box. 'I learned more about society hidden behind a black-silk mask than I ever did sitting quietly in a corner while the women gossiped.'

'And what costume am I to wear?' He shifted behind her and wrapped his arms around her waist to peer over her shoulder. His cheek rested against hers as she folded back the tissue paper to reveal the garments beneath.

'I decided to make it simple.' She lifted a flowing dark green cloak with a hood and matching silk mask out of the parcel. 'Cloaks and masks.'

Justin reached out and slid the mask from her fingers. The silk gliding over her skin raised a line of goose bumps along the length of her arm. 'If the wine business fails, we can take up careers as highway robbers.'

'It'd certainly be an interesting way to fund a venture and quite thrilling.'

'Until we're hanged.'

'I didn't say there weren't risks.' She grinned at him over her shoulder. 'And you'd make a dashing rogue.'

'I like the sound of that.' He flicked the mask on to the bed and turned her around, pressing her to him so she could feel the stirring of his manhood against her stomach.

'That's not all you like.' She twined her arms around his neck, drawing him down to her, eager to be close to him and enjoy the comfort and peace of him. It would banish the worry still hovering inside her.

There was no careful removing of clothes or the slow unlacing of stays tonight. Their garments were discarded in a hurried frenzy of tugging and pulling with one or two snapped buttons plinking to the floor before Susanna and Justin tumbled naked and needy on to the bed.

Against her skin Susanna felt the discarded mask. Pulling it out from under her, she drew it across the span of his back.

'What are you doing, my little minx?' he

growled in her ear, his fingers pausing in their tracing of her thighs.

She didn't answer as she draped the silk over the top of his shoulder and then down his chest, pushing it over the solid ripples of his stomach and the sides of his waist. He sat back on his knees and she rose to hers, never allowing the silk to leave his skin as she worked it lower. She slid the softness up and down the length of him, drawing from him a low, deep moan.

'Do you like it?' she asked in seductive innocence, tilting her head down like a coquette.

'What do you think?' he murmured, his fingers tight on his thighs as he closed his eyes, delighting in each stroke of her hand. He grew stronger beneath her palm until at last he pulled her hand and the mask away. 'Careful, we don't want to end things too soon.'

He gently pushed her down into the coverlet and arched over her to take one taut nipple between his teeth before pressing a kiss against the space between her breasts. He moved lower, tracing circles on her stomach with his tongue before he placed a kiss at the top of the hair between her thighs.

'Don't tease me,' Susanna gasped, wanting to be one with him at once.

'I must.' He smiled like the devil before his head dipped down and his mouth pressed against her most intimate parts.

She gripped the coverlet as he tasted her until she thought she could take no more. Arching her hips against him, he slid his hands beneath her buttocks, his fingers gripping her tight as he continued to pleasure her. She sighed, not ashamed to surrender to him in this most delicate way. It would have embarrassed her a few days ago to be so vulnerable with him, yet she welcomed it tonight, lost in the desire he raised within her, trusting her whole being to him. She knew he would never betray it or her. She cried out as he slid one finger inside her, caressing her with a gentle pressure. Never in her life had she imagined so much passion and intimacy could exist with a man.

She whimpered, eager for release and at the same time holding back, wanting all of him. When at last she thought she might shatter, he withdrew from her and sat up. She rose to her knees and feeling quite bold, pushed him back down against the coverlet. She straddled his thighs until the tip of his hardness pressed against her. He took her hips with his wide hands and eased her down over him, filling her body as he had her heart since the day they'd wed.

He clutched her by the waist and rolled so she was under him. She grabbed his buttocks, pulling him deeper into her as he lay down on his elbows, his chest hard against her breasts, his mouth firm on hers as he thrust into her. Bound together as one, they raced towards their pleasure, each pushing the other higher until at last their release crashed over them like waves against the rocks of the shore.

'I love you...' Justin breathed, his face buried in the silky curls which had slipped from their pins to spill across the pillow.

'I love you, too.' She held on to him, refusing to let him slide away from her, still so afraid this bliss between them wouldn't last. All her life she'd wanted this closeness, this beautiful experience of being cherished and loved. To think it might end with only a few nasty words broke her heart nearly as much as his love had mended it. Tears filled her eyes and one slid down her cheek to wet his.

'What's wrong?' he asked, touching his forehead to hers.

'I'm so happy with you. I don't want anything to ruin it.'

'What could?'

She closed her eyes and inhaled his musky scent. She loved him and she didn't want to lose him. Despite the joy of the last few days, she was still deceiving him in the worst way a woman could. How something wouldn't come from it to ruin everything, she didn't know, but she couldn't reveal her fears.

'Have faith, Susanna, in me and us,' he murmured in her ear.

She pressed her lips to his, struggling to share in his belief all would be well. Perhaps it would and their love would never end. It was a beautiful dream and she would cling to it, and his heart, for as long a she could.

The bell over the wine shop door chimed as Justin entered. From the room behind the counter, Susanna appeared, a welcoming smile spreading across her pretty face like the light falling in through the windows. It heightened the blush of her cheeks and the sparkle in her eyes. He'd been called away at daybreak by Philip, denying him the pleasure of waking with her and perhaps enjoying something more of the delight which had kept them both from sleep for the better portion of the night.

'Do you like what I did with the front window?' she asked, coming around to offer him a kiss which was both welcoming and inviting. If she continued with such sweet greetings, he might have to set up a private room in the back with a bed, or find a way to make the squabs of the chaise much more comfortable.

'I adore it. You're beautiful *and* clever. How did I get so lucky?'

'I jumped in your carriage instead of some buck-toothed old man's.'

'How fortunate for both of us.' He nuzzled her neck, ready to pull her into the room at the back, send away the assistant and the apprentice, slip the lock and while away the hours when the bell over the front door clanged.

Justin straightened, his hand freezing on Susanna's back at the sight of Helena striding through the door. Susanna looked from Justin to Helena, scrunching up her brow in question.

'Good morning, Mrs Gammon. To what do we owe the pleasure of this visit?' Not even Justin's skills at jest could keep the edge from his voice.

'I'm Mrs Preston now,' Helena corrected. 'Mr Preston and I were married a few days ago.'

'Congratulations,' Susanna offered in a sweet voice, but Justin caught the slight hesitation.

'The Chartons told me of the shop and your wedding. I wanted to meet the new Mrs Connor and see your establishment.' Helena fixed her scrutiny on Susanna as though she were an elegantly crafted bottle of fine port with a hefty price affixed to it. If Helena appreciated the vintage, it was difficult to tell through the jealousy which stiffened her stance beneath the red silk pelisse she wore.

'And now you have.' Justin rapped the top of a cask with his knuckles, making it clear it was time for her to take her leave, but it was obvious her curiosity was not completely satisfied. It could kill her for all he cared.

'Mrs Connor,' the bespectacled assistant said, coming out from the back room. 'There's a discrepancy in the ledger I'd like you to see.'

'Yes, I'll have a look.' She glanced back and forth between Helena and Justin as if debating whether or not to leave them alone together. Justin nodded at her. He was more than capable of facing his old lover and seeing her off. 'If you'll excuse me.'

Susanna followed the shop assistant through the far door and into the storeroom behind.

'She's very pretty,' Helena grudgingly admitted, clearly disappointed at finding Susanna beautiful and not horse-faced or buck-toothed.

'I'm not you, Helena. I don't sell myself to the highest bidder to achieve my goals.'

'I didn't marry Mr Preston only for his money. We care a great deal for one another.' She wasn't convincing and she knew it. She lifted a bottle of wine out of the straw-filled crate beside her and read the label, nodding approvingly. 'I'll have to send my man here to purchase a few bottles. Mr Preston does love his Madeira.'

She practically dropped the bottle back in the crate and Justin knew it wasn't all marital bliss at the Preston residence. A part of him felt sorry for her. They'd been friends once, but she'd made her decision and now she would live with it.

'I must say I'm surprised. I didn't think you'd make a go of it.'

He crossed his arms over his chest to keep

from tossing the woman out on to the street. 'I'm glad I exceeded your expectations.'

'I never thought you one to take responsibility seriously, especially not all the endless details like inventory and bills.' She flicked a glance around him to the door leading into the back room. 'Or have you left those things to your wife while you enjoy the more pleasurable aspects like sampling the merchandise?'

'He hasn't left all the work to me.' Susanna's voice echoed from behind the counter as she came to stand beside Justin, linking her arm in his and facing the widow. 'It's to Justin's credit we purchased this shop. Without his hard work in securing the merchandise, and our clients, we would've been forced to abandon the venture long before we'd begun.'

'I'm sorry, Mrs Connor. I didn't mean to insult you or your husband,' Helena stuttered, her round face as red as her pelisse with her embarrassment.

'Yes, Mrs Preston, I believe you did.'

Justin held his head a little higher at his wife's response, heartened by her courage. If she could stand up to a woman like Helena, she could face anyone who cast aspersions at her about her background.

'Yes, well, I apologise again, Mrs Connor. Congratulations on your success.' With her head lowered, Helena hurried out the door, all the confidence she'd walked in with gone.

'Quite a charming woman,' Susanna observed, sliding her hand down his arm to lace her fingers in his. 'Whatever did you see in her?'

'Not nearly as much as I've seen in you.' He claimed her mouth, drawing out her tongue with long, smooth caresses. She pressed her body to his, fitting against him perfectly.

'Come.' He pulled her towards the door.

'Where are we going?'

'Home. Mr Spinner, the shop is yours for the afternoon,' he called over his shoulder.

'Yes, sir.' The assistant's voice trailed out of the door behind them.

Justin bundled her inside the chaise. 'Home, Mr Tibbs, as fast as you can.'

Justin climbed inside beside her, smiling to find she'd already drawn the shades. Without a word they were in one another's arms, exploring each other as best they could through the wool and cotton covering them. He slipped his hands under her skirt and traced the line of her calf up behind the curve of her knee, slipping one finger in between her skin and the ribbon holding up the stocking.

It wasn't physical need which drove him forward now, but her belief in him. Never had a woman made him feel so capable of achieving every goal he'd set out to achieve, or stood beside him as Susanna had just now. All the others had considered him only for sport or an evening of pleasure and laughter. They'd never seen him for more, or believed in his dreams.

Sliding his hand up her thigh, he found her centre, his restraint threatening to buckle as he discovered her readiness for him. This would be no rushed fumbling in a carriage, but merely the prelude to an hour or two in which he would pleasure her entire being. She clasped his lapels, breathing hard against his cheek as his fingers worked her tender flesh, stoking a need which had sparked long before they'd entered the carriage.

'Please stop,' she begged, her wanting clear in her strained voice, but he continued with the relentless pace of his strokes, eager for her to reach her release more than once today.

The noise of the streets muffled her cries as she fell against him. He cradled her, playing with the soft skin of her thighs, his member throbbing with impatience beneath the buckskin of his breeches. He could open the fall and be inside her at once, give in to the urgency near strangling him, but he held back as the chaise came to a rocking halt in front of his house.

Together, they hustled to straighten her skirts and she was just composed when the driver opened the door. Jumping out, Justin pulled her along behind him. They rushed past Walter, who held open the door, and up the small staircase, reaching Justin's room and slamming the door closed behind them.

Together they toppled on to his bed. With deft fingers she slid his buttons through their holes and tugged his breeches down over his hips. The cold air of the room hit him and he closed his eyes, opening them in surprise when Susanna's gentle lips brushed the tip of his hardness. He moaned as her mouth slid over him. With her tongue she teased him and he grew tighter with each satiny caress until at last she sat up and he groaned his frustration, opening his eyes to pin her with a look of pent-up need he could feel deep inside of her.

Pulling her skirts up around her waist, she straddled him, sliding down to take him inside her. He let out a low, guttural sound as she ground her hips against his. He raked her thighs with his fingers and her stocking-clad feet curled beneath her on the bed as she moved with a steady pace over him. As her body began to tighten around him, he clasped her thighs, his strokes coming faster and faster until his cries joined hers and she collapsed on his chest, the ripples of her pleasure caressing his.

She laid down over him and rested her cheek against his chest, closer to him than anyone had ever been. For all his jokes and humour, for all his teasing and pretending not to care, there'd existed inside him a loneliness she now filled. He didn't want to lose it any more than he wanted to let go of her now.

They laid together in silence for some time, Justin tracing lazy circles on Susanna's still-exposed thigh. She fingered the line of his uncovered hip, her gentle touch increasing the contentment their lovemaking had brought him. Helena's insults had struck a nerve he thought his father's condemnation had long made him blunt to, but Susanna's sure belief in him had eased the sting.

'I couldn't have managed the start of my

business so well without you,' he admitted, breaking the quiet punctuated by birds and a maid calling to someone across the street.

'You could have. You have a way with people. I've seen how you handle the men who deliver the wine and the ones at the docks who you buy it from. You're a natural charmer.'

'But Helena is right, I don't have a head for the details.' It nearly choked him to say it. 'It's why I've left them to you.'

She lifted her face to his, resting her chin on her hand on his chest. 'And I have no gift with the importers. It's why we do so well together.'

He pulled her closer. 'I lied to you when I said nothing ever troubles me.'

'I know.' She slid down beside him and rested her head on his shoulder.

'Ever since my mother died, it's killed me to see my father drinking himself to death. He used to be like me, capable of charming anyone. It's what my mother said she loved so much about him. I barely remember what that man was like.'

'Perhaps if you talk to him,' she urged.

'I've tried, many times. I'm always polite when we're together, but it never makes a difference.' He wound one of her loose curls around his finger, hating to admit his failure with his father. It was as devastating as the loss of his ship and much more lasting because he couldn't overcome it. 'No matter what I do, it doesn't make a difference to him.'

'Don't be so sure, Justin.'

'It's hard not to be. What hurts the most is what he says about me. Sometimes, I think he's right.' He stared at the ceiling and the small crack in the plaster snaking over the bed, unable to face her, despising how weak and sad the admission made him.

She propped herself up on one elbow to sit above him, caressing his face with her hand. The light coming through the cracks in the curtains glittered in her eyes and caught the wispy strands of hair cascading down the side of her face. 'Don't let others define you, or set your value. It's something I've allowed people to do to me for years and it's never made me happy or changed their opinion of me.'

He stroked her cheek with the back of his fingers. 'You're as wise as you are beautiful.'

He drew her down and her hair fell over him as he tasted her lips, the sweetness of them driving back, but not silencing, the foul insults he'd endured for years and the failures which followed on their heels. He was a better man than all those people believed, one worthy of his wife's love. In time, with her help, he'd silence everyone who thought otherwise.

The clock on the mantel chimed one o'clock. With a sigh, Justin disentangled himself from Susanna. He wanted to linger here, but numerous details now demanded his attention.

'Where are you going?' she asked.

He stood, tugged his breeches up over his hips and did up the fall. 'Your father is expecting me and I have a great deal of charming to do.'

The glow from their lovemaking faded from her face and she chewed her lower lip in worry. 'Be careful with the Rocklands. I don't trust them.'

'What can they do except renege on their word?'

'More than you realise,' she murmured as if she knew something he didn't.

'Such as?'

Apprehension drew down the corners of her lips before she regained her smile. 'Nothing. I'm sure you'll dazzle my father with all the charm you use with your other contacts.'

'Indeed, I will.' He pressed a kiss to her

forehead, ignoring the strange sense there was more to her worry than she was revealing. 'I'll be back soon.'

Susanna watched him slip out the door, leaving her alone in the semi-darkness of the room. She drew her knees up to her chest and wrapped her arms around them, wishing she'd gone with him. It wouldn't stop Lady Rockland from lashing out at them if she chose to, but at least it would prevent her from worrying about what might happen while Justin and her father were together.

Swinging her legs over the side of the bed, she rose and made for her room to change her dress, determined not to fret. Nothing would happen. All would be well, just as Justin had promised last night. Selecting a new dress from the wardrobe, she shrugged out of her old one. The faint smell of Justin clinging to the muslin might be a comfort, but she could hardly go through the rest of the day so dishevelled.

An hour later, dressed in a simple white gown with green sprigs and with her hair confined once again to its coiffure, she sat at the writing table reviewing the week's menu. The satisfaction of her lovemaking with Justin had long since eased and had been replaced by the anxiety which continued to prick at her like a pin left in a dress. She didn't want Justin anywhere near the Rockland house, or her stepmother and the secret she held. It would be a long few hours before he returned and she learned if her secret was safe, or everything was coming to pieces.

She was so distracted with worry she didn't hear the elder Mr Connor until he sauntered into the sitting room unannounced.

'A good day to you, Mrs Connor.' He swept off his hat and handed the dented Wellington to Walter.

'And you, too, Mr Connor.' They went to the dining room where Mrs Robinson laid out the tea and set before him the half-full bottle of port. Mr Connor's hands still shook as he poured out a measure of the drink, but he didn't appear as rumpled or careworn today as he had during his first few visits. His coming to the house had become a habit over the past week. He seemed to know with unfailing canniness when his son wouldn't be home.

'Thank you for treating me as you do. I

haven't felt this well in a long time.' He patted her hand in the fatherly way which had developed between them during their teas. 'I sometimes think, if my wife had lived and with her the little girl, she might have grown up to be like you.'

Susanna struggled to maintain her smile. He wouldn't wish for a daughter like her if he learned what kind of woman she really was. She settled her hands over her stomach, noting the slight thickness where the child was growing inside her. For all her kindness to Mr Connor and his son, she was still a charlatan, a fallen woman who hadn't had the sense to remember herself in the face of a man's false promises.

'I'd like to tell Justin of our teas and have him join us one of these days,' Susanna offered.

'Don't go ruining a man's meal with such unpleasant business,' Mr Connor chided her, taking a long drink before setting the teacup back in its saucer.

'If you both spoke civilly to one another, you might be surprised how different things could be between you.'

Mr Connor scratched his head, mussing his

already wild grey hair. 'Gets to be so many years, a man doesn't know where to start.'

'The simplest, most direct approach is best.'

'But not always the easiest.' With a wink reminiscent of his son's, he held up his cup to her, then took a hearty sip. 'But I suppose nothing worth doing is ever easy.'

'Then you'll see him?' Susanna asked.

'Let's see what time brings.'

It wasn't a promise, but she felt sure he would soon face his son just as she was now certain how much port to place in the bottle, or which tarts were his favourites. There was no denying the change in Mr Connor and even Mrs Robinson had remarked on it. Whether it would last or result in any peace between father and son, she still couldn't say, but she'd continue to try and mend the rift between them. She owed this much to Justin in thanks for all he'd done for her, known and unknown.

Chapter Ten

'Here you are, Mr Connor, a complete list of the wines I require for Lady Rockland's masque.' The duke handed a sheet of paper across the wide oak desk to Justin. The entire room was grand, imposing, meant to make a man like Justin cower before the wealth and influence of Lord Rockland, but it did nothing to intimidate him. Today the duke might own the world, tomorrow his debts might consume him and force him to sell off the full-length Van Dyke hanging on the wall behind him.

Justin took the paper and examined it, careful to conceal his true reaction at the sheer number of bottles and vintages required. It would take all his connections throughout London, and quite possibly in the countryside, to acquire everything on the list. It'd be even more of a challenge given he had only a few days to achieve it, but he wasn't about to fail. Despite Susanna's worries about Lord Rockland's support, Justin was confident a man impressed was a man he'd continue to do business with. 'I'll have this to you in time, Your Grace.'

'Are you sure?' Lord Rockland regarded him with more shock than admiration at the alacrity with which Justin answered. 'It's quite an extensive selection.'

The sense the list was something of a test nagged at Justin, but he wasn't about to give Lord Rockland a gentlemanly way out of their bargain. 'I assure you, I'll have everything delivered in time.'

'Of course you will,' he answered with some disappointment. 'You do understand, after the masque, the two of you cannot expect further invitations or help from me in regards to your business. A man of my station can hardly be expected to meddle in the affairs of merchants. I've done my best to be responsible, as I have with all my other obligations, giving Susanna a most generous dowry which an enterprising couple could make more use of than my limited influence.'

It was then Justin understood why the duke

had taken Susanna in, but shown her no real love or affection. She was a duty, not his daughter. He was honourable enough to assume those duties laid at his feet, but once they were discharged, he would wash his hands of them, as he would Susanna and Justin after this order was fulfilled.

'You've been very generous with Susanna and you needn't worry about us. I made my way in the world before I married your daughter. I will again.'

Lord Rockland silently regarded him with, if Justin dared to think it, respect, the kind his father hadn't even grudgingly shown him. 'I have no doubt you will.'

Lord Rockland rose and nodded to Justin, bringing their meeting to an end. 'Good day to you, Mr Connor.'

Tucking the list in his coat pocket, Justin followed the waiting footman out of the high-ceilinged study, down the wide avenue of the hallway and to the expansive space of the entrance hall with the tall double doors set in the far end. For all his bravado in Lord Rockland's presence, the clear understanding there would be no more patronage was a blow. Susanna had tried to warn him, but he'd held out hope she might somehow be wrong. He should have listened to her. This must have been what she'd attempted to caution him about before he'd left. She knew the Rocklands better than he did, but still Justin wanted the great man's business. Lord Rockland's support would've smoothed the way to quicker success and the ability to rub it in the faces of his detractors sooner. Without the high-born patronage, Justin would once again be left to make his own way.

'Here to beg from my husband so soon?' A voice from somewhere above Justin made him stop. He turned to watch Lady Rockland descend the stairs, eyeing him as though he were a bug scurrying across her dinner plate. 'Has your business failed already?'

'I'm here at Lord Rockland's request.' Justin struggled to maintain his smile, seeing first-hand the wickedness Susanna must have suffered under the woman. 'My shop is doing well, thank you. Susanna is proving quite an asset.'

'It's fitting since she was born to such a low station in life.' Lady Rockland came to face Justin in an imperious rustle of black silk, her tight curls unmoving against her head. 'And she's brought you such a great deal beside her support, hasn't she? Money, connection to my husband, a child.'

Justin cocked his head at the woman. 'I have no doubt there will be children in the future.'

'There'll be a child sooner than you think, Mr Connor, one with a bloodline more distinguished than yours, but condemned to life as the common offspring of a wine merchant.'

The house rocked around Justin. He stood still, summoning up everything he'd ever learned from his father, Philip or at the pugilist club to centre himself and keep a hard restraint on the anger, disbelief and confusion rising inside him. Susanna hadn't deceived him. It was this wicked woman trying to cause trouble.

'Saying such a thing can be of no benefit to a woman of your rank and manners.'

'It is if it means you won't pollute my house with your or your wife's presence ever again.' Her tight face sharpened the jut of her square chin. 'My husband might welcome you here, but I won't have you set foot in this house again. He may want to wallow in his sins, but not me. I suggest you don't assist him in the endeavour by not attending the ball.'

Justin didn't answer, but executed the same

bow which had shocked her the first time they'd met. Then he turned on his heel and made for the door.

'Through the back door, Mr Connor, where the rest of the tradesmen call.'

Justin didn't break his stride as he marched towards the front door. The butler moved to step in front of it and block his exit, but Justin pinned him with a scowl to nearly fell him dead. The man drew back, leaving Justin to pull open the tall wooden doors and step outside. He left it to the hired man to close them behind him and, with his head held high, climbed into the chaise.

The streets of Grosvenor Square passed on either side of him in a blur as he stared at the empty seat across from his. It wasn't Lady Rockland's slight which had followed him out of the house like the stench of beer from a brewery, but her accusation.

Susanna is carrying Lord Howsham's child.

Justin banged his fist on the side of the chaise. He wouldn't let this consume him, not until he reached home and heard from Susanna it wasn't true. It couldn't be. He wouldn't put it past the old carthorse to lie in an attempt to cause trouble between the two of them, or ensure Justin was so disgusted by the duchess he stayed away from her husband, the house and the masque. Yet the instinct he'd relied on to keep himself and Philip safe prickled along the back of his neck. He'd trusted his senses too many times to his benefit to shake the feeling off as a mistake now.

Justin trilled his fingers on the squabs. Susanna's attempt to speak to him in Gunter's the day before the wedding added to his torment. Something had pressed on her enough to dull the usual sharpness of her eyes and make her appear as worried as a pickpocket before the magistrate. Justin's stomach dropped. She'd been intimate with Lord Howsham and when she'd tried to elaborate, he'd refused to listen, believing with too much glibness nothing from his past or hers could trouble them. By cutting her off, he'd made it easier for her to deceive him, or abandon whatever guilt her conscience drove her to relieve.

Self-disgust whirled in him to muddle with his anger. He should've listened, he shouldn't have been such a starry-eyed fool, too focused on the shop and the future to see what was in front of him. Assuming what Lady Rockland had said was true. He didn't know, but he'd soon find out.

The streets outside grew more familiar as the chaise rumbled down Fleet Street. Justin tugged at his cravat, irritated by the cloying heat inside the carriage. He pulled down the window, but the thick air outside, rank with horses and the river's stench, was no better. He fell back against the squabs, hands tight on his thighs, trying to regain his calm, but one thought kept stealing it from him. What would his father and Helena say if the rumours reached them? They'd laugh and call him a cuckold, and every damning thing they'd thought of him would be proved right by the one woman he'd come to rely on and love more than any other.

He tapped his heel against the floor, pulling back his condemnation. Before he'd left, Susanna had worried Lady Rockland might strike at him and she had. This had to be a lie, it needed to be. With his street coming into view, he'd soon have his answer and surely all his worries would be for nothing.

The chaise hadn't even stopped before he tossed open the door and jumped down.

'Good evening, Mr Connor,' Walter greeted him as Justin strode into the house.

'Where's Mrs Connor?'

'In her room,' Walter stuttered, surprised at Justin's curt query. It wasn't like him to dismiss the man, but he wasn't interested in the butler, only his wife and her reassurance all was well.

He took the stairs two at a time as he continued to chew on Lady Rockland's pronouncement. The woman was probably driven by jealousy at seeing her husband's illegitimate daughter married while her daughter languished for another Season. Justin wouldn't believe her story until he heard it from Susanna herself.

He flung open the door to her room. She looked up from whatever she was working on with Mrs Robinson at the writing table. She smiled at him, bringing Justin to a halt. He could say nothing and trust in this woman who regarded him with an eagerness and faith few had granted him before.

She set down her pen, her pleasure at his return changing to worry. 'What's wrong? Did my father renege on our agreement?'

He glanced to Mrs Robinson who, without

a word, excused herself, drawing the door shut behind her.

'No, he's purchasing the wines, but he made it clear there'll be no further help after the masque.'

She drummed her fingers on the desk. 'We never negotiated for any and we should have. That was my fault.'

'It wouldn't have made a difference. He and Lady Rockland are quite eager to see the back of us, as you expected.'

She didn't gloat over having been correct, but seemed to mourn with him Lord Rockland's lack of support. Again he considered biting his tongue, but the uncertainty tearing at him wouldn't allow it.

'There's more, isn't there?' she asked, twisting the pen between her fingers.

'I encountered Lady Rockland as I was leaving.' He pressed his fists to his hips, unable to hold back the question which had tormented him since leaving Grosvenor Square. 'She said you're carrying Lord Howsham's child.'

The colour drained out of her cheeks as she dropped the pen to clatter against the table top.

'Tell me it's a lie,' he demanded, wanting to

hear the words from her mouth, to soothe the anger roiling inside him. 'Tell me.'

Her shoulders slumped in a defeat he felt in his soul, and everything between the two of them shattered as the truth rippled through her eyes.

'Did you know before the wedding?' he demanded, wishing for a leather dummy from his pugilist club so he could pound out the rage rising inside him. She'd deceived him, all the while pretending faith.

'I tried to tell you at Gunter's, but you wouldn't let me.'

'So this is my fault?'

She jumped to her feet, reaching for him before pulling her hand back. 'No, of course not.'

'I think it is, for letting you and your entire damned family take me for a dupe.'

'They aren't my family and it wasn't about how I could fool you. It was never about that.' She raised her voice to match his, balling her hand at her sides. 'I was afraid I'd lose you or you'd reject me and the child. You don't know what it's like to be a bastard, to have people scorn you for something that isn't your fault. To bear a bastard would've meant being condemned twice and subjecting the child to an even worse childhood than I knew. Lord Rockland would have thrown me out if I hadn't gone through with the marriage and then where would I have been? Where would the child have been? I couldn't condemn a baby to a future in the gutter because of my mistake.'

'I wouldn't have turned my back on you.' Justin stared into the fire, following the rise and fall of each flame as it consumed the coal. 'I know what happens to women who end up in the streets. I see it each time I visit Moll Topp's to investigate a potential client's debts. I see the gaunt, disease-ridden women devoid of hope or happiness, with their daughters washing the filthy sheets until they're old enough to earn their keep on their backs while their brothers are stuffed up chimneys until they contract soot wart. I know Lord Howsham forced himself on you, taking advantage of your loneliness and lack of experience to satisfy his own lust. If you'd believed in me enough to tell me the truth, I wouldn't have consigned you or the child to such a fate. Instead you took me for a fool and it burns more than your deceit.'

She laid one hand on his arm. 'I'm sorry, Justin. I'm sorry I hurt you, I'm sorry I deceived you and didn't give you the chance to decide.'

He shrugged off her touch. 'Apologies aren't enough.'

'I don't know what else to say, or do.' Susanna stared into the fire, the pain etching her face touching him. He hardened himself against it. He didn't want to pity her or understand her suffering, not with the storm of emotions surging inside him and the new worry eating at him.

'You're not to do anything which might endanger your life, or the child's, do you hear me?' He wouldn't have them solve their problems that way or lose Susanna to the darkness of death where nothing, no conversation or the passing of time, could ever bring her back. The idea tore at his insides with claws as sharp as her dishonesty.

Susanna nodded. His insistence she not risk her life or the baby's spoke to his integrity and increased the shame draping her like a shroud.

'What will happen between us?' she asked, as though he was as much a stranger to her now as he'd been the morning they'd entered into this agreement.

'I don't know.' Without another word he turned and left, the door lingering open behind him. Then she heard the back door slam and him call out in the mews for the chaise.

In the dim light of the bedroom, she dropped down on her knees to the rug, buried her face in her hands and wept.

Justin jabbed his fists at Philip, first one, then another, each time missing his friend. Justin didn't back up, or try a new position, but swung blindly, his failure to strike anything fuelling the rage hollowing out his innards.

'You're sloppy tonight. What's wrong?' Philip dodged another hit and Justin growled with his frustration. He shouldn't be taking out his fury on his friend, but on the punching bag in the corner. With so many other men crowding the club, he wasn't about to beat the thing into a pulp of leather and feathers in front of everyone.

'I'm experiencing some marital difficulties,' Justin admitted through gritted teeth as he shuffled forward to try and land another hit on his friend who easily dodged him.

'I remember you telling me once to go home and deal with my woman troubles instead of pounding them out.' Philip leaned away from Justin's swing. 'Why aren't you taking your own advice?'

Justin ceased his mindless jabbing, but didn't

lower his fists, unable to unclench his hands. 'I can't go home.'

'Why not?'

Justin dropped his arms to his sides, his muscles screaming from his exertion, but not as loudly as his heart. He stared at his best friend, the man who'd seen him cry the day he'd lost his mother, who knew every trouble and grief his father had caused him. He didn't want to reveal this deepest of all his shames, but he had to tell someone. 'Susanna is pregnant with Lord Howsham's child.'

What Justin's fists had failed to accomplish this pronouncement managed, knocking his oldest friend silent.

'Are you sure?' Philip asked after a long pause, lowering his fists. The fight was over.

'Yes.' Justin briefly explained his encounter with Lady Rockland and coming home to have Susanna confirm it. He'd spent years fighting his father, now it would be his wife. This wasn't how he wanted to live. The choice had been torn from him by Susanna and the Rocklands.

'What'll you do?' Philip handed his friend one of the towels draped over the ropes of the sparring ring.

Justin rubbed the stinging sweat from his eyes, then flipped the towel over his bare shoulder. 'What can I do? We're wed. In the eyes of the law the child is mine no matter what villain sired it.'

At once he understood why his father drank. What he wouldn't give to crawl into a gin bottle tonight and forget everything—his mother's death, his father's insults, his business failures and his wife's betrayal.

'Then treat it as yours and never let anyone aside from us think any differently.'

'And the Rocklands? The duchess won't be content to let this secret go.'

'If she sees her vileness hasn't troubled you or driven a wedge between you and your wife, then she will.'

'It has driven a wedge between us.' He tugged the towel from his shoulder and threw it to a passing boy. 'Any other bastard and no one would care, but she's the Duke of Rockland's daughter foisting her child off on another man. It'll give everyone from Mayfair to Seven Dials something to talk about.'

'The better sort don't care what we get up to.'

'They do when it involves the illegitimate daughter of a duke.'

'Then walk away from them and never have anything more to do with them. Then nothing they or anyone else of their class says will ever matter,' Philip suggested.

'I can't, not yet. It would mean missing the ball, forfeiting the chance to cultivate clients and getting stuck with a lot of inventory instead of selling it to the duke.' It wasn't so much the wine motivating him now, but the craving to stick a finger in Lady Rockland's eye by attending. He'd have to do so with Susanna at his side, the two of them grinning like idiots and pretending she hadn't hurt them. It'd be worth it to spite the old dragon. 'I refuse to let him out of his agreement, or to allow his wife to sneer and look down on us.'

'And Susanna?'

'I don't know.' Justin opened and closed his fingers, the knuckles smarting beneath the bruises forming there. He didn't want to care about how facing the Rocklands might affect her. She hadn't shown him the same consideration when she'd marched up the aisle to meet him, giving him no say in a future so carefully planned out with the Rocklands. They'd all thought him stupid enough to accept a woman carrying another man's bastard and like a dolt he'd fallen in neatly with their plans. 'I love her, as you love Laura.'

It made her betrayal hurt so much more, dragging him down further than the day he'd learned the ship had sunk. Failure dogged him again, predetermined by forces he couldn't control or account for, just like before.

'Which gives you more reason to overcome this. I've seen the two of you together. You get on well and are good for one another. You can be happy if you find a way to move past this and you must.' Philip dropped a steadying hand on Justin's shoulder. 'You know what might happen when she's brought to bed.'

'I do.' Justin shrugged off his friend's hand, not wanting to face the truth the way he had the morning his father had told him about his mother's passing along with the infant they'd anticipated for so many months. His mother's loss had ruined his father. What might Susanna's do to Justin? Nothing. Her lie had already destroyed everything.

Justin pinched the bridge of his nose with his fingers. Spite for the Rocklands burned a hole in his chest, not just because of what they'd torn from him, but what it meant for the future.

'What'll I do if the child is a boy?' Another man's son would be heir to everything he might build. He could amend his will to cut the child out, give his rightful heirs their due, but it would mean admitting to the world their secret and tainting the child the way Susanna had been tainted. Given what Susanna had suffered, and having been scorned by his own father, he couldn't visit such misery on an innocent boy. He would have to bring himself to love this child, as much as he disliked it and its mother right now.

'You'll have time to figure it out. Nothing needs to be decided tonight,' Philip reminded him, but it didn't help.

He needed time and distance, a chance to reclaim the centre which had been knocked out of him by Lady Rockland's nastiness and Susanna's grudging honesty. With the masque only a few days away, it was a luxury he didn't possess. He couldn't walk away from the Rocklands' wine order any more than he could from his marriage. He'd see to it the duchess didn't win, but to do it he'd have to choke down his pride, especially where Susanna was concerned. It was a vintage he wasn't ready to swallow.

* * *

Susanna sat listlessly by the fire in the sitting room, her eyes sore from another night spent crying alone in her bed. She hadn't seen Justin in two days. He'd come home well after dark and risen before dawn. She didn't know where he went. She was afraid to ask and powerless to stop him. All she could do was continue with her routine, going to the shop every day and seeing to the endless tasks. Every time the bell over the shop door rang or the back room door to the alley opened, she held her breath, waiting to hear Justin's voice, but it was never him.

Coming home to the empty house again today, the stiff upper lip she'd tried to maintain in the presence of the shop assistant and the servants began to flag and her spirits ebbed nearly as low as they had in the days after her mother had died. She sat in the window seat, trying to read, but tears kept clouding her eyes. She dropped her head in her hands. It was too much and she hated herself for what she'd done, but she despised Lady Rockland more. There'd been no reason but sheer spite for her to tell Justin of the child and ruin everything.

The front door knocker banged and she

raised her head, unable to see who was waiting outside from where she sat. Rubbing the tears from her eyes, she hoped it was just another messenger with a note for Justin. She picked up her book, attempting to appear composed to whoever might happen to see her, but the pages blurred through her unshed tears.

'Mr Connor,' Walter announced.

Old Mr Connor stepped around the man and beamed at her, a new fullness about his crinkled eyes and beneath his square chin. His clothes appeared neater today, though they were still near threadbare around the elbows and collar. He wore his old Wellington, which he swept off his now combed hair and handed it to Walter. In the entrance hall, Mr Green even smiled as he left Mr Connor in Susanna's care to seek out Mrs Robinson.

'You look very well today, Mr Connor,' she remarked, his transformation lifting her for a moment from her own sorrows.

'Good food will do that to a man.' He patted his fuller stomach before taking her in with a critical eye. 'You aren't looking very well. Justin isn't running you ragged with the shop, is he?'

'No, he—' The brave face she'd worn the

entire day began to crack. She wouldn't cry in front of him, she refused to, but the tears fell in steady streams down her cheeks to drop on to the front of her dress.

'What's this, then?' Mr Connor sat down next to her in the window seat and wrapped his arms around her.

She buried her face in his soft dun-coloured coat. It smelled of tobacco and the coal-filled London air. The scent was as comforting as his large hand rubbing her back, soothing her as she'd wished her grandfather would have done so many times as a child.

'Tell me what's wrong, lass. There's no reason you should be crying.'

His sympathy made the tears come harder for herself, Justin and everything she'd never had in her life and wouldn't have in the future. For a few short days she'd discovered what it was to be loved and through her own weakness she'd ruined it all. She wished she'd never enjoyed such happiness with Justin so that losing it now wouldn't be so bitter.

'Come now, tell me what's wrong,' he urged.

The story came tumbling out, all of it, as she cried against him. He'd find out about it soon enough and the patient way he listened made it so she couldn't hold back the words. While she spoke, he never once stopped in his comforting or pushed her away. Instead he continued to hold her, calming the sobs until only the dried tears on her cheeks and the sense of being wrung out like a rag remained.

She rubbed her wet face with a small handkerchief from her pocket. 'You hate me now, don't you?'

He shook his head. 'I don't hate you and what's done is done. I'm not saying it's right, 'cause it ain't, but I understand why you did it.'

'Do you?' It didn't seem possible.

'I'm a man of the world. I know how it works. Why, Justin was almost born on the wrong side of the blanket. Molly and I were so in love and young and foolish. We couldn't wait for the church's blessing, so we did what nature drives a man and woman to do. I hadn't thought of marrying yet, but when she told me, I did right by her. Never regretted it because I loved her and she loved me.'

'But that wasn't how it was with me and Justin.'

'It's how it is now.' He patted her hand with his calloused one. 'You have a good heart and you did what you did because you care for a child which ain't even here yet. You treat me kind because you are kind and you care for my son.'

'I love him. And now he hates me.'

'No, he doesn't, but you've given him a shock and it'll take time to gain back what you two had before.'

She twisted the handkerchief between her fingers. 'Do you think he'll give me another chance?'

'All the times I've come in here cursing at him like the devil and still he hands me money, keeps me fed and housed, talks to me with a respect I should show him.'

'But you're his father.' She didn't have the same claim on Justin's affection.

'There's plenty out there who don't give a fig for the hardships of their folks, or their children.' He rubbed his chin, a pensive look coming over him. 'I've been hurtin' so bad these many years, ever since I lost my dear Molly. I took it out on him and he didn't deserve it. Still, he treats me as a son should treat his father. He'll do the same for you.'

It wasn't Justin's regard she wanted, but his love. 'There's no reason for him to be kind to me.'

'Yes, there is. You're his wife whether it's been for three weeks or twenty years. He'll do right by you, but you'll have to work for it, keep the anger from festering like you've done with me. Don't let him pull away as I have, but hold him close and cherish him. He loves you. Bring it out and I promise you, all will be well.'

She hugged him, hoping he was right.

It was well after dark by the time Justin returned home from another day of scouring London for Lord Rockland's libations. His father's gig sat out front and whatever brief ease he'd found in his work today vanished as his shoulders and neck tightened. He was in no mood for his father's acid tonight. He thought of turning around, climbing back in the chaise and going to the Rathbones', but he wasn't a man to run from his problems. He'd face them, as he always did, but with a little less humour tonight.

Justin strode into the sitting room, dug some coins from his pocket and held them out to his father. 'Here, take the shillings and be gone.'

His father waved the money away. 'I don't want money.'

Justin pocketed the coins, eyeing his father suspiciously. Something about him seemed different tonight. 'What do you want?'

'To talk to you.'

Ice crept through his veins. The last time his father had sought him out to talk had been to tell him his infant sister hadn't survived and neither had his mother.

'Is Susanna all right?' Panic nearly sent him hurling from the room and up the stairs to check on her.

'She's well, but she ain't all right.' He sounded weary and for once his hands didn't shake, nor did the agitation which usually marked his visits send him grumbling and pacing across the room. He was the calm, steady man Justin remembered from his youth and for a moment Justin saw the shadow of his childhood, before his mother had died, when the three of them had been happy and his father had been his hero. 'I spoke with her this afternoon.'

The fact his father and wife enjoyed a confidence startled him as much as his father refusing the coins. 'I didn't think you two were on such intimate terms.'

'I've been coming here for tea for a while

now, always when you're gone. We decided not to tell you. Wanted it to be our secret.'

'Yes, she's good at keeping secrets.' He wondered what else she was upstairs hiding. If he hadn't seen the bank account for the dowry, he'd wonder if the fifteen hundred pounds were real or another one of her lies. 'She's told you, then?'

'Aye, she has.'

Justin crossed his arms. 'Go ahead, belittle me for trying to rise above my station, tell me I deserve to be made to look like an idiot by the better sort.'

'I won't, because you don't deserve it. She's been telling me about your shop and the clients you've got.' Pride coloured his father's words. 'I went there once and she showed me the cellar and the front room. She's done it up very pretty, tells me you're to supply Lord Rockland with wine for his masque.'

Justin lowered his hands. He couldn't believe after so many years of insulting him for wanting to better himself, his father was praising him now. 'I thought you said I wasn't good enough for such things?'

'I was wrong to say it,' his father admitted, knocking Justin more off centre than any of Philip's or his trainer's punches. The man he'd once admired was standing in front of him again. 'I was jealous of you, afraid if you made something of yourself, you'd look down on me. I was wrong to treat you the way I did, to blame you when it was me who was at fault. The young lady made me see it. It's why I can't condemn her for what she's done. She was kind to me when I was making my mistakes. I can't help but be kind to her and you.'

Justin stared at his father in disbelief. He'd waited years to hear this kind of apology, hoped his patience would bring it about, but it hadn't. Susanna, the woman who'd deceived him, had caused this. He should be glad for it, but it was tainted by everything else he was mired in.

'What you're dealing with ain't easy,' his father offered. 'But don't let this trouble come between the two of you. You're a good and caring man, keep being one where she and the child are concerned. She's already worn thin worrying about how you'll treat her. Such a thing is dangerous to a woman in her condition.'

The worry which had gripped him at Philip's similar warning seized him again. She might die in childbirth, whether it was with his baby or another man's. He couldn't shake free of the possibility, or how much losing her would reopen the hole in his life he hadn't realised existed until he'd met her. It didn't move him to forgiveness, but increased the cut of her deception. All the time he'd been falling for her and coming to rely on her support, she'd been lying to him.

'Put aside your anger like I should've done all those years ago after your mother died. Instead, I wallowed in my grief and you suffered because of it. Don't turn into me.' His father tapped his hat over his grey hair and made for the door. Mr Green rose from his place in the hall to follow him out into the night.

Justin didn't stop him, he couldn't. He hadn't expected this any more than what Lady Rockland had told him about the child. The change Susanna had wrought in his father was nothing short of a miracle and an answer to at least one of his long-held wishes. Whether she'd done it to ease her guilty conscience or for a nobler reason he wasn't sure and he wasn't ready to find out.

He wandered to his study and dropped down into the leather chair, catching Walter's curious glance from the doorway before the valet hurried away. They knew. Servants always knew gossip first and now his father did, too. Yet the one man he'd expected to laugh the loudest at his misfortune had pitied him and advised him with as much insight as Philip.

He took up the whisky and poured himself a healthy measure, then drained the glass. It didn't matter how much the smoky liquor fogged his brain tonight, it was already muddled beyond reason. He grabbed the decanter and filled the glass again. If she'd told him the truth before the wedding, he could have recommended her to Philip's charity. They would have looked after her and the child as they did all the other unfortunate women whose husbands and fathers had fallen into debt and left them in dire straits. It would've meant leaving her and all the hope he'd felt in her presence behind, abandoning the one person who'd believed in him and his dream.

He stared into the tawny liquid, his thirst gone.

She'd made him happier than he'd been in years, working alongside him in the shop. He'd accused her of not caring for him and lying simply to save her own hide and that of the child's, but she'd befriended his father before Justin had discovered her secret, working to bring about a change not to redeem herself, but to help him. It made the veracity of his accusation difficult to maintain. If nothing else, he owed her for this kindness.

He finished the drink, then set the glass on the table with a clunk. He might have been taken for a dupe, but he'd be damned if he'd prove himself any less of a gentleman than the duke. She was his wife and he'd honour the commitment he'd made to her and do right by her and the child the law would view as his. Whether it meant loving them both, especially her, he couldn't say, but he was stuck with her and would make the best of it, as he'd made the best of his losses after the ship had sunk. He wouldn't give up and he wouldn't let this ruin him. He was too good a man and if others couldn't see it, it didn't matter. He knew and so did those who cared for him the most, even his lying wife.

The sound of whispering pulled Susanna from a restless sleep. Light flooded the room and made her blink as she opened her eyes. Justin stood at the foot of her bed. At once she sat up, but the trials of the past few days, the lack of sleep and a proper meal made her stomach rebel and the room spin. She closed her eyes and took a deep breath, glad when she opened them to see everything as it should be, except for Justin.

His face was drawn as tight as it'd been the night she'd first met his father. The time he'd spent away from her hadn't changed anything between them or brought him any closer to forgiving her. It was evident in his hard expression and the stiffness of his hands by his side.

She tugged the coverlet up a little closer to her chest when she noticed the distinguished older gentleman standing behind Justin and carrying a black leather bag. He was tall with grey hair along his temples and vivid blue eyes which took her in with a strange sort of curiosity.

'Susanna, this is Dr Hale, Philip's father-in-law from his first wife.' Gone was the laughing, smiling Justin she'd come to love. She barely recognised this taciturn man.

'Good morning,' the doctor said brightly. 'Justin tells me you might be with child.'

She let go of the coverlet, stunned someone would announce it in such a merry tone. She'd greeted the news of her pregnancy with nothing but dread.

'Yes, I believe so,' she stuttered, amazed Justin would reveal this to a near stranger, even if he was a physician.

'You two have wasted no time,' Dr Hale teased as he pulled the chair from the dressing table next to the bed and sat down beside her. He took her wrist and slid a watch out of his waistcoat pocket to check her pulse. 'When were your last courses?'

Susanna exchanged an uneasy glance with Justin, looking to him for what to say, unsure if she should tell the truth, or try to concoct some lie. If the doctor examined her, he'd know at once she was further along than simply the three weeks since her wedding. 'The week of Lady Day.'

Dr Hale's fingers stiffened on her wrist before he released her. He slipped the watch back in his pocket, all business as though he hadn't calculated the date and realised exactly what it meant. 'I see.'

Shame weighed on her as much as a lack of rest. This wouldn't be the first awkward encounter Justin would have to endure because of her mistake. There'd soon be many more when her condition could no longer be hidden, though if he'd wanted to avoid this one, he shouldn't have brought the doctor here. It didn't lessen her humiliation at the embarrassment he was forced to endure thanks to her. She was sorry and would have told him so if Dr Hale hadn't been there. Although no apology could undo the damage her lie had wrought or make him look at her as he had the morning before he'd gone to the Rocklands'.

Dr Hale asked her a few questions and she answered honestly, all the while conscious of Justin's presence. There was no pretence during the exam to their being a happy couple, not for her sake or Dr Hale's. If the physician noticed the tension between husband and wife, he never revealed it, maintaining his courteous chatter until, at last satisfied she was well, he snapped his black bag closed.

'Now get some rest. I'll return in a few days to see how you're doing.'

'I'll see you out,' Justin offered.

'Justin,' Susanna called, unwilling to let him go. Something had drawn him to her this morning, a care or concern which, for the first time in days, offered some hope of lifting the darkness which surrounded them. If she could draw it out, like the long-buried goodness in his father, perhaps they could begin to repair the rift between them.

Justin hesitated, but didn't answer. It was Dr Hale who made the decision for him.

'I'll wait downstairs.' Dr Hale strode into the hallway, his steps fading off down the staircase.

'Why did you summon him?' Susanna asked, confused.

'Mrs Robinson tells me you've been tired and you haven't eaten much.' He might not have seen her these past few days, but he'd taken an interest in her well-being. It should've comforted her, but it didn't. It was probably Mrs Robinson who'd informed him of Susanna's lack of rest and food, rather than he who'd asked about her.

'But now he knows.'

'You're my wife. It's my duty to see to your well-being.'

'Your duty,' she whispered, understanding why he'd endured humiliation to summon the physician. Like her father, he'd honour his obligation, but there'd be nothing more, no love or the affection they'd shared during the past three weeks. The loneliness of the years when she'd lived with her grandfather and uncle, tolerated instead of cherished, was suddenly fresh again. Bitter tears stung her eyes, but she fought them back, wishing he'd been this way from the beginning. The joy they'd found in one another was gone, leaving nothing but the cold, empty shell of what might have been to taunt her.

'I must see the doctor out.' He left before she could stop him. She wasn't sure he would come back unless some other obligation drove him to it.

She laid her hand on her stomach, trying to summon up the resolve which had carried her through the long years in Oxfordshire and then with the Rocklands. She could endure the heartache and disparagement of a cold spouse. It was the child which worried her. Justin would look on it as her grandfather had looked on her, with grudging acknowledgement, not love, never love. Lady Rockland had stolen the chance from her and the baby. At least the child wouldn't endure the suffering of being illegitimate. Having lost the love of her husband, it was Susanna's only consolation.

* * *

'Congratulations, Justin.' Dr Hale held out his hand as Justin came down the stairs.

Justin gritted his teeth as he shook the man's hand. Whatever Dr Hale suspected about the parentage of the baby, he'd decided to ignore it, as he suspected most people would. It was what they'd say behind his and Susanna's backs he wondered about. Dr Hale wasn't one to gossip, but many others would. Justin had never cared before, having created more rumours than he could recall, but this burned along the back of his throat and there was nothing to do but silently tolerate it.

'Is she well?' Justin asked.

'Many women suffer from fatigue in the first months of pregnancy. A few days of rest and some good food will see her set to rights very quickly.'

To Justin's ire, the doctor's proclamation sent a wave of relief through him. He shouldn't care whether she felt well or not. She'd never considered his feelings once in the matter. 'When do you think she'll be brought to bed?'

'Early winter, I'd say, though babies have their own schedule and will arrive when they're good and ready.'

'Do you think she'll be delivered safely?' Justin asked, though there was no physician who could predict such a thing. It was up to nature which women survived and which didn't and whether the infants joined them or not, just as it'd been up to nature to sink his ship and his last business.

'She's young and healthy. I'm sure she'll come through her confinement. I shouldn't worry.' Dr Hale clapped him on the arm. 'Summon me if there are any problems, though I don't think there will be.'

'Thank you, Dr Hale.'

Justin watched Walter close the door behind the doctor. He would go through the motions of being a dutiful husband as he'd gone through the motions of being a dutiful son for years, all the while fighting back the bitter bile of the situation which at his lowest times would creep up to almost consume him.

The whisper of a lady's step on the stairs made him turn. He expected to see Mrs Robinson, but it was Susanna. She stopped, the hem of her wrapper fluttering around her legs. Over one shoulder her hair fell in a long braid, its darkness echoing in the circles beneath her eyes. In their time together, he'd never thought of her as frail, but seeing her leaning heavily on the banister, Philip's warning about what might happen if she were brought to bed seared through his mind. Despite Dr Hale's assurances, Justin worried about her.

'What are you doing up?' Justin demanded.

'I have too much to do to sit in bed all day.'

'It can wait until tomorrow. You need rest.' He marched up the stairs, took her by the elbow and gently turned her around. She didn't fight him, but allowed him to lead her back up to her room.

Her exhaustion was evident in her slow pace and the heaviness of her arm beneath his palm. Dr Hale had said it was to be expected but it raised the worry which had tormented him all night until he'd been forced to summon the physician early this morning in order to put his mind at ease.

They stopped outside her room, Justin making it clear he wouldn't follow her inside.

'Will I see you tonight?' The sadness marking her questions reminded him of the times she'd talked of her childhood. For a moment, he wanted to banish it, but he couldn't. Nothing right now could make him take her in his arms or forget how she'd deceived him.

'No, collecting the wines for your father's party will keep me occupied for some time.'

'And will we attend the ball?'

With her so tired and pale, he couldn't imagine forcing her through the rigours of the ball, or the strain of facing her dragon stepmother. Nor could he stand before Lady Rockland and act like some Drury Lane leading man, grinning like an idiot and pretending all was well. Lord Rockland had made it clear there'd be no more support for Justin's business so there was no point pressing the flesh with the better sort, or putting either of them through the strain of a long evening which might garner them nothing. 'No. We need to distance ourselves from the Rocklands for good.'

Her shoulders relaxed with a relief he couldn't share. This one difficulty might be surmounted, but there were many others facing them, along with disappointments. Despite her warning about cultivating the patronage of the *haut ton*, he'd held on to the hope of securing more clients at the masque. The plan was now as good as dead.

'I must go.' Without another word or a kiss goodbye, he made for downstairs. Things might be all confusion, but the simplicity and focus of his work remained. He had a job to do, wines to procure. Even if he despised his client, he'd be damned if he'd fail. He'd never let Philip down in all their years of business. Now he was in charge and he would fail no one, least of all himself. Everything else could wait.

Susanna dragged herself back to bed, thankful for the soft sheets and pillows. She was tired, wrung out by crying, worry and the demands of the infant growing inside her. Nothing with her and Justin was settled, but a small relief made resting easier. They weren't going to the masque. He would fulfil her father's order and then their time, her time, with the Rocklands would finally end. Lady Rockland had done her worst and now Susanna never had to face the evil woman again. Even if she continued with her whispers, the distance between Fleet Street and Grosvenor Square was vast enough to keep Lady Rockland's vinegar from tainting her life more than it already had. Insulated by his friends and his business, she and Justin would find some way past this. They might never enjoy again the closeness of last week, but they'd find a way to live with one another and make the best of the union. Sleep began to creep over her as she snuggled down beneath the coverlet. No matter what happened between her and Justin, the Rocklands would never be there to trouble them again.

Chapter Eleven

Over the next three days, Justin had paid a call on every contact he possessed and made a few new ones in the processes of assembling the required vintages. He had even managed to secure a case of the Spanish port which had nearly eluded him and left the order unfulfilled. The morning of the masque, he personally saw to the wine's delivery, unwilling to trust even Mr Tenor with its safe handling.

As he finished going through the list with the tart Netley, Lord Rockland joined them in the wine cellar. He inspected the casks and crates of bottles stacked up in the dank, dark room with a critical eye, as though looking for any reason to reject the wines, or deny Justin his money. After what Lady Rockland had done, Justin wouldn't put it past the man to leave Justin on the hook for the stock and the bills which went with it.

Lord Rockland picked up one of the bottles of Spanish port from the shelf where the butler had set them. His eyebrows rose with admiration before he set it down, offering no congratulations for the effort it'd taken to secure it. It was as if he was owed the thing simply because he'd asked for it and had been given by providence the means to pay for it. His surety in himself and his place in the world nearly made Justin sick. The man's wife had thrown Justin's life entirely off kilter and yet nothing mattered more to this man than whether or not his guests could drink themselves into a stupor. Neither he nor his wife had done a day's work in their entire lives, or knew what it was to scrape by on little more than ambition, yet they thought nothing of ruining those people who worked hard. Despite hating to admit it, Susanna was right. These weren't the kind of people to build a business or a future upon and he couldn't be free of this sort soon enough.

'Well done, Mr Connor. I'm impressed.' Lord Rockland at last faced him and Justin made sure to maintain his deference. He didn't want the man to suspect the loathing he carried for him and his wife. 'I'm very impressed.'

Whether it was because Justin had procured the wine or defied his low expectations he wasn't sure, although he could well imagine. 'Thank you, Your Grace.'

'See to it Mr Connor receives his payment, then set things up as we discussed yesterday,' he ordered Netley, who didn't work to hide how he felt about having to pay Justin as he dropped a leather bag of coins into his palm.

With the matter concluded, Justin tucked the pouch in his coat pocket and picked up the crooked lid of a crate to straighten it, ready to see this strange part of his life laid to rest.

'Lady Rockland tells me you and Susanna won't be able to attend tonight,' Lord Rockland observed. 'She says Susanna isn't well.'

Justin's fingers tightened on the rough wooden edge of the crate lid as he set it down over the bottles. His determination to walk away now and leave the Rocklands to their lives while he and Susanna went about theirs came rushing back. He could agree with the duchess, graciously bow out of tonight and heed her warning to not sully her precious party with their presence. Until this moment, it was exactly what he'd intended to, but he couldn't. He didn't want her or Lord Rockland to think they'd triumphed over them. Lord Rockland had agreed to their invitation to the ball as part of the marriage contract. If Justin declined to attend now it would relieve the duke of this last duty and Lady Rockland would win. Justin wasn't about to allow her to think she'd defeated them, or to let Lord Rockland out of even one of his obligations, no matter how small. Nor was Justin about to surrender his own ambitions and miss the opportunity to acquire a few new clients. With his marriage in tatters, Justin's work was the one thing remaining to lift him up. He would succeed, despite what anyone, even Susanna, thought.

'I'm afraid Lady Rockland is mistaken.' Justin brushed the wood and dust from his hands. 'Susanna is quite well and we will be there tonight.'

'Good, I'm glad to hear it.' Lord Rockland hummed. If he was surprised by the answer, his laconic demeanour didn't change to show it.

Justin realised it didn't matter to him one way or another. It was Lady Rockland who'd seethe like a cornered cat when he and Susanna appeared tonight. He wanted her to fume; she deserved it.

Lord Rockland reached up to a nearby shelf and ran one finger over the embossed label, the one Susanna had designed with the printer. Then he turned to face Justin with a strange kind of scrutiny. 'I think a man of your ingenuity will do well tonight with my guests in establishing your name.'

Justin stilled. At least there was one person who saw something of worth and promise in him. He hadn't expected it to be Lord Rockland. 'I hope so.'

'Until tonight, then.' Lord Rockland made his way back up to the kitchen, his business done and other needs awaiting his attention.

Justin didn't linger in the cellar, but gathered up his men and made for home. It would be a press to prepare for the masque. Susanna wouldn't be pleased, but it didn't matter. It was time for her to resume her duties as a wife and stand beside him.

Susanna sat curled in the chair by the fire, trying to read, but not one of the sentences she'd skimmed in the past half hour had remained with her. In the three days since Dr Hale's visit, she'd seen less of Justin than she had in the days after her secret had been revealed. She knew he was securing her father's order for the masque, and understood once the delivery was made she and Justin would be free of the Rocklands at last.

It seemed such a strange idea and at the same time it was the only one which gave her any joy. For years she'd wished them to be a part of her past as much as her grandfather and uncle. Soon, they would be. Despite the fact Lady Rockland had risen up one last time to destroy all chances of a happy future for Susanna, she was glad to never have to face her again. She would remain here, quietly living her life with Justin in whatever shape it decided to take, while the duchess and her father lived theirs.

The door to the room swung open and Justin stepped inside. She set aside the book, her heart fluttering not so much with hope at his arrival, but in anxiety over the stern set of his jaw. Had her father rejected his order or refused to pay? She knew the cost of the wines Justin had procured. She'd taken a glance at the list during one of the many nights she'd been awake, pacing in her worry. There was more than one bottle only a man like Lord Rockland could afford, the cost of which would ruin Justin if Lord Rockland didn't pay.

'Did all go well?' she dared to ask, almost afraid to hear the answer. She wouldn't put it past Lady Rockland to try and ruin Susanna's livelihood as well as her marriage in the hopes she and Justin would sink from all society for good.

'It did. Your father was very pleased. So much so, he believes I can cultivate some of his friends as clients.'

Her stomach dropped. They weren't supposed to have anything more to do with society. 'What brought about his change of heart?'

'I impressed him. There's no reason why I can't impress his friends.' He marched to the wardrobe and flung open the doors, then plucked from inside the green domino and gown. 'We're going tonight and we have to make a good show of it.'

'We can't.' She jumped to her feet, rocking a little with dizziness before the room settled around her. 'Lady Rockland won't allow us to walk in there without finding a way to punish us. You saw what she did when you were alone in the house. Imagine how she'll strike if we dare to show ourselves at her ball.'

'Lady Rockland can go hang. Her guests are the only people I care about.'

'You used to think nothing of them before. Now, because you want their patronage, you're willing to risk being insulted or humiliated by Lady Rockland to curry their favour.'

He whirled to face her, the domino hanging limp in the hand by his side. 'I want to succeed and if that's how I can make it happen, then so be it.'

'There are other ways to do it without them.'

'Not tonight, there isn't. With everyone there enjoying their drinks, I can slip among them and spread the word about my business.'

'You won't win these people over, especially not if Lady Rockland is set against it. These aren't merchants who appreciate the effort it takes to procure things they believe their due. They won't admire you like the duke, but look down on you for meddling in trade.'

His fingers played with the sagging cape while he considered what she'd said. He knew she was right, but it was plain something more than ambition was driving him tonight. He'd told her in Hyde Park not to care about these people; now he was willing to set aside his pride to wander among them and it frightened her. This wasn't the Justin she'd come to love, the man she wanted so much to be with again.

'I understand your desire to prove wrong all those who've doubted you,' she sympathised, desperate for him to give up this course. 'But I don't want to see you ridiculed for my mistakes.'

He reached into the wardrobe and plucked out the mask, the one she'd so carefully laundered after their intimacy together, a closeness they might never take pleasure in again. 'You didn't mind so much the idea of ridiculing me when we wed.'

She swallowed hard against his insult. 'If you're determined to attend, then you'll have to do it alone. I won't face them or their insults and snide remarks again.'

Especially not on the arm of a man who could barely stand to look on her.

He marched up to her, coming toe to toe with her, but with nothing of the adoration or care he'd shown her the first time they'd stood so close. 'Whatever discomfort you experience tonight, it isn't even a measure of what I've been forced to endure, what I'll continue to endure because of your lie. We will arrive there together and appear like the happiest of couples.'

'How will we, when we aren't?'

He started and in his silence she caught the regret before his anger buried it. 'You lied to me to get me to the altar and for all the days afterwards. Surely you can lie as convincingly for one more night.'

'I lied about the child, but I never lied about how I felt about you. I love you, very much.' She reached up to touch his face, but he flinched away.

'Then it shouldn't be too difficult for you to act like it tonight.' He flung the domino across the foot of the bed as he made for his room. 'Be ready within the hour.'

Chapter Twelve

Susanna entered Lady Rockland's masque on Justin's arm. There was no footman at the door to announce the names of each arriving guest. Instead, they strolled in with their costumes, some with their hair powdered in the fashion of a few decades before, others with togas draped around the men's shirts and golden asps wound around the ladies' arms. Each one paraded through the main floor of the house in the guise of a different historical figure, laughing and drinking the wine, unaware of how hard a man had worked to procure the libations they enjoyed. They didn't care. This was all for their amusement and tomorrow it would be forgotten as they moved on to the next, trying to fill their vapid lives with meaning.

Elaborate masks covered many of the guests' faces, and Susanna wished she'd opted for something more substantial than the thin silk covering her eyes. Despite the cape allowing her to blend into the shadows along the edges of the room, it wouldn't be long before someone recognised her. Then it would all begin again, the whispering behind fans, the reminders she wasn't one of them, but someone to be pitied and ridiculed. This time the rumours would be more cutting, for surely Lady Rockland had let Susanna's secret slip and it was now making the rounds through the sitting rooms and dressing rooms of society.

At one time it would've been a comfort to have Justin walking beside her. Tonight his hardness added to her isolation. He'd all but ignored her when she'd come downstairs to join him, offering a stiff arm as he'd led her to the chaise. They'd sat beside one another in the darkness as it'd rattled towards Grosvenor Square, more tension icing the air between them than the night when she'd first jumped into his vehicle at Vauxhall Gardens. The silence had left her to wallow in her fears about what might happen both tonight and in the many more days to come. She hoped like most worries the reality would pale in comparison to what she imagined, though at present it didn't seem likely.

'At least try to smile,' Justin demanded from beside her.

'Why? It doesn't matter to these people whether we're happy or crying in some corner.'

'It matters to me.'

She forced herself to smile as wide as he did, hating this act. She'd pretended so many times in places like these to be honoured when some lord evaluated her to determine whether a connection to the Duke of Rockland and a thousand pounds was worth marrying a bastard. She'd appeared gracious as she'd danced with men who'd thought her as loose as a cyprian because of her illegitimacy. She'd stood behind Lady Rockland and Edwina, pretending not to notice how they ignored her. She never imagined she'd be here pretending to be happy with her husband while her entire world was falling apart.

Her smile sagged and she didn't bother to bolster it. She was tired of play-acting for these people and longed for tonight to be over and to finally leave this rotten, ugly world behind.

'Please, Justin, let's leave,' she begged, tightening her hand on his arm. 'There's nothing we can gain here.'

His smile stiffened, turning as hard as his

muscles beneath her palm. 'Of course there is. There's Lord Pallston. Introduce me to him.'

He pulled her through the crowd to where Lord Pallston stood stuffed into a doublet as red as his nose and near bursting at the seams under the strain of his bulk. The earl finished his drink, depositing the empty glass on a passing footman's tray and taking another. He tossed it back, then grabbed the tall footman's arm to stop him so he could take one more before sending him on his way.

'Lord Pallston—' Susanna began, enduring the nasty curl of his fat lip in displeasure as she introduced him to Justin.

'The champagne is a fine vintage, isn't it?' Justin plucked a flute off a passing tray and handed it to the man. He regarded Justin suspiciously as he finished his other glass and exchanged it with Justin for the full one.

'Definitely better than many I've enjoyed at such gatherings,' Lord Pallston mumbled through a tongue thickened by his enjoyment of the duke's hospitality.

His confidence buoyed by Lord Pallston's appreciation of the champagne, Justin produced one of the engraved calling cards Susanna had printed for him and held it out. 'I'm the man who procured it and I can acquire more for a gentleman who appreciates the finer vintages.'

Lord Pallston took the card with two sausage-like fingers and eyed it as if it were a biblical tract condemning strong drink. Then he flicked it away. 'I don't trouble with merchants. My steward deals with them. Talk to him.'

He waddled off in the direction of another footman with a full, glittering tray of drinks.

Justin snatched the discarded card from the floor and stuffed it back into his coat pocket, then dropped the empty glass on a passing footman's tray.

'Go ahead, gloat over my failure, tell me you were right and how I'll succeed in the pubs of Fleet Street, but not in the ballrooms of Grosvenor Square,' he said, the knock to his pride so palpable it made Susanna's chest hurt.

She wouldn't gloat. She couldn't, because his failure didn't feel like a victory. She wanted him to succeed as much as he did. 'You're determined to continue?'

'I'm not leaving here without one good contact.'

She studied him. It was difficult to read his expression behind his mask, both the silk one and the one he'd worn in her presence over the last few days. She wanted so much to be with the laughing man she'd come to love during their marriage, the one who didn't care about what all these people thought of him or her or their situation. But that Justin wasn't with her tonight and she'd have to do her best with this sullen one.

'Then speak to Lord Felton. He's a baron and not as rich as Lord Pallston, but his mother was a merchant's daughter. He might be more inclined to patronise us. Come, I'll introduce you.'

Without waiting for him to agree, she wound her way through the crowd to where a man draped in a cape and hidden by a mask similar in simplicity to Justin's leaned against a column. He watched a set of masked ladies and gentlemen move through the tortuously slow steps of the minuet, the long notes of the violin accompanying them grating on Susanna's nerves.

'Lord Felton, it's a pleasure to see you tonight.' Susanna held her hand out to the man who recognised her at once, responding to her greeting with enough charm to almost raise her fallen spirits.

'Miss Lambert, I thought you'd left us for a better place,' the distinguished older gentleman drawled, his enthusiasm for the night's festivities lacklustre.

'I have.' She told him of her marriage and her new name, speaking of it with as much pride as if she possessed as grand a title as anyone here, hoping Justin might notice. Then she introduced Justin to the baron and explained about their business. Lord Felton listened with an interest not usually seen in great men unless they were discussing hunting. By the time the man was summoned away by his wife, Justin had given him his calling card and extracted from him a promise for an order for a dinner party the man was hosting next week.

'That was unexpected,' Justin remarked with a touch of his old humour, their accomplishment appearing to have tempered his foul mood.

'You mean his not flinging your card away?'

'No, you helping me, even after I dragged you to this sixth level of hell.'

It wasn't an accusation tossed in her face, but almost a surrender of some of the vitriol he'd carried against her since learning her secret. It was as if for a moment he'd been able to see the love she still held for him. She wished she could work another miracle for him, demonstrate again the depth of her dedication to their union and remove some of the anger still clinging to him, but there wasn't another man here with Lord Felton's background or a soft spot for merchants.

'You asked me in Hyde Park to help you and I said I would. I might not have told you of my condition, but it doesn't mean every other promise I made to you was false.'

He didn't respond, but looked past her to focus on the room, his brown eyes behind the mask thoughtful, as if he was considering not just the guests, but also what she'd said. It gave her some hope, not for tonight, but for their future.

'My father says the two of you have been taking tea together,' he said at last, fixing his eyes on her instead of the room.

She pressed her lips tight together, regretting her decision to keep even this seemingly innocent secret from him, especially in light of her more nefarious one. 'I'm sorry I didn't tell you, but I thought if I waited a little while longer, I might make some progress with him.

I'd hoped by showing him some kindness, he might return the favour with you.'

'He did,' Justin admitted, the stiffness which had marked him since they'd left for the ball easing around his lips and in the set of his shoulders. 'We spoke the other night. It was the first civil conversation we've had in years. Thank you.'

'It was the least I could do after all you've done for me.'

A couple passed behind him, forcing Justin to step so close his chest nearly brushed against Susanna's. Standing over her, his breath sweeping across her cheeks, he regarded her not with the stern distrust of the last few days, but as if realising for the first time since learning of the baby she hadn't acted to trick him and didn't think him a gullible fool. She'd done her best tonight, despite the strain between them, to demonstrate how much she still cared for him. In his acknowledgement of her efforts both tonight and with his father, there lingered something of what they'd once had together. Their love wasn't dead, only hidden beneath his resentment and distrust.

'I think we should go.' He held out his arm to her.

With relief, she wrapped her hand beneath it, allowing her fingers to rest in the crook of his elbow. Nothing was settled between them, or forgiven, but in the tenderness with which he laid his hand over hers, she felt in time it would be.

They were not two steps towards the door before a sight across the room riveted her to the spot.

'What's wrong?' he asked.

'Lady Rockland.' She nodded to where the duchess held court near the windows leading out to the garden. Edwina stood beside her, her roundness stuffed into a black Tudor dress with a high ruffle behind her which did nothing to flatter the increasing size of her waist. Susanna's half-brother stood beside his sister, looking as bored and sallow as he always did at these events, less interested in displaying himself to a future wife than sneaking off to his club to drink away his evenings along with his health and a good bit of Lord Rockland's money.

It wasn't so much her family together which chilled her, but Lady Rockland speaking with Lord Howsham. She recognised him by the red hair peeking out from beneath his domino.

'Let's leave before she spies us,' Susanna insisted, eager to avoid both Lady Rockland and Lord Howsham, but Justin refused to move.

'Let her see us.' He drew himself up taller beside her, the tenderness which had marked him a moment before gone as he stared at the woman in defiance. 'I want her to see she hasn't won.'

At last, sensing their scrutiny, Lady Rockland slid aside the mask she held on a stick, her eyes narrowing in disgust as she spied them.

Susanna shivered, for the first time truly afraid of Lady Rockland. Having realised the depths to which the duchess was willing to sink to strike at Susanna and Justin, she could only imagine what damage she intended to inflict now. Her intentions revealed themselves when she turned to Lord Howsham and levelled her mask at Susanna, drawing his attention to where she stood.

A wicked smile broke beneath his elaborate white-plaster half mask, the same conquering jeer he'd pinned her with after he'd taken her innocence. She could practically hear him laughing at having been relieved of any consequence for what he'd done.

'Please, they've seen us now, let's go.'

She tugged Justin towards the door, but he wouldn't move.

'Who's the man in the white mask?' Justin asked as Lord Howsham started towards them.

A slight sweat broke out on her neck beneath the cloak. She didn't want to be here or face the earl and endure the nasty things he might say. 'Lord Howsham.'

Justin's jaw ground beneath his mask and a new fire burned in his dark eyes.

'Let's go.' Susanna begged. 'Please.'

'No, we'll face him.'

'We can't.' If Justin had been willing to come here tonight simply to spite Lady Rockland, she could well imagine what he'd do to Lord Howsham. The man deserved it and more, but not here, not when his title gave him privileges Justin could never hope to possess, or use to protect himself.

Lord Howsham cut a deep swathe through the guests until he was in front of them, as arrogant as ever as he swept Susanna's body with a disgusting, lascivious look. 'Susanna, what a pleasure it is to see you here tonight.'

'Her name is Mrs Connor,' Justin corrected, the same force she'd seen in him at Vauxhall Gardens curling through him now.

Susanna slid her hand down his arm to intertwine her fingers with his. Even after everything that had happened, and all the doubts and heartache still lingering between them, he was standing beside her, defending her, making her and everyone see she was worthy of respect. Neither Lord Howsham nor anyone else here had the right to look down on her and she'd allow it no more. She wasn't the bastard daughter of a duke any longer, but the wife of an honourable man she loved.

'I'd forgotten you married her,' Lord Howsham snorted. 'Quite convenient for me since it relieved me of not one, but apparently two very minor problems.'

Justin's hand tightened in hers and she noticed many masks turning to face them. She let go of Justin and came to stand toe to toe with the earl, defiant against his haughty triumph.

'It isn't you who was relieved of a burden, but me. To think I nearly saddled myself with a man so deep in debt he must chase after every heiress from here to York or lose his estate,' Susanna shot back, noting with pride how Lord Howsham's eyes widened in surprise beneath his mask before they darted to those around them who moved in closer to gather more gossip.

'Such words from a bastard married to a mere merchant,' Lord Howsham sneered, colouring beneath his mask at this first public confirmation of his debts and all the rumours surrounding them.

'I'd rather be the wife of a merchant than countess to a man like you whose estate is mortgaged to the rafters, yet who still doesn't have the fortitude to work hard to save it. While you sweat and worry about your bills, afraid to lift a finger to do anything more than turn over a few cards and waste even more blunt, I'll be far from here and happy. I'll never, ever give you another thought.'

Stepping back, but not flinching from the hate in Lord Howsham's eyes, she took Justin's hand, bolstered by the pride in his gaze. It was the same pride he'd shown her the day they'd ridden through Hyde Park, when she'd faced Lady Rockland's wilting sneer on the stairs, refusing to back down. She never would again. These people and their opinions of her were nothing and when the door to the Rocklands' house closed behind her tonight, they'd never matter to her again.

Without a word, she and Justin turned to make for the door, the show of solidarity he'd craved on display for Lord Howsham, Lady Rockland and all society to see. It wasn't a lie or an act, but as genuine as the diamonds around Lady Rockland's thin neck.

'How does it feel to have married my whore?' Lord Howsham called out to their backs.

A gasp of shock rippled through those around them.

Justin spun on his heel and rammed his fist into the earl's face. Lord Howsham's mask cracked in two, falling away as he staggered back to hit a pillar. Blood slid down his nose and stained the front of his shirt as he blinked, trying to recover from his shock. The commotion brought the music to a halt and the dancers stopped, craning their necks to see what was going on.

'I demand satisfaction for your insult to my wife,' Justin cried, drawing the attention of the entire ballroom.

From her place near the window, Lady Rockland turned a deep shade of red with a fury Susanna had only witnessed once before—the day Lord Rockland had brought Susanna to Rockland Place. Back then, Susanna had cowered before the imperious woman; tonight she stood strong beside her husband, her defiance further darkening the crimson blotching her stepmother's cheeks.

'You're no gentleman to be challenging me.' Lord Howsham blanched more at the challenge than the blood on his fingertips.

'Too big a coward to face me?' Justin prodded, tearing off his own mask so everyone could see his face.

Lord Howsham looked around at all the masked people watching him, as if hoping one person with a cooler head might step forward and settle the matter. No one, not even Lord Rockland, who must have been among the disguised merrymakers, moved. Justin was backing him into a corner. Lord Howsham would have no choice but to accept. Without the anonymity of his mask, everyone would witness Lord Howsham shying from a challenge, one from a man beneath him in rank no less. He'd never be able to show his face in society again if he didn't agree to the duel.

'I accept your challenge,' Lord Howsham declared for everyone to hear, but there was no mistaking the flutter in his voice. For once he'd have to deal with the consequences of his actions. If the man he was facing wasn't Justin, Susanna would cheer for the duel. Instead she stared back and forth between the two men in horror. This wasn't how she wanted this to end. 'We'll meet at dawn with pistols.'

'My favourite weapon.' Justin smiled darkly at Lord Howsham, who cringed back, hiding his fear behind the handkerchief he pressed to his still-bleeding nose. 'Bring your physician. You'll need him.'

Justin grabbed Susanna's hand and pulled her towards the entrance. People parted to let them pass, gawking in disbelief. Behind them the crowd closed and the whispers rose to drown out the now playing violins. They were the talk of society, a spectacle to amuse and disgust all the lords and ladies and for the first time in her life Susanna didn't care. All she could think about was Justin and the danger waiting for him tomorrow morning.

Susanna nearly tripped in her effort to keep up with Justin's hard stride as they marched down the pavement outside the Rocklands'. He pulled her along the line of carriages until they found his chaise, the small vehicle obscured by the massive town coaches filling the street. She climbed inside, struggling to breathe against her stays and the panic making her heart race.

Justin thudded into the seat beside her and banged on the roof to set the vehicle in motion.

'Maybe he'll send his second to apologise, then you won't have to meet. He's a coward. He might do it.' Susanna rushed on. This wasn't how she wanted things to end, for Justin to put his life in danger for her honour or his. 'He can refuse you and he might since you aren't—'

'A gentleman?' Justin finished in a tone as hard as a grinding stone.

She didn't care if his ego was bruised. She wanted him alive, not dead with his pride intact, especially not in defence of her. 'He won't lose face if he does, at least not among his class.'

'I struck him, he can't refuse me now.' Justin crossed his arms as if welcoming the coming fight, so sure he wouldn't die, but she knew better. A duel was an unpredictable way to settle a matter of honour.

'At one time you didn't care what these people thought of you and urged me to do the same. Now you're willing to risk your life to prove yourself to them?'

'I won't be mocked, not by Lord Howsham or by anyone.'

'What good is your dignity if you lose?' Susanna pressed, refusing to allow the darkness filling him to make him risk his life. In the ballroom when he'd thanked her for her friendship with his father, it'd seemed the beginning of a fragile peace between them, one Lord Howsham's insults had killed. If she could call it back, build it and him up again, maybe he might not meet the earl in the morning.

'Dr Hale will be there,' Justin scoffed, focused on the quiet London streets passing by outside the chaise. The late hour had drained the lanes of traffic and any impediment to a quick journey home.

'He can't put your head back together if Lord Howsham shoots it off.'

He jerked upright, his hands tight on the edge of the squabs. 'Still you have no faith in me. You think I'm nothing but a reckless idiot. He insulted you. Don't you care?'

'No, not any more. I only care about you and keeping you alive.'

'Don't fret too much. If I die you'll get everything for yourself and the child,' he mocked.

'I don't want it if it means losing you.' She

was determined to remain steadfast in the face of his derision. This wasn't the Justin she'd come to love, the one who met adversity with an easy smile and a quick wit, but one driven by a pain she understood. She wouldn't allow it to consume him as it'd once consumed his father or her so many times. 'Everyone I've ever loved and who ever loved me has ended up in the churchyard—my grandmother, my mother. I won't see my husband buried there, too.'

He stared at her, the mockery knocked out of him by her honesty. His eyes softened, but not his tight grip on the leather. She waited, hoping her words were enough to help him see beyond this crisis to the future they'd planned and the love they could rebuild.

The chaise slowed, leaning to make a turn before rocking to a halt in front of their house.

'It might not have come to this if you'd thought me a better man and not hidden your child from me,' he said at last, throwing open the door and stepping out of the carriage.

She climbed down into the sharp cold of the night, facing him on the pavement.

'I did it because I was afraid and I didn't know you as I do now.' She took his hand and raised it to her lips to press a tender kiss against the skin. He didn't jerk away from her or accuse her of playing him for a fool, but allowed her to hold him and it gave her hope. 'I love you and I'm certain you still love me. Forget the duel and society and everyone. They don't matter, only we do.'

His fingers curled around hers and she held her breath, praying the man inside him, the one whose optimism had captured her heart, would win against the one so determined to fight.

Then his fingers eased and he withdrew his hand. 'I have things to see to before tomorrow morning.'

He climbed back into the chaise and without a second look set off.

With a heavy heart she watched him go, his demons driving him on. She prayed clearer heads, or Lord Howsham's cowardice, might prevent their meeting at dawn.

'Is that all, then, Mr Connor?' Mr Woodson, Philip's solicitor, asked, looking up from the will he'd been summoned to draw up according to Justin's instructions. As sure as Justin was of his aim, he still needed his affairs to be in order before sunrise.

'No.' Justin ceased his pacing of Philip's office to stare out at the moonlit garden and the dark corner of the portico where he and Susanna had first kissed. The roses had faded since then, leaving only a few buds clinging to the thorn-ridden stems. Susanna's pale and worried face from across the chaise haunted him, as did her pleas for him to end this, but he couldn't. He wasn't about to allow Lord Howsham's insults to stand or to prove himself the gullible idiot they believed him to be. 'In the event I die, all is to be left to Susanna, including the care of my father.'

'Might not Mr Rathbone be a better guardian?' Mr Woodson asked. Having fought to make Justin his father's guardian, he knew something of Mr Connor's reputation.

'Susanna will do. She and my father have become friends.'

The man nodded in surprise. 'I suppose every man has it in him to change.'

'I suppose he does.' His father's apology and the contrition and regret which had lengthened the lines of his face came back to him. If Justin hadn't been wallowing in his own pain and heartache, he could have hugged his father and put to rest for good the turmoil between them. His father had changed for the better under Susanna's influence. How different things might be now if Justin had allowed her influence to work on him.

Shifting, he caught his reflection in the window pane, the serious man who met him in the glass barely recognisable. She was right, he wasn't the same person who'd driven with her through Hyde Park as if nothing in the world could diminish his spirits. He was a hypocrite, telling her not to care what others thought while he left their insults and derision to fester until he was willing to risk his life to prove they were wrong about him.

'Is that all, then?' Mr Woodson pressed him again, covering a large yawn with the back of his hand, not the only person in the room feeling the late hour.

Justin opened and closed his fingers by his side. The memory of Susanna's warm hand, and the faint brush of her lips against his flesh, crept through him more than the fury which had driven him away from her. On the pavement, she'd almost made him believe she truly cared for him. He'd wanted to believe it, but he'd ignored his intuition one too many times before and it'd cost him. Whether his instinct was still worth employing as a guide he wasn't sure. Everything was clouded by his hate of Lord Howsham and everyone who'd ever looked down on him. 'Yes.'

'Mr Rathbone, I'll need your signature as a witness.' Philip stepped forward from where he'd been observing from behind the desk, took up the pen and put his name to the will. Then the solicitor held out the pen to Justin who, without much thought, scrawled his name above Philip's. The solicitor rose and tucked the paper into his satchel.

'Good luck to you, Mr Connor.' He left, taking Justin's will with him.

With any luck, neither Justin nor Susanna would need the cursed document.

'Is everything ready?' Justin asked, sagging down into his usual chair by the window. Beside him a decanter of port shimmered with the candlelight, but he ignored the tempting liquor. This was no time to indulge.

'It is. We're to meet at dawn on Primrose Hill. As we have no duelling pistols, Lord Howsham will provide them.'

'Make sure to check them before I fire.' He didn't trust Lord Howsham to fight fair, even when it was in his best interest to do so. If the earl tampered with the weapons, it'd be society's judgement, not Justin's he'd have to face when this was over. He knew how cruel the toffs could be, especially when it came to matters of honour.

He laced his fingers over his stomach. Seeing Lord Howsham disgraced wouldn't amuse Justin if he was shot dead by the man.

Philip took his chair behind the desk, rested his forearms on the blotter and fixed on Justin. 'Are you sure you wish to do this?'

'No, but if I walk away, they'll call me a coward. No one wants to do business with a coward. Besides, my honour is about the only thing I have left.' He clung to his distrust of Susanna, despite her tempting words of love which had played on him in the chaise. There'd been nothing in them, or in the faint tears shimmering in the corners of her eyes, to tell him her love for him was false, yet still he refused to believe it. 'You'll be sure to look after Susanna if anything happens to me.'

'I will.'

'And the child?'

'The child as well,' Philip agreed and the relief which eased Justin's tension surprised him. He'd spent so many days despising the baby and what it meant to her and him and their future. He couldn't despise it any longer. It was as much a part of its mother as her beautiful voice, or the smile which had eluded him for the last several days, the smile he missed.

'Have you made your peace with her?' Philip asked.

'No.' He couldn't. Even if the hardness he'd born against her had begun to soften beneath her love and concern for his life, his suspicion of her motives continued to play on him. 'Why do you think she kept her pregnancy from me?'

'She was afraid of losing you.'

Justin banged his fist against the arm of the chair. 'Because she thought so low of me.'

'Because everyone has always thought so low of her. I imagine she couldn't conceive of a man she barely knew standing by her when those bound to her by blood never have.'

'No, I don't suppose she could.' Yet she'd believed in herself tonight, standing firm against Lord Howsham, proclaiming her faith in herself and Justin to everyone.

He picked at the thick stitching of the chair's covering, unable to ignore the pride he'd felt when she'd stood up to Lord Howsham, defying the man who'd treated her like an old coat to be worn and then discarded. In doing so, she'd demonstrated to him and everyone her deep belief in herself and Justin. It wasn't the first time her faith in him had prevailed during the masque. She could have stayed silent after Justin's failure with Lord Pallston, refused to offer any assistance and let him blunder his way through who knew how many more meetings. Instead, she'd demonstrated to him the manners it took to win the influence of a baron, as well as the necessary information to target the right man.

He wished she'd gloated. It would make shunning her easier. She'd stood beside him against Lord Howsham and Lady Rockland exactly as he'd asked her to do. He couldn't even promise to come home to her without a hole in his stomach.

Philip rose, coming around the desk. 'You'd better get some rest.'

'I'd like to stay here.' It almost seemed an easier thing to face an earl at dawn than to go home and face his wife. He possessed enough concerns about tomorrow without adding Susanna's to them, and he couldn't face her pleading green eyes and expect to stand firm. She'd nearly swayed him on the pavement with her tender kiss, her chestnut curls glistening in the carriage light until he'd wanted to twine his hands in the locks and draw her lips to his. As much as he tried to ignore his instincts, tonight they told him she loved him. It was as disquieting as the coming duel.

Chapter Thirteen

A soft mist settled over the green grass covering Primrose Hill and wound through the few trees near the bottom of the rise. In the distance, London spread out, its chimneys spewing thin tendrils of black smoke into the air, which the wind carried away to obscure the orange of the rising sun. It wasn't high enough in the sky to cast off the early-morning gloom and Justin stood in his greatcoat, gloved hands in his pockets to protect against the chill air. Behind him, horses tossed their heads and jingled the equipage of the many carriages lining the road. Inside the vehicles sat those brave or curious enough to rise early after a long night at Lady Rockland's to watch the duel.

'I've drawn quite a crowd,' Justin remarked to Dr Hale who stood beside him, looking over his shoulder at the people standing along the edge of the field waiting for the spectacle to begin. What little sleep Justin had snatched in the Rathbone house hadn't eased the anxiety tightening his muscles, or the second thoughts which continued to fight with his determination to see this through.

'Not too late to reconsider,' the doctor advised. 'Better to go home to your wife in a chaise than a coffin.'

Justin let out a long breath and it curled like smoke in front of him before fading away. If he came home unscathed, Susanna would be waiting for him and with her every ambition for his business and a long life ahead of them both. Whether it was one of happiness or marked by the bitterness which made Lady Rockland such a prune he wasn't sure. In the end it would be up to him. She'd made her love and belief in him clear, and during the few dark hours of last night, as he'd lain in the Rathbones' guest bed contemplating the past few weeks, he'd come to realise, like his father had, it was time to choke down all the hate and hurt and cross the wide chasm separating him from Susanna. No matter what secrets she'd brought to their marriage, she was his wife for better or for worse and he'd prefer better, assuming he survived the morning.

'Lord Howsham made the first insult. It's up to him to apologise.' Justin rolled his head against the stiffness in his neck, eager to get on with this business.

Across the field, Philip stood talking with Lord Sutton, Lord Howsham's second. Justin wasn't surprised to find one coward standing beside another, Susanna's half-brother throwing in his lot with the man who'd stood against his own sister's husband. A small part of him wished the arrogant earl would relent and apologise. Judging by the sneers he tossed at Justin from out of his two blackened eyes, it wasn't likely.

While they waited for the seconds to finish their conversation, Justin didn't pace. He wasn't about to fret in front of all these people, or his opponent. As much as he might dream of a life with Susanna after this morning, once the duel was over, there could be other problems to face. He didn't doubt he could kill Lord Howsham. Every time he thought of what he'd done to Susanna, Justin wanted to put a ball through the earl, but duelling was illegal. He might drop the man for his crimes, then find himself on the long end of a short rope for murder. He'd been audacious enough to challenge a peer to a fight, he didn't want to risk execution. It meant winging the earl and hoping he didn't die of gangrene. He should have sent Mr Tenor to book passage for him on a ship out of England, just in case. Fleeing was safer than avoiding the constable, assuming Lord Howsham didn't get off a lucky shot. They might both be dead before noon.

Justin glanced at the carriages along the ridge, wondering which unadorned one carried Lady Rockland. No doubt she was here to watch her son stand with Lord Howsham against Justin with great pleasure. In a short while, Justin would see to it Lady Rockland choked on her relish.

Susanna wasn't amongst the crowd. He hadn't seen her since leaving her on the doorstep last night. There'd been no note, no good wishes or sudden appearances before sunrise to talk him out of the duel. She'd pleaded her case with him last night and he'd ignored it, so there was no reason for her to be here and nothing she could say which would stop him. It was too late.

The conversation between the seconds

ended and Philip strode back across the moist earth to Justin and Dr Hale.

'Well?' Dr Hale asked, more anxious than Justin when Philip returned.

'He won't apologise.'

'Good.' Justin tugged his gloves off, then stuffed them into the pocket of his coat. 'Time to satisfy my honour.'

He marched across the grass, the soggy earth giving way beneath his boots as he approached his adversary. Dr Hale and Philip followed behind him in the silence which swept through the waiting crowd at the sight of the two men coming together.

'I didn't think you gentleman enough to appear this morning, Mr Connor,' Lord Sutton taunted.

'How's the stomach?' Justin smiled coldly at his despicable brother-in-law.

'You'll get yours this morning.' Lord Sutton glowered.

'Let's begin,' Lord Howsham demanded, but not with his friend's bravado. His hand shook as he waved his manservant over, his eyes darting to Justin's, then everywhere around the park as he shifted from foot to foot.

Justin stood straight as an oak, his eyes

boring into the earl's as the manservant approached with the burled wooden case carrying the pistols. If sheer bravado could force an apology out of Lord Howsham, he'd stare him down until sunset, but the earl, with his honour at stake, refused to yield. Good, Justin wanted a fight.

The manservant opened the case, revealing two shiny pistols resting on blue velvet. Justin picked up the closest and examined it, looking for any evidence of tampering. He wouldn't put it past the man to rig the duel, but with so many of his peers watching, it seemed he'd decided to rely on his talent instead of more nefarious methods to win this challenge. If so, it wasn't a fair fight.

He handed the pistol to Philip who looked it over and, silently agreeing with Justin's assessment, handed it back to him.

'The pistols are acceptable, then?' Lord Howsham questioned.

'Quite.' Justin dropped the weapon to his side, adjusting his fingers on the handle and getting a feel for the weight of it. He'd handled many weapons, none as fine as this, but in the end they were all the same whether they were polished to a gleam or tarnished with grime.

The manservant closed the case, then handed it to another. 'Twenty paces, gentlemen. The first to draw blood wins. You have both met here and proven your bravery. Mr Connor, do you feel your honour is satisfied?'

'No, not unless Lord Howsham publicly apologises to me and my wife.'

The man paled before seeming to revive what little courage he'd mustered for the morning. 'You'll have to shoot me first.'

'If you insist, though I want it noted, he demanded it.' Justin turned his back on the earl, waiting for him to do the same.

The grass shifted behind him and he heard more than felt Lord Howsham's back meeting his.

'You'll regret this, Connor,' Lord Howsham hissed.

'If I do, it won't be because of your bad aim.'

'Twenty paces, gentlemen,' the manservant announced. 'One—'

With each call of the number, Justin and Lord Howsham moved away from one another.

Justin cleared his mind, caressing the trigger with his finger, figuring out the distance between him and the earl and where best to aim. The calculations would come together in an instant the minute the manservant reached twenty and Justin turned to fire. He didn't know much about the earl, but he'd heard more rumours of his debt than his duelling abilities; yet even a poor shot could get lucky once in a while.

In the distance, where the field met the road, a gig came racing up the hill. Justin was about to look away, to centre himself again on the weapon and what he was about to do when he noticed his father at the reins. Susanna sat beside him, gripping his arm as his father pulled the gig to a stop. She jumped down and with Mr Connor close behind her, hurried across the grass, the hem of her white dress growing dark from the dew wetting it. She stopped as close as she dared, but she was so near Justin could see her green eyes made more vivid by the red of many shed tears.

'Ten, eleven—'

Justin's pace didn't slacken, but his grip on the pistol tightened. Around her people whispered and pointed, but she saw none of it, focused on him with a worry which could melt a man's heart.

I love you. Don't do this, she mouthed as he continued to step away from his opponent.

His determination threatened to desert him and he struggled to maintain his grip on it and the weapon. It was too late, he couldn't back out now and hope to save face. Once the two men turned, fate would decide if one, both or neither of them walked away. If Justin died, what would it be for? These weren't his people. He'd never given a fig for their opinion or approval before, yet he'd allowed his pride, his need to prove himself to her and everyone, to drag him to this field. There was no reason for him to do it. He already possessed her faith in him and he always had. She'd believed in him enough to help him, not just with the business, but with his father. She'd cared for him. Yes, she'd deceived him, but it'd been to protect her child and because she'd been afraid to lose him and the life he'd offered her.

The pain in her green eyes in the chaise when she'd told him about losing everyone she'd ever loved echoed between them now. She clung tight to Justin's father's arm, his skin as pale as hers with worry. They both loved him and he was hurting them by risking his life. His death would crush his father like his mother's had and it would destroy Susanna, too.

Her eyes held his and it wasn't pride in what he was doing which wrapped around his heart, but shame. Nearly everyone who should have loved her had failed her and Justin was throwing his name on the heap, shoving her aside and risking their life together for his own selfish means. The toffs might respect this display of honour, but this wasn't who Justin was or the kind of man he wanted to be.

'Eighteen, nineteen—'

'Stop. I withdraw my challenge,' Justin announced, sending a gasp racing through the crowd. He saw Susanna sag against his father in relief before he turned to Lord Howsham and lowered his pistol.

'Are you too much of a coward to face me?' Lord Howsham taunted, puffing out his chest in victory.

Justin flung the gun away and marched up to the earl. The man shifted one foot behind him and raised his pistol as though he expected Justin to fall upon him. Justin had no such designs. He brought his chest right up to the snub, the cold metal hard against his shirt.

'Go ahead, shoot me. Show everyone here what a brave man and how superior you are by killing me,' Justin growled.

'No!' Susanna cried, her voice carrying over the mist of the morning settling on the grass.

The silent crowd watched, mesmerised.

'You should listen to your wife,' Lord Howsham suggested, but Justin sensed the tremble in his hand through the barrel of the pistol.

He continued to stare down Lord Howsham until the arrogant sneer he'd worn since last night began to fail. The earl's attention darted from Justin to the spectators then back again. Beneath Lord Howsham's red hair, a small bead of sweat slid down to his round jaw. He wouldn't kill him, Justin knew it as well as he knew the bookseller would never come back. Everything Lord Howsham had done, from his relationship with Susanna to his smearing of Justin's character, had been executed either in secrecy or from behind the anonymity of a mask. Now he was in front of everyone who mattered to him, his deed made public for all to see. If he killed Justin, he'd be killing an unarmed man. If society didn't shun him for it, the law would certainly hang him.

Somewhere behind him a horse whinnied and the sound was joined by the faint call of a bird far off in the high grass.

At last, Lord Howsham lowered his gun. 'I'm sorry for the offence against you and your wife.'

'Say it again and this time so everyone can hear,' Justin insisted.

Lord Howsham took a deep breath, screwing his lips tight in defiance before he at last spoke up, silencing the birds in the trees. 'I'm sorry for the offence against you and your wife.'

'Apology accepted.' Justin turned his back on Lord Howsham and strode across the field towards Susanna.

She let go of his father and raced to him, the same joy he felt in his chest making her glow.

She threw her arms around him and buried her face against his neck as he hugged her tight, her love more precious than even his honour.

'You're safe, you're safe,' she sobbed, her tears as tender as her body against his.

'You doubted me?' Justin laughed as he curled his arms around her, inhaling her jasmine scent as though he'd come back from the dead.

'I've never doubted you, I couldn't.' She shifted back within the circle of his arms, her tear-stained face wrinkling in displeasure at his carefree smile. She clutched at his lapels and pulled herself up on the balls of her feet to better face him. 'Don't you ever scare me like that again. He might have killed you.'

'I knew he wouldn't.'

'How could you have known, you arrogant fool?' she hiccupped.

'The same way I know I love you.'

She let go of his jacket as two tears spilled down her cheeks kissed with red by the morning chill. Justin slid his hand behind her neck and bending down, took her warm lips with his, not caring for anyone or anything except the flutter of her pulse beneath his fingers and her hot breath mingling with his.

Epilogue

Four years later

'Did the delivery to Lord Pallston go well?' Susanna asked Justin as he stepped through the door of her bedroom.

Pausing on the threshold, he took her in, as awed by her beauty today as he'd been the night she'd first climbed in his chaise. She sat in the chair by the window, nursing their infant son. Behind her the sheer curtains softened the light which fell over her chestnut hair and danced in her green eyes. Beside her on a small stool sat Emily, reciting her letters from her horn book, her hair as dark as her mother's and bound up in a large red bow.

'Exceedingly well, as always.' He dropped his hat and gold-tipped walking stick on the table by the window, then made for his wife. 'I told you a thirst like his could make us rich.'

'His and all his friends,' Susanna added with a lopsided grin. 'I'm quite impressed with your ability to make the lords pay their bills. You're the envy of every merchant in London.'

'I suppose my reputation for collecting money for Philip precedes me.' After the duel, most of London had read of the incident in the paper and even the toffs had gained a new respect for Justin, leading to a flood of orders which had poured in from every corner of London, including the better parts.

He placed his hands on the arms of the chair and leaned in to lay a swift kiss on Susanna's lips. Between them, their infant son gurgled and fussed before settling back to his suckling. Justin pushed himself up, ruffling Emily's big bow.

'Daddy, don't!' She swiped away his hand and he reached in again, truly mussing her hair this time, much to the girl's amused irritation. 'Daddy!'

He tapped her on the nose, then straightened. 'I think it looks better that way.'

'Daddy, are you going to take me for a drive in the new chaise like you promised?'

'I will. I'll even show you the new shop with its cavernous cellar.' He picked her up and whirled her around, making her squeal with laughter. 'Perhaps we can convince your mother and brother to come, too.'

'Grandpa,' the girl screamed in Justin's ear.

Justin came to a stop at the sight of his father in the doorway. A wide smile drew back the wrinkles at the sides of his father's mouth and made his faded brown eyes twinkle. His coat was well tailored, if not a little large to accommodate the fullness of his body.

'Spin a young lady around like that and you'll bring up her nuncheon,' he warned. His grey hair was as wild as ever as he entered the room, with his arms held out to Emily. 'Besides, that's what her Grandpa is for.'

'Good afternoon, Father. We weren't expecting you until supper,' Justin greeted him as he set his daughter down and she ran to hug her grandfather.

'I had to bring you this.' He withdrew a slender newspaper from his coat pocket and held it out to Susanna. 'Have you seen it?'

Susanna took the paper with her free hand and read the headline, then gasped. 'Lord Rockland is divorcing Lady Rockland.'

Emily let go of her grandfather's leg and rushed to her mother's side. She peered at the paper with her green eyes, her mother's eyes, studying the words she couldn't yet read before she wrinkled her freckled nose. 'Who's Lady Rockland?'

'No one of any importance.' Susanna rubbed the small girl's back. They hadn't had anything more to do with the Rocklands after the morning of the duel, each family leaving the other in peace.

'But I want to know,' the child insisted as only a three-year-old can, as unaware of her mother's heritage as her own.

'You're too little to hear about grown-up things,' Justin chided, hoping she never learned the truth. He loved her as if she was his own and he never wanted her to learn the truth.

'Come on, young lady, we'll leave your parents to talk and see if Mrs Robinson has any of those mince pies we love.' Justin's father took Emily by the hand and led her out of the room in search of a treat.

Justin turned to his wife, who continued to read the paper, her lips twisting into a small frown. Reaching the end of the piece, she laid the paper on her lap and shook her head. 'Lady

Rockland cheated on her husband with the Earl of Colchester and Lord Rockland has brought a suit of divorce against her in Parliament.'

'He certainly has the means and influence to do it.' He took the paper from her and skimmed the story. 'Makes for quite salacious reading. I suppose what is good for the goose is forbidden of the gander.'

He handed the paper back to her, but she didn't finish the story.

'It serves the nasty woman right to taste the poison she spewed on so many for so long.' Susanna did up her bodice and laid the squirming boy on the pillow across her lap. 'She can have her troubles. I don't care.'

She tossed the paper in the glowing fire beside her. In a rise of flames it ignited, the story turning black beneath the curling paper.

Justin knelt beside her chair, perching his elbows on the arm and laying a kiss on the top of his son's head. 'How's he doing?'

'He's hungry, as always, like our daughter was.'

He rose up, taking Susanna's face in his hands. 'And how are you?'

'In love with you, as ever.'

'As I am with you.'

As their lips met, the fire crackled in the grate, consuming the gossip and all the memories attached to it, the sound of it eclipsed by the contented snore of their infant son in his mother's arms.

* * * * *

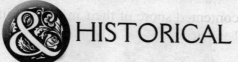

MILLS & BOON®
The Billionaires Collection!

This fabulous 6 book collection features stories from some of our talented writers. Feel the temperature rise with our ultra-sexy and powerful billionaires. Don't miss this great offer – buy the collection today to get two books free!

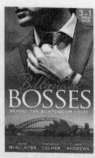

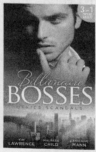
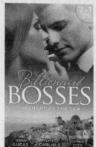
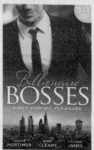

Order yours at
**www.millsandboon.co.uk
/billionaires**

MILLS & BOON®

Let us take you back in time with our Medieval Brides...

The Novice Bride – Carol Townend

The Dumont Bride – Terri Brisbin

The Lord's Forced Bride – Anne Herries

The Warrior's Princess Bride – Meriel Fuller

The Overlord's Bride – Margaret Moore

Templar Knight, Forbidden Bride – Lynna Banning

Order yours at
www.millsandboon.co.uk/medievalbrides